"Combining mystery with a bit of romance and a peek into Hollywood's obsession with being thin, Laybourne creates an interesting commentary on society's addiction to weight loss and diets."
—Booklist

"Delivers a candy-coated horror novel that alternates between increasingly violent scenes and Laurel and Tom's poignant romance."
—Publishers Weekly

"While maintaining an exciting, fast-paced, terrifying narrative, Laybourne manages to weave in details that highlight friendship, the culture of celebrity, and addiction."
—Asheville Citizen-Times

"A finely knit narrative in which romance pairs perfectly (somehow) with societal horror."
—School Library Journal

"Celebrities, romance, and carnage on the high seas . . . Fast-paced."
—Kirkus Reviews

"There is a healthy dose of humor, some romance, a critical look at modern culture, and heart-stopping, sometimes disgusting, violence. . . . Give this to teens looking for fast-paced action and adventure."
—Children's Literature

"Laybourne's masterful novel opens as a comical potential romance, becomes suspenseful, then horrific, and ends as a gripping, action-adventure survival story sure to enthrall readers across abilities and interests. Distinctive prose reveals strong characters with engaging voices."
—VOYA

sweet

EMMY LAYBOURNE

sweet

Solu

SQUARE
FISH

FEIWEL AND FRIENDS
NEW YORK

SQUARE
FISH

An Imprint of Macmillan
175 Fifth Avenue
New York, NY 10010
fiercereads.com

Our books may be purchased in bulk for promotional, educational, or business
use. Please contact your local bookseller or the Macmillan Corporate and
Premium Sales Department at (800) 221-7945 ext. 5442 or by e-mail
at MacmillanSpecialMarkets@macmillan.com.

Library of Congress Cataloging-in-Publication Data

Laybourne, Emmy.
Sweet / Emmy Laybourne.
pages cm
Summary: "The luxurious celebrity cruise launching the trendy new diet
sweetener Solu should be the vacation of a lifetime. It takes a horrifyingly wrong
turn when the gig becomes an expose on the shocking side effects of Solu"—
Provided by publisher.
ISBN 978-1-250-07999-2 (paperback)   ISBN 978-1-250-07906-0 (ebook)
[1. Cruise ships—Fiction.   2. Celebrities—Fiction.   3. Sweetners—
Fiction.   4. Drugs—Side effects—Fiction.   5. Survival—Fiction.   6. Science
fiction.]   I. Title.
PZ7.L4458Swe 2015
[Fic]—dc23
2014049283

Originally published in the United States by Feiwel and Friends
First Square Fish Edition: 2016
Book designed by Véronique Lefèvre Sweet
Square Fish logo designed by Filomena Tuosto

1   3   5   7   9   10   8   6   4   2

AR: 9.0 / LEXILE: HL560L

For my father.
I became a novelist
because you love story.

sweet

LAUREL

A GUY WEARING SKINNY JEANS and a neon-blue fedora is leaping into the air, vaulting up onto the backs of the people in the crowd, waving like crazy and shouting, "Baby Tom-Tom! Baby Tom-Tom!" like a man on fire calling for a bucket.

The dock is a zoo. Fans, maybe two thousand fans, are crammed into the space on either side of a red carpet that extends from the limo drop-off point, all the way up the dock, up a narrow gangplank and onto the luxury cruise liner, the *Extravagance*.

It's dawning on me that I've made a terrible mistake: I walked.

My parents dropped me off way back at the ship terminal after besieging me with last-minute instructions about everything from cell phone usage to alcohol poisoning.

I should have come with Vivika. She begged me to join her in the limo her dad rented for her. But, eh, I felt like I didn't want to show up like some pseudo-celebrity in a rented limo.

Well, it turns out that when you're boarding a cruise that's filled to the brim with wannabe rock stars and reality-TV almost-rans, you want to be chauffeured. A limo means you wind up on the right side of the security guards and the red velvet cords.

I see a curvy, tan girl with a razor-straight brown pageboy haircut get out of a Hummer limo (yes, they make them) at the start of the red carpet.

It's Sabbi Ribiero, the Brazilian heiress from *Teens of New York*, along with several wealthy sidekicks. They all look polished and gorgeous, but not quite as polished and gorgeous as Sabbi, herself. Of course.

The fans go ballistic.

Uniformed bellmen start unloading stacks of leather matchy-matchy suitcases and hanging bags and valises and, God, hatboxes (hatboxes!) out of the trunk of the monstrous Hummer.

The lanky fellow in the blue fedora yells, "Sabbi! Sabbi, we love you!" and puts his hand on my head, to push off me like you would a fence post.

"Hey!" I shout. "That's my head!"

But he doesn't care. He's yelling to some off-site friend on his phone. "This scene is insane! I'd give anything to get on that boat!"

Hmmm, I feel the exact opposite way. I sorta feel like I'd give anything *not* to get on that boat. How did I let my best friend talk me into coming on this—the Solu "Cruise to Lose"? The most famous cruise since the *Titanic*?

I have to get onto the carpet. Vivika's already on board and her texts are getting apoplectic in tone. I don't blame her. I'm late, as usual.

If the ship is going to leave on time it's leaving in the next, yikes, twenty minutes.

Okay, I tell myself. You can do this. I close my eyes and take a deep breath.

Being pushy is not really in my wheelhouse. But I told Viv I'd come with her on this freak show and unless I get through this crowd and onto the other side of the red stanchions, it ain't gonna happen.

So I start shoving.

"Out of the way! Make way! Coming through!"

I elbow and push, dragging my mom's rolling suitcase behind me and using my extra-large handbag (which Viv calls "the Boho beast") as a kind of very soft and lumpy weapon. My guitar, safely strapped to my back in its hard shell, isn't helping, although I do thwack a few irritating people on the head with it (by accident, mostly) on the way.

Finally, I make it to one of the guards standing at the left side of the red carpet.

"Hi!" I say.

He nods.

"I need to get in."

He eyes my guitar.

"You gonna play for change?"

"Oh," I say. "That's funny. No. I'm actually a passenger."

He arches his eyes in surprise.

"Yeah, I know," I say. "Strange, but true."

"You just walkin' up, huh?"

"Yep."

He's enjoying this now. "Just walkin'. You a local?"

I nod. He's really having fun. People are pressing up behind me and cursing my luggage.

"Couldn't get a lift or nothin'?"

I rifle in my purse and come up with my ticket case, a slim padded leather case embossed with the single word: SOLU. Some kids behind me jostle forward as another celebrity passes on the carpet. I think it's a famous chef guy.

"Ease up, now," the guard bellows to the crowd behind, "this girl here has a ticket!"

I feel like Charlie Bucket for a second as people around me gasp and stare.

"Who is she?" a girl whispers.

"I don't know . . . Nobody, I don't think," her friend answers.

Nice. (True, of course.)

I flash the man my ticket. The people around me are now taking my picture with their phones as the guard inspects my ticket.

"Maybe she's a rock star!" somebody guesses.

Yeah, right. (I'm an amateur classical guitarist.)

"It's legit," the guard says, regarding my ticket. People around me literally *gasp*.

The guard unhooks the stanchion and lets me onto the carpet.

"Hey!" he yells. "We need a bellman over here!"

I shoulder my handbag and pull my mom's rollaway bag onto the red carpet and stand there like the dork of the century.

Here's the picture:

- Awkward, slightly chubby girl.
- Most of wavy, strawberry-blond hair escaping the "Easy Crown Braid" hairstyle I tried-really-hard-and-failed to copy from *Seventeen* magazine.
- Guitar on back.
- Freckles. Too many. Everywhere.
- Combat boots on feet with wool socks my grandma knit peeking out the top.
- Cool white Indian tunic from India Bazaar now crushed, sweaty, and ripped at hem.

- Jeans shorts looking dumb when I thought they'd look rocker classy.
- My face blushing beet red under the numerous freckles.
- My expression clearly showing that I would like to sink into the red carpet and disappear forever.

Also, I should have worn more makeup than Carmex and mascara.

Then, fate intervenes in the form of a slim black man with a magnificent handlebar mustache, dressed in a fashionable seersucker suit with a pocket square in a calming shade of lavender.

He strides toward me, holding a clipboard and looking like he was born and raised to run a red carpet.

"Darling! It's me, Rich. Rich Weller, the publicist for the cruise," he says, feigning some prior acquaintance. (As if anyone on earth could ever have met him and then *forgotten* him.) He kisses me on one cheek, then the other. I think we're through, then he kisses me again on the first cheek. Three kisses.

"Come with me, sugar," he says. His tone is intimate and friendly and clearly conveys that he knows I am a fish out of water and is doing his best to try to help me not make an ass out of myself. (Ass-Fish? Fish-ass?) "Leave your bags."

When I don't move immediately, he says, "Just drop them."

I let go of the handle of my mom's suitcase and, of course, it plonks over onto its belly with an awkward *thomp*. A grinning Indonesian bellman sweeps in and lifts the bag onto a cart.

"May I carry your instrument, miss?" the bellman asks, gesturing to my guitar. He gives me a friendly smile.

"That would be loverly, Imade," Rich says for me. Rich takes the guitar off my shoulders and hands it over.

Now I'm conscious of the sweat stains on my back. The tunic, well, it's a little see-through when you sweat like you're facing the guillotine, so everyone can now see the back of my bra where the sweat has made my shirt transparent and the chub that flows over and under the band. This just gets better and better.

Behind us, there are screams as a new celebrity (an actual celebrity, I should say) arrives. Thank God, the attention's off me.

"Tootsie pie, listen to me." Rich murmurs. "Shoulders up, now. That's good. Now you go and walk that carpet, sis. Come on, stand up straight or they'll eat you alive."

I gather myself up and square my shoulders to the carpet and the banks of photographers on either side.

You can do this, I tell myself.

I take two steps forward, and *whack*, Rich spanks me on the butt.

"Go get 'em, girl," he tells me.

The photographers, God love them, don't take my picture! Oh, a couple do, but most of them are angling to snap some shots of the guy coming up the gangplank behind me (he's a reality-show God—survived on nothing but grubs for two weeks on some island where apparently all they have to eat is grubs).

At the top of the gangplank, a line is forming—the boarding passengers are backed up.

It's a check-in line, where you give them your ticket and they hand you some kind of ID card, but that's not why there's a backup.

There's a weigh station.

You hand them your card, then hop on a scale. They record your weight and swipe your card.

Okay, so I knew that this cruise had a weight-loss contingent. The Solu Cruise to Lose has been all over the talk shows and tabloids for months now. Solu is this new diet sweetener that not only sweetens your coffee, but makes you lose weight. And when the divorce between Viv's parents became final, it seemed pretty clear that Vivvy's dad would give her pretty much anything she wanted. Well, this was what she wanted. To go on the cruise. (She's been unhappy with her weight since preschool. I remember her love-hate affair with graham crackers and apple juice.) They say that each of us will lose 5–10 percent of our body weight during the cruise's seven-day trip.

So I knew all that. And I agreed to go because—well, a luxury cruise? For free?! And living in Fort Lauderdale, we're always seeing the big ships come and go. I was so excited to actually be on one. To wave good-bye from the prow is something I will never get to do again in my life, I am sure!

But I did *not* know that we'd be publicly *weighed* before we were allowed to board the ship!

I fumble in my giant purse for my cell phone. I'm going to do some angry texting to Viv. At least, she could have warned me! She knows I'm shy about stuff like this—weight is private. And, yeah, I could stand to lose five pounds (okay, fifteen) but that's nobody's business but my own.

To be weighed in public seems like a big fine to have to pay to go on the cruise.

Then I hear the deep, raspy, heavily accented voice all of America would recognize. Sabbi Ribiero: the infamous, hard-partying, and Maserati-wrecking Brazilian heiress.

She is talking. To me.

"Can you believe this?"

"No," I say. "It's so demeaning. It's insulting. I mean, are we to be weighed like cows? Like luggage?"

Sabbi blinks her twenty-inch-long eyelashes, looking at me like I'm speaking a foreign language.

"I haven't *waited in line* since I immigrated to America, when I was six years old," she says pointedly, like I'm an idiot. To tell you the truth, I kind of act like an idiot because I'm mesmerized by her mouth. She forms each word like it's a little masterpiece. And her voice is like a jaguar purring.

She cocks a perfect eyebrow at me, waiting for a response.

"I wait in line all the time." I shrug.

One of her groupies laughs, then cuts it short when he sees

no one else thinks I'm funny.

Sabbi tosses her hair and turns her back on me, without another word.

When Sabbi is motioned up to the scale, she removes her aqua-colored leather jacket and hands it to one of her people. She's wearing a curve-hugging aqua-colored sweater and aqua pants with a little gold belt. She kicks off her gold stilettos and steps onto the scale. (It could be that her shoes are made of solid gold. That would not surprise me at all.)

Sabbi looks right at me, holding my gaze steadily and proudly, as a lady checks the scale and enters the figures onto a laptop, then swipes Sabbi's ID card and hands it back.

Two uniformed crew members thank Sabbi, help her down, and hold her hands as she slips back on her gold stilettos.

What the hell has Vivika gotten me into?

It's a relief when I get up onto the deck. Some of the people are super-famous, like Sabbi, and then there are the fat wealthy people. Those are pretty much the two categories—young, gorgeous semi-famous people who look like they are probably here for free, and wealthy people who want to lose weight. I guess there's a third category—people like me who don't look like they belong in either category. And jeez! There's a fourth— people serving the passengers. There's an awful lot of them!

Waiters in white jackets are circulating champagne flutes on trays lined with lavender-colored linens. The deck looks like a five-star hotel, tricked out in polished wood, brass, and crystal. There are bouquets of lavender-colored flowers here and there. (What's with all the lavender?)

An elderly man and a frumpy-looking Asian lady are making rounds, shaking hands and welcoming people on board. They must be executives from the Solu Corporation. Standing a few steps behind them is a bald guy with a clipboard who is incredibly muscly, like, about to burst out of his suit. It's like the old guy has Drax the Destroyer for a personal assistant.

I see "Baby Tom-Tom" with a TV crew, over by the railing.

Okay, so I am now looking at my childhood crush, Tom Fiorelli. With my own eyeballs.

Once upon a time, he was the tubby child star of everyone's favorite sitcom, *The Magnificent Andersons*. We all watched him grow up on screen. (By "we all" I mean the entire United States of America.) They canceled the show when he hit fourteen and his voice started cracking. Since then he lost weight and tried to be a serious film star, but his films were bad. Really bad. So bad that I had to leave the theater during *Double Fang*.

It was about a gang of teen boys who turn into were-vampires at night. (Yes, werewolves who are also vampires. And the film was not a comedy.) Baby Tom-Tom was their leader. His name in the film was 'Cisor. (The film should have been a comedy.)

Maybe he couldn't make it as a film star because he chose dumb movies to star in, but maybe it was because everyone still calls him Baby Tom-Tom. There's just no way to take that name seriously.

And there was the whole thing with the pop singer Bonnie Lee Finn. That horrible breakup and the leaked voice-mail messages he left her where he sounded really sad and kept telling her that he *did* know how to have fun. He could *learn* to loosen up.

I felt really bad for him.

I crane my neck to get a better look at him, over the heads of the small crowd gathered around him.

He's only eighteen or nineteen, but he's handling the large crowd like a pro, grinning and jovial. This is what he does now—hosting stuff. He's always on a red carpet or talking about who wore what. He's good at it.

He sure looks like he knows how to have fun, right now.

"Now, lots of people have asked why Solu decided to hold their launch event on a ship. Do you know?" Tom holds the microphone out to a pretty girl in a halter dress. She shakes her head and giggles.

"Anyone?" He offers the mike out.

"Because cruises are awesome?" the girl suggests.

"True! But not just that," Tom says. He gestures over the edge of the ship.

"Look down here. See those crewmen waiting down there?"

I peer over the side of the boat, with everyone else.

There are two workmen in overalls waiting on a wooden platform that's been lowered down to sit just above the level of the water. They have cans of black paint with them and large rollers.

"Once all the passengers are on board," Tom continues, "those crewmen are going to paint a line indicating the ship's weight. When we come back to this port, in seven short days, the ship will sit at least ten feet higher in the water! That will indicate a combined weight loss of at least five thousand pounds from the *Extravagance*'s five hundred passengers! And it could be even more!"

The people around Tom cheer. He beams at them all.

I sort of want to raise my hand and say, "What about the weight of the food we will eat? What about the fuel? Won't those things affect the weight of the ship?"

But I'm not going to be some kind of lame whistle-blower on their promotional idea.

I have to say, it's weird to look at him.

It's Baby Tom-Tom, grinning that grin we all know so well.

I feel like I can see ghost images of him over his face—there he is as a toddler, as a saucy seven-year-old, as a chunky eleven-year-old wiseass, and then there's the present Tom.

The baby fat's gone now—he has a hard, etched jaw and his body's lean and muscled. You can see his pecs kind of straining at the fabric of his shirt. He's not that tall, but he has an electric charm coming off him. And hotness. (Coming off him in waves.)

Have I mentioned the hotness? Because he is scorching hot.

Then something surprising happens: Someone I can't see says, "Cut," and the smile drops off Tom's face. One minute, he seems to be having a great time and the next, he's totally serious. Over it. Huh. (Maybe he doesn't actually know how to have fun, after all.)

"Laurel! There you are!" Viv crushes me in a giant hug from behind. "Stop gaping at Baby Tom-Tom like a dork."

"I wasn't gaping!" I protest.

She drags me away from the little crowd.

"You have to see our room!" Vivika exclaims. "You're going to D-I-E die!"

TOM

HI, I'M TOM FIORELLI and I'm sweating through my third shirt
of the day.

Very classy.

It's hot. I don't know why the heat is taking me by surprise—it's
June and we're in Fort Lauderdale. But there's no airflow and I'm kind
of sweltering here on the deck.

My producer, Tamara, is checking something off on her iPad, scowling as usual. I like Tamara. No one else treats me as poorly as she does
and I like that. She doesn't handle me with a bunch of flattery. I imagine she treats me like she would any one of her seven brothers and
sisters.

We've been working together for over a year. She's my producer and
also my manager for my hosting gigs. Tamara has big ambitions for
me—the VMAs, New Year's Eve, *The Voice.*

There are about five girls in bikinis just "hanging around." I guess
they're hoping I'll pick them to interview.

I will. I should. I'm pretty sure they've brought on a bunch of attractive "ringers" for us to use. But I duck back toward the cameraman,
Cubby, and take a sip of water. Just taking a break while Tamara's
distracted.

"Gotta hydrate," I say.

Cubby's mopping his head with a handkerchief. Sweat has made dark stripes on his brown T-shirt.

"Heck yeah. Feels like a hundred and ten in the sun. Seems to me like the whole deck's acting like a magnifying glass or something."

I like Cubby. He's friendly, but not needy. When you're shooting with a one-man crew, you want to like the guy you're working with.

"Maybe once the ship starts moving it'll cool down," I say.

It's been go-go-go since we boarded. First we did red carpet stuff down on the dock. Now these interviews on deck. We're shooting for another hour or so and then I get to go see my room and hit the gym.

The ship is really nice. Tamara said it was world-class and, I have to say, she was right.

This is nothing like the Carnival cruise my mom took me on when I was fourteen. I had always wanted to go on a cruise when I was a kid. It was one of those things my mom would dangle over me when I didn't want to do another take. Then they canceled the show and we went and it was a nightmare. Every time we tried to go to the pool, drunk frat boys would chant "Tom-Tom, Tom-Tom, Tom-Tom!" I spent most of that week in my room playing Xbox.

This is different.

The ship is sweet. White glove. Done right.

Most of the passengers are wealthy people desperate for thinness. I'd say a quarter of the passengers are minor celebrities and attractive "set dressing" party people. There's no one really A level. Luka Harris and Sabbi Ribiero, I guess. And that grub guy from *Survivor*. I'm sure all three of them—possibly all the celebrities—are getting paid to be here.

There is more than a fair share of pretty girls. We haven't even set sail yet and a bunch of them have busted out bikinis. I don't know, maybe they had them on under their clothes.

It's been suggested to me that I use this cruise as a way to remake my image when it comes to girls.

The way Molly, my publicist, put it was that people saw me as a tender heart, but now it was time for me to show them all how cocky and wild I could be.

Tamara, my producer, was less politic. "The thing with Bonnie made you look like a loser. You gotta party on this ship. Flirt. Grab ass. Get laid."

Cubby elbows me.

"Hey, what are the chances this shit works? The Solu?" Cubby asks, surveying the crowd. He's got a sizable belly. He's probably thinking about becoming a customer. "I'll tell you what I'm going to do," he tells me. "I'm going to wait a year and then try it. By then we'll know if it works."

"If it does, I bet they'll give the inventor a medal," I say.

"A Nobel Peace Prize," he adds.

"Claire, quit dawdling!" says a bossy lady wearing tons of jewelry and a large, floppy hat. She's dragging along a girl whose on the obese side of obese. The poor girl is wearing a giant nautical striped outfit and looks profoundly miserable.

I tap Cubby on the shoulder, nod toward the girl.

He doesn't quite get my meaning. I guess he thinks I'm telling him to check her out because she's fat.

"It's a shame," Cubby says, not meeting my eye. He thinks I'm about to say something mean about her.

"No, no," I say. "That's not it. Tape me."

Here's why I want to tape her: We should interview the people who Solu might actually, really *help*, not just pretty girls and petty celebrities.

"Excuse me, miss," I say. I reach out and tap her on the shoulder. "I'd love to hear your thoughts about the cruise."

The girl's face is polite at first, then goes slack, as she realizes that it's me doing the asking, then she turns beet red.

Cubby has the camera up and is taping.

"Are you excited about the cruise?" I ask her.

Her mother doubles back for her.

"Claire, come on!" she says. Then she sees me and the crew, taping. Her mouth drops, too. "Oh."

"How would you describe the boat?" I ask Claire.

She's looking at me, then back to her mom, then to me again. I'd put her at around twelve maybe. She's definitely the youngest passenger I've seen so far.

She's quiet for so long I start to regret this. There's an expression on her face that says she thinks I'm screwing with her.

"I really do want to know," I tell her. I give her a wink, smiling, encouraging.

"I guess . . . it's amazing!" she says, finally. "All the famous people and the ship's really nice."

"Do you think Solu is going to deliver on its promises?" I ask.

"God, I hope so," she says. And it's funny, the way she says it. Makes me laugh.

And she laughs, too.

There's a sparkle in her eye.

I think I just made her day, which makes me feel good. She reminds me of my cousin, Lizette. About the same age and everything.

"Of course Solu will deliver!" says a creaky old guy in a suit. He walks right into our shot.

Tamara is right behind him, mouthing something to me. I can't understand what it is.

"I'm Tom Fiorelli," I say, extending my hand.

"Timothy Almstead. And this is Dr. Elise Zhang." He gestures to a cherubic Asian woman with tortoiseshell glasses.

I get what Tamara's mouthing to me: *OWNER*.

Of course! Almstead is the CEO of Pipop, the country's most famous beverage company and favorite soda of almost everyone on the globe, at last survey.

"Mr. Almstead, what a pleasure to meet you," I say. "And Dr. Zhang, congratulations."

Dr. Zhang is short and wearing an ill-fitting dress and smiling like she alone knows the secret to happiness. She pumps my hand five times.

She should be happy. Zhang's the mastermind behind Solu—the one who got the formula right. Her face is on the cover of this week's *Time* magazine.

Tamara is not so gently edging Claire and her mom away from us.

"Young man, I had the idea that you should interview me," Almstead says. "I think people will want to know about Dr. Zhang and myself, don't you think?"

"Of course," Tamara answers for me. "It was on the schedule for tomorrow. We have a room booked. But, um, if this is convenient for you, we can do it right here—"

"Carpe diem!" Almstead chirps. "When you get to be eighty-three, like me, you don't set stock on 'see you later'!"

He smiles. I think I like him. He's a bit dotty, and a bit mischievous.

I take another swig of water. I need to get this right. From what Tamara told me, Almstead wanted to hire Ryan Seacrest to do the coverage, but the cruise's publicist, Rich, sold me. Told Almstead I would appeal to both the American youth culture, and to the older generations, who had watched me grow up on *Andersons*.

Tamara also made it clear that this was a big break for me and I'd better not blow it.

I take a breath, run my fingers through my hair, and reset my position, gesturing for Almstead and Zhang to step closer to me, against the rail. A small crowd has gathered.

I nod to Tamara.

She says roll, Cubby says rolling, and we're off.

"I'm Tom Fiorelli, coming to you from the deck of the *Extravagance*, and I have the pleasure of speaking to the two people who've brought us all here today: Mr. Timothy Almstead, America's 'Soda Pop King' and the president of the Solu Corporation and CEO of Pipop; and Dr. Elise Zhang, the chief scientist of the Solu Corporation."

They answer with some "pleased to be here"s.

"Tell us, Mr. Almstead," I continue. "What's in store for the five hundred people who've come aboard today?"

"Fine dining. Shuffleboard. Some snappy shows featuring half-dressed showgirls."

He's playing with me.

"Really? Is that all?" I ask, pimping him a little.

"Why no. Funny you should ask. Every single passenger aboard is going to lose five to ten percent of their body fat, Tom. That's a guarantee."

The people around us give a little cheer.

"People on board are pretty excited about it," I say.

"As they should be!" Almstead replies.

Time to get Zhang in.

"Dr. Zhang, you developed the formula for Solu. Tell us, what makes Solu different from other weight-loss products?"

"The first difference is that Solu works," she says. More cheers. "Solu safely and effectively shrinks fat cells. These excess fat molecules are voided harmlessly through normal physical elimination. Most importantly, once the subject has taken Solu for a period of six weeks, three doses a day, those cellular changes are essentially locked in for as long as one year and more for some people."

"So every year, people will need to eat Solu for another six weeks?" I ask.

"Pretty savvy, don't you think?" Almstead says with a wink.

I laugh.

"Yeah, that's pretty clever," I tell him. "But judging from the excitement of the people on board, you're not going to have any trouble selling Solu. In fact, I've heard that stores around the country have already sold out."

"Well, now, no," Almstead says, a stormy look coming over his features. "No one's allowed to sell it until Sunday, a week from today. The product doesn't launch until next Sunday! Until then, the Lux Lines here have an exclusive on the stuff."

"I misspoke," I say.

"Anyone sells it before Sunday, they're breaking the law. I mean it."

"I meant to say pre-sales. From what I understand, Amazon and all major U.S. retailers have pre-sold millions of boxes of Solu."

Almstead is still frowning.

"You, young man, should say what you mean. And I'll repeat this, for anyone who needs a reminder: If you sell one box of Solu before next Sunday, you'll be hearing from our lawyers. I mean it."

Dr. Zhang puts her hand on Almstead's shoulder.

"I think Mr. Almstead is looking forward to seeing the response of the passengers to Solu on this cruise. Everything is just as he wants it," she says.

Almstead looks at her and nods.

"I can certainly understand that," I say.

"Did you know we painted a mark on the side of the ship?" Almstead asks me. "And they'll paint another one when we return home. I came up with that idea myself!"

"It's a great idea," I say with maybe more enthusiasm than necessary. His reaction about the sales thing threw me off my game a bit. "And I think the world is going to be thanking you two for a long time. In fact"—I pause for effect—"there's a rumor that if Solu really is the solution to the obesity epidemic, you two will be on the short list for a Nobel Prize."

Almstead and Zhang grin at each other, surprised and delighted.

Cubby's too much of a pro to laugh aloud, but I see his shoulders shaking just a bit.

This is how rumors get started.

You just start them.

LAUREL

I FOLLOW VIV INSIDE THE SHIP.

There is a central staircase that is all gleaming wood and sparkling brass. It's open to the decks below, so you can see down into the ship. Three glass elevators run in the center, and on each side is a staircase that loops around as it lands on each floor.

"This is the most beautiful stairway I have ever seen," I murmur.

"Yeah, yeah. Come on!" Viv says.

She pulls me away from the landing and down a hall.

Uniformed maids and bellmen smile as we pass. I see that the bellmen are delivering our luggage to our rooms.

Viv taps her ID card twice on the door and it opens.

"Whoa!" is about all I can say.

The room is just totally gorgeous. The carpet, the bed, the twenty fat pillows arranged just so. Everything is cream colored. And there are these blond wood accents striped down the walls at intervals and the other furniture—the mirrors, the bed frame, the coffee table—they all match the wood.

"This is like heaven but made into a little ship cabin," I say in a hushed tone.

"I know," Viv says.

We look at each other and . . . we shriek!

I take a flying leap and jump onto the bed. Viv lands beside me, bouncing up and down on her knees.

"Oh my God—my boots!" I say. "Ack!"

I've tracked dirt on the plush, creamy carpet.

I sit up and slip them off.

"Ugh, those clodhoppers!" Viv complains.

I hold them in my hand, looking around for something . . . well, something not cream colored to put them on.

"Here," Viv says, holding open the bottom door on the nightstand.

I plunk them inside. Viv slams it shut. We laugh.

Together we lie back on the king-size bed.

I run my calloused fingertips over the duvet.

"I think my fingers are going to faint from how soft this is," I say.

"And look," Viv says, hopping up. "There's a minibar."

"Really?" I say. "With liquor?"

I mean, we're both seventeen . . . (Born four days apart, actually, in the same hospital.)

"What do you think?" Viv scoffs.

She opens it and I see it's fully stocked with juice and soda.

"It's like they knew we were minors," I say.

"Dur! They *do* know we're minors. They know everything about us. I even told them about your allergy to kiwi fruit."

"Well, we should definitely lay off that minibar stuff," I say. "My folks told me to be really aware of things like the minibar and, like, excursions. There can be a lot of hidden charges . . . "

What I'm *not* saying comes through loud and clear—I am not

allowed to spend any money. Vivika's dad, Mr. Hallerton, is footing the bill for our trip. My mom and dad would *never* be able to afford a cruise like this. They're saving every dime for a down payment on a house. I mean, I think my ticket probably cost a year's *rent* for our two-bedroom condo. (And our rent is more than two thousand dollars a month!)

Viv rolls her eyes.

"Sweet love, this ain't a Princess cruise. This is all-expenses paid. My daddy says we don't have to worry about a thing."

She grabs a bottle of OJ and tosses it to me. "If you want to, take a bath in fresh-squeezed orange juice."

"Bathing in orange juice. Sounds very sticky," I say.

I peel the top off the plastic bottle and take a swig.

"Oh my God, even the *juice* tastes luxurious. Thank you, Mr. Hallerton!" I shout up to the ceiling, like he's up in heaven or something.

"Thank you, Daddy!" Viv shouts.

I set the juice down and jump up on the bed.

"Thank you, Vivvy's daddy!" I yell, bouncing.

Viv hops up beside me.

"Thank you!" we call up together, bouncing like little kids and feeling like a million bucks.

So, Viv hates my clothes. She always has.

And I have to say, as we unpack into the frickin' walk-in closet (walk-in closet!), my duds are looking like . . . duds.

"Tell me you brought some regular shoes," she complains as I set out my other boots.

I shake my head no.

"You know, there are *clubs* on board. That's plural. As in more than one," she scolds me. "And all you brought is boots?"

"I brought my fancy boots," I say, offering up my white, prairie-style lace-ups.

"There is nothing fancy about boots!" Viv complains. "I'm going to get you into heels if it kills me."

Vivika's clothes are already hanging up in the closet and (really, even for Viv) it's a lot of clothes.

For example—I am not kidding—she has eight bathing suits.

"Viv," I say, holding up a silver one-piece. "It's a seven-day cruise. You have one too many."

"Oh, ha-ha. *Tres* funny," she says. "You don't understand my plan."

She steps back and gestures to a bunch of clothes on her side of the closet.

"These are the size I am now. Fourteen. Blech."

She gestures to the next set.

"And these are all new—one size lower."

And she gestures to the last group.

"And these are eights! Oh God, if I could fit into these by the end of the tour, I feel like my life would be complete. I even brought one dress that's a six! Though that's just insane . . . "

She stands there fingering the material on a little black dress.

Viv's weight is her now-and-always obsession. I've known her since she was six, and even back then, she was pinching her belly and scowling at her reflection.

Over the years, I've listened patiently (and sometimes not so patiently) while she laid out a hundred new "eating plans" or "ways of eating" (she read somewhere you shouldn't use the word *diet*). I've tried to share her enthusiasm when these new don't-call-them-diets let her lose five or ten or twenty pounds. And I've held her hand while she wept (every single time) when after a month or two, she'd gained back all the weight plus ten.

The messed-up thing is that Viv and I weigh around the same. I think we look fine. Like normal young women with curves in more or less the right places.

But Viv hates her body. And sometimes I can tell she thinks I should hate mine, too.

Maybe the reason Viv and I feel so different about our weight can be explained by our parents—or by the shape of our parents.

Viv's dad is built like a fireplug. Short and fat. Exudes wealth, and perhaps because of that, he could care less about his weight. Viv's mom? Even though she counts calories with a microscope, she's still a wee bit oversize. She's always wearing "foundation garments" and trying to get Viv and I to wear them. I think she might even wear Spanx to bed.

My dad? Regular height. Regular-dad beer belly. And my moms? Exactly like me. We're both 5′ 7″. Both size fourteen. Ample breasts, belly, and rear.

So genetically, both Viv and I are set up to have the bodies we have.

But here's the thing: My Dad loves the way my mom looks.

My mom will come home from a day at the bank with her hair frizzy, her suit jacket rumpled, her bust straining the buttons on her blue button-down shirt, and my dad will take her in his arms and gaze at her like she's the most beautiful woman on earth. He thinks she's sexy and perfect the way she is. (I know this because he tells her. Frequently. Often in public.)

So I know it's *possible*.

It's *possible* to find a guy who will find me attractive. I could even find one who finds the overflowing scoopfuls of me sexy and perfect.

Viv, on the other hand, has had to watch her dad grow steadily disgusted with her mom's body over the years.

Right before the divorce, maybe a year ago, I was at their place, out at the pool, and Viv's mom came out in just her bathing suit. Her dad said, "Jesus, Nadine, put a sarong on or something."

Her mom put her hands down over her thighs like they were some monstrosity and apologized, "I couldn't find one anywhere. Where does Maria hide my beach cover-ups?!"

Then she went back inside and she didn't come back out for the rest of the afternoon. She never came back out to swim.

Vivika kept on reading her *Vogue* like nothing had happened, but I couldn't get my mind around it.

Viv's mom didn't swim that beautiful, sunny Saturday afternoon because her husband thought her legs looked too fat to cross their lawn unveiled.

Is it any wonder Viv is always trying to slim down? (Her mother is thinner than she is.)

"I'm going to say what I always say—" I warn Vivika.

"Don't say it."

"You're beautiful the way you are."

"You said it." She sighs. One of her open suitcases is sticking out from under a rack of clothes and she nudges it with her foot.

"Because it's true."

In the suitcase, I catch a glimpse of a bag of Oreos. I dart my eyes away just as Viv leans over to shut the suitcase with her hand.

So she brought Oreos. No big deal.

A woman with a voice like a kindergarten teacher comes over the PA and welcomes us all aboard. She explains that she's our cruise director and talks about the welcome dinner at seven sharp in the Aurora Restaurant (I guess that's the main dining hall) and that there is a mandatory muster drill at four.

"A muster drill?" I ask Viv.

"They show us how to use lifeboats and stuff," Viv tells me.

"Oh," I say. "That's cool."

She shrugs. "We had to do it on the Regent cruise I took last year. It's boring, but it's over fast. And we can scope for hotties. Sabbi Ribiero brought her whole entourage!"

I should probably mention my brush with famousness, but, eh. Viv will get so into it and I'll have to recount every breath I spent in the presence of her Brazilianess.

Viv digs through a folio of papers from the concierge that was set on top of the desk.

"I signed us up for all the *best* excursions!" she says. "Snorkeling in Roatan, which has real pirate ships, and we can take dune buggies out in Belize!"

"I will drive!" I tell her. "You drive like brakes don't exist."

"What is this word *brakes?*" she says.

I cross to read over her shoulder.

She's looking at a little shipboard guide with information about the cruise. It's printed on heavy stock.

She traces a map of our route with her finger.

"Tomorrow is Key West, then we hit Cozumel, Belize, then Roatan, which is this tiny island off Honduras!"

"Viv," I say. "I'm not going to thank you like a million times and drive you crazy, but really . . . thanks for bringing me."

"Please. Shut up," she says. And she hugs me.

There's a kind of a lurch underfoot.

"What was that?" I ask.

"The ship's finally moving!" Viv exclaims. She grabs me by the arms. "It's happening! We're on our way!"

I'm distracted by the engine's rumbling and the slight, slight sensation I feel—the floor is moving.

Hmmm. Not so sure I love that feeling.

"Hey, my stomach feels . . . like . . . it doesn't like the floor moving," I say.

Viv turns to me, a gleam in her eye.

"Come on," she says. "The air up top will take that feeling away."

She puts her arm through mine.

Oh God, the room lists gently to the side. My head feels weird.

"Let's go mingle!" Viv says.

T O M

AFTER THE INTERVIEW, TAMARA escorts Almstead and Dr. Zhang toward the entrance to the elevator.

The ship's moving now and I was right—the breeze is cooling it down.

We're up on the top deck, which runs around the pool deck, sort of like a track. There's a small swimming pool below, as well as tables and chairs set in the shade, and a long, fancy appetizer buffet.

My stomach growls.

"I'm getting hungry," I say to Cubby, stretching.

"Me, too," Cubby says.

My trainer, Derek, says on days like this I need to eat every four hours to keep my metabolism amped. Stoke the fire, he tells me.

Protein and greens, ideally. I can see some shrimp cocktails in crystal dishes set into a bed of ice near an ice sculpture of a giant *S*. It takes me a second to realize the *S* is for Solu. Duh.

Tamara hustles back.

"Okay, we need more teens, a few more celebs, and then we're done for the afternoon. Having fun?"

I hate that question.

The answer is no. I'm working.

Work doesn't have to be fun. It's work. That's the idea.

"Yeah," I lie. "Sure."

Tamara has wrangled three giggling girls in bikinis. They'd better watch it with the Solu—I don't see where they're going to lose any weight from.

I ask them some questions and they laugh and answer. I flirt with them and they respond. It's easy when I'm on camera—I know my role.

But off camera . . . I don't know what to talk about with girls.

I don't know where to look. It's like they're always gazing into my eyes, trying to tell me something, and it just makes me want to leave and go work out.

Especially after what happened with Bonnie. It was . . . not good.

I should have known what was coming. What an idiot.

I liked her, in the public eye.

I pursued her, in the public eye.

The whole thing was under some kind of publicity dome—every night out recorded and tweeted about and blah blah blah.

So, of course, the breakup would be public. Of course, she'd leak my voice mails to *TMZ*.

But the thing is that I thought it was real.

I really liked her so I thought she really liked me. The way we'd talk about being sick of the cameras and wanting privacy. It all seemed real to me.

I kept telling my publicist, "Molly, please. Get the paparazzi off our trail. Bonnie and I want to be alone." And she promised—she swore to me that she'd stopped leaking any of our itinerary to them. Yet there they were. Photographers shouting our names anywhere we tried to go. Hiking in Laurel Canyon. Getting tacos down in Manhattan Beach. At La Parilla in Silver Lake.

So, duh—obviously Bonnie lied to me. Bonnie hadn't told *her* people to let up on us. Her publicist, Shane, was feeding them everything.

Anyway, ancient history.

A girl who leaks your voice mails is an a-hole. Plain and simple.

She can send me apologetic texts all she wants. She can blame it on Shane. On being drunk. Whatever.

She's cut off.

"Where are you, Tom?" Tamara asks. "You're fading."

"Sorry, what?" I say. "I'm just a little hungry."

"Have you met Sabbi yet?" Tamara asks.

I shake my head.

"I got an interesting text from Rich. Apparently her people are wondering if you two might want to hang out on the cruise."

I eye Tamara.

"Are you kidding?"

"Not in any way."

I exhale and turn out to sea.

"Hang out" is code for a planned romance—something that our publicists can use to push us onto the front pages of *People* and all the rags.

"Rich Weller thinks Almstead would be very happy about it," Tamara says. "And God knows your image would benefit. Not sure why Sabbi's interested, frankly. Unless, gasp, she actually thinks you're an intriguing person she'd like to get to know."

"No. Absolutely not," I say. "I can't believe you're even asking me."

"Most guys your age would leap at the chance to be Sabbi Ribiero's boyfriend, even if it's only pretend."

"Yeah, well, most guys didn't just have their heart stomped on by a teen pop princess."

"Bonnie Loo was a skank."

"It's Bonnie Lee," I say.

"You have to move on. She certainly has."

Bonnie's dating the lead singer of the band Creeping Phlox. Stupid name for a band. Creeping Phlox is a flower used for ground cover. I looked it up.

"I really need to eat," I tell her.

"Okay, let's get those two and then we're done," Tamara says. She's pointing to two curvy girls standing right at the tip of the bow. One of them's wearing combat boots.

That's a good sign. Maybe she'll give me something besides "Oh my God, I'm so excited to be here! This cruise is awesome!"

We head over. Cubby elbows me.

"I'll give you ten bucks you get one to say, 'I'm the king of the world!' " he says.

I laugh.

Cubby brings the camera up to his eye and rolls tape.

"Hi," I say to the girls. "Excuse me, how are you two finding the *Titanic* so far?" I pimp. Can't give a better setup than that . . .

One of them turns and flashes me a broad grin.

"Oh my God!" she says. She elbows her friend in the ribs. "This cruise is so amazing! I can't believe we're getting to meet you!"

Then the other girl turns.

She's got strawberry-blond hair that's coming out of some kind of braid up-do. She's pretty. Not too skinny at all. Her face is covered in freckles and her skin . . .

Her skin is green.

"How do you like the view?" I ask.

Then blondie hurls.

She pukes up her lunch all over the deck and all over my feet.

Tamara says, "Cut."

LAUREL

IF ONLY I COULD JUMP OFF the boat and become a mermaid and swim out into the sea.

Or sprout gossamer wings? Take to the air like a vomity fairy? Or keel over and die?

Anything to not have to look up from the puke-covered, really-nice leather loafers of my childhood TV crush into the incredulous, really-gorgeous hazel eyes of my childhood TV crush.

But there's no magic I can call to power and so I just have to look up.

Baby Tom-Tom is horrified.

His cameraman has dropped the camera down to his side.

"Wow! This is—I'm so—God, Laurel—" Viv is mortified (for me or by me?).

"Seasick," I say to Tom, as way of apology.

"Yep, I'd say so," he answers.

And now the smell is hitting the people around us and, of course, they're turning to stare.

I grab Viv and stagger toward the door to go inside.

So much for mingling.

A waiter came up and gave me a linen napkin to dab my puke-face with, and he gently suggested I visit the medical center, which was a very good idea. So, after reassuring Viv, like, a million times that I would be okay and I could find my way to the medical center alone, I set off alone. (She was so excited to mingle.)

Now I am lost.

I took the elevator (terrible choice—lurch much?) and now I'm on Deck 4, where the waiter told me I'd find the medical center, but I don't see it. Just a bunch of doors that look like I'm not supposed to go through them and then some big empty rooms with stuff stored in them like stanchions and deck chairs.

A leggy, tan girl comes out from a hallway door, holding some costumes covered in plastic dry-cleaners bags.

She holds the door open for me, looking a bit irritated.

"Thanks," I say softly.

I should ask her directions, but she seems so crabby.

But now the whole look of the hallways has changed. The carpeting is plain and the doors aren't wood—they're gray painted metal.

Ugh, the boat keeps doing this slow roll.

Obviously I'm in the wrong place.

But, oh, I need to rest. Just for a second. I lean against the wall.

Don't want to puke again.

"You all right there?" a really kind-looking guy asks me. He's fixing a name tag onto a red vest. He's slender, has dark skin, doesn't look much older than me. I think he's Indian.

"Is this your first cruise?"

I nod, miserable.

"Seasick?"

I nod again.

"You must be a performer," he says.

(Okay, how on earth can he tell I play the guitar just by the look of me?! Do they hire *psychics* on this ship?)

"I'm Jaideep. I'm a waiter. You must be the new singer."

"No," I say. "No."

I flush.

"I'm a passenger."

"Oh!" he's embarrassed. "Excuse me, miss. It's just—"

"I know, the way I'm dressed. I look like a bum."

"No! No. You—you are in the staff quarters. I assumed—"

The ship tilts slightly and my stomach rolls. I groan.

"Let's get you back where you belong," he says. "You're really not allowed down here."

"I was looking for the medical center," I mumble.

"They need to put a bigger sign on it! Come on, I'll help you there."

He bends down and slides an arm under my shoulder, helping me to stand.

The voice of that nice lady comes over the PA. In a singsong voice she announces, "Attention, crew members, Code Ingrid in suite 826. Code Ingrid, suite 826."

"Who's Code Ingrid?" I ask.

Jaideep laughs.

"It means that someone in suite 826 is in need of medical attention," he tells me. "Ingrid is for 'injured,' that is how I remember it. There are many codes, for different situations."

And as he escorts me to the medical center (I am on the totally wrong end of the ship), he distracts me by listing the codes.

Code Ernie—environmental hazard (something's
gone over the side of the boat).

Code Frieda—fire.

Code Sherman—security breach (!).

Code Rosa—bomb threat (!!).

Code Oscar—man overboard (!!!)

Code Matthew—fatality (um, !!!!!!!).

"God," I say. "Do you get a lot of bomb threats and deaths and people falling overboard?!"

"No!" he laughs. "Never! But we are prepared. We run drills."

"Well, thank you for being prepared," I say.

"Here you are," he tells me, depositing me at the medical center doors.

"Thanks," I say. "I really mean it."

"Give it a day or so. You will soon be a regular sailor," he tells me.

I'm in there just long enough for them to press some Drama-mine into my hand when that super-peppy lady comes back on the PA and tells us all it's time for the muster drill.

TOM

SO I SAW SABBI AT THE MUSTER DRILL.

We all had to file into the Celestial Lounge—which is a big theater where they do the shows at night, and sit around while safety procedures were explained to us by the cruise director, a woman named Lorna somebody.

She kept on saying things like "Now, I'm not used to giving these directions to big celebrities like Luka Harris and Sabbi Ribiero, but just bear with me!"

Sabbi was seated at the back of the room and people kept turning to check her out when the cruise director mentioned her name. I felt like Sabbi was looking at me, waiting for me to turn around and nod or something.

I didn't. I just stared ahead at Lorna what's-her-name.

I guess I hadn't made up my mind yet about what to do about the "discreet" offer made to my people by Sabbi's people.

We learned about the "abandon ship" signal—one long blast, followed by seven short ones. We also heard about the life raft capabilities—some of them have motors and some of them don't; we were called in groups and led single file down through the boat to Deck 6.

They had us put a hand on the person in front of us and make a human chain.

Two heavily made-up cougars were joking around, elbowing each other out of the way so they could be in front of me.

"He's mine!" said one.

"You're married! Give him to me," the other one cackled.

"There, there," I said. "I can put one hand on each of you."

I didn't really feel like joking around with them. They were pretty worn-out looking, but I guess it's a part of the job.

A beefy man in a polo shirt was behind me.

He put his hand on my shoulder.

"Lord, get a load of the traps on this fella!" he called, massaging my back.

Yeah, yeah, yeah. Manhandle the celebrity.

"Didn't you used to be tubby, like the rest of us?" he joked.

I pretended it was funny.

On Deck 6 there are open areas where the lifeboats are on these giant braces, suspended above us. In case of an evacuation, they are lowered down and we board right from the side of the deck, then the whole thing gets lowered to the water level.

"What say we give it a test drive?!" the beefy guy called to the perfectly nice crewman supervising us.

"I'm afraid that's not allowed," the crewman answered with a bright smile. "We're just waiting to hear that everyone has arrived to their stations and the drill will be over."

There was a small cheer from the guests.

One of the cougars pinched me on the arm.

"I'd like to get you alone in one of those," she said, indicating the lifeboat with a lift of one of her penciled-on eyebrows.

Just then the crewman got an all clear from his walkie-talkie. "That's it! Thanks, everyone," he called out.

I got away as fast as I could.

Gross.

Tonight's dinner is Black Tie Optional. Optional for everyone except me.

"Are you kidding me?" Tamara gasped after I asked Rich if I could, maybe, just wear a sports coat. This was after our guided tour of the ship and I was feeling pretty wired out.

Rich patted Tamara's hand with an unspoken "I'll take care of this," and turned to me. He threaded his arm through mine.

"I know you've had a long day, Thomas," he said. "But I want you to think of yourself as an ambassador on this trip. When you show up looking fine, it elevates the whole event. These people are here for romance and transformation—and you're like an angel, standing at the pearly gates of gorgeousness and fitness and luxury, welcoming them in. Can you see that, baby? Can you visualize it?"

I like Rich, with his crazy mustache, so I worked hard to nod and look like I was really letting his words sink in.

I did not roll my eyes.

Tamara didn't feel the need to be so "inspirational."

"I think you're forgetting how lucky you are," she scolded me. "Solu selected you, and you alone, to do the media coverage for this cruise. I mean, this is the exclusive of the century. You're it, Tom. So if Rich asks or if I ask you to show up in a tux, I expect your question to be 'Zenga or Armani?'"

"Okay. Zenga or Armani?" I asked.

"Whatever makes your ass look better," she snapped.

Nice, very nice.

I wore the Armani.

And I'm glad I did.

Because as the maître d' leads me to my table in the Aurora Restaurant, I see he's going to seat me right next to Sabbi Ribiero.

Sabbi's dressed in a glittering green cocktail dress. She kind of looks like a boa constrictor.

I greet everyone, introducing myself where I need to, and then sit down. Luka Harris is seated on Sabbi's other side. His shaggy blond do must take hours to get like that. Jenny Palmer, who was a Bachelorette in 2014, is there with the guy who won her—can't remember his name. And there's Tamara, scowling at me, and the grub guy from *Survivor*, who looks like he's been making up for lost time.

Sabbi extends her hand to me palm down and I have no choice but to kiss it.

I hope I look calm and collected. Inside I'm shouting at myself for not figuring out what I wanted to do about Sabbi.

It's too late now, I realize. I've lost the chance to back out.

"You know what they call you in Brazil?" Sabbi asks.

"What?" I say.

"Tomazino. In Brazil, they hate abbreviations for names. Nicknames. I don't know why, but it's true."

"That's strange," I say. Tamara gives me the evil eye. "I mean, in an interesting way."

Jenny interrupts, "To me, you'll always be Baby Tom-Tom!"

"Well, I actually prefer Tom—" I try to say.

"It's just the cutest name and when I think about you as a toddler . . . "

Her eyes are welling up with tears. We're not being filmed, so I think they are actual tears. She turns to the rest of the table.

"Oh my God, remember that episode when he got his pants caught in that elevator and they ripped off! What were you? Four?"

Everyone gushes about the episode.

I was six. I didn't want to do the bit and my mom made me. The elevator doors closed on my pants. I got tipped over so I was upside down, on a rig, of course, facing the elevator doors.

As my pants got pulled up, my body started slipping down. That wasn't a part of the plan.

I tried and tried to hold those pants on and that's what made everyone laugh so hard.

"Television history!" Luka Harris bellows.

I tell you, as a six-year-old boy, I just didn't want my pants to fall off.

I just didn't want my butt to show.

If my smile looked fake before, I'm sure it looks forced now.

"Baby Tom-Tom! Dude. You'll always be Baby Tom-Tom!" Luka crows. He pats me on the back.

It's all I can do not to grab Luka Harris by his trademark blond shag and slam his head into the table.

"Didn't you hear him?" Sabbi says, her voice suddenly cold. "He prefers Tom."

"Yeah, but—"

"No," she says. And that's that.

Luka mumbles an apology and starts a conversation with the Grub Guy.

I look at Sabbi and she gives me a wink.

Saved by Sabbi Ribiero . . . Maybe she's not so bad?

There's the sound of microphone feedback and all eyes turn to the bandstand.

"Excuse me, ladies and gentlemen," says the captain, who's now standing in front of the band. "I'm Captain Kevin Hammonds and I'd like to take this moment to welcome you all aboard."

I see Cubby set up, taping, nearby.

"It is my privilege to welcome you to the *Extravagance*. My crew is going to take special care of each and every one of you. We are honored to host the momentous and historic launch of the new sweetener, Solu."

Big cheers from the audience.

"Please welcome Timothy Almstead and Dr. Elisa Zhang to the stage."

Almstead and Zhang come to his side.

"Hello, everyone," Dr. Zhang says, way too loud. You get the feeling she doesn't know her way around a microphone. "When I was growing up in Shanghai, I never dreamed I would be on a ship like this, talking to people like you. Much less did I dream that I would create a new substance that would bring such important change to the world. Science is all about change. And our world needs change. I think."

Everyone applauds. She has a unique charm to her. An I-don't-get-out-much thing going on.

Almstead takes the mike.

"That's right, Elise. Hey there, everyone! You know why we picked the name 'Solu'? Well, research and development, of course. They said people liked it the best, so there you go. But why did people like it best? Solu. It's short for 'solution'! We got a problem—people don't like to be fat. And Solu's gonna fix it. Solu-tion! Maybe that sounds like an oversimplification, but I'm a simple guy!"

Cheers for this. People love this guy.

"You know, we picked the *Extravagance* because it could seat all of you at the same time. It's the only cruise ship that can do it. Dinner for five hundred! Imagine that!" Almstead says, grinning. "We wanted you all to get your first taste of Solu at the very same time. So without further ado . . . here we go, folks."

At this point, waiters swarm out of the kitchen with trays loaded with pastries.

They set a dessert plate in front of each of us.

"Ladies and gentlemen, you are the first people in the public to taste . . . Solu!"

And everyone goes nuts, applauding and cheering.

Now the only sound you can hear is the tinkling of cutlery as people cut into their cream puffs.

This is the moment I had hoped would not come.

'Cause I'm not taking Solu.

I discussed it at length with my trainer, Derek. Several times. Diet pills can backfire. I've seen it a hundred times.

I've worked too hard to get my body the way it is. Every pound I lost, I lost the hard way. Clean eating and exercise.

I'm not going back.

I cut up the pastry and move it around on my plate.

"Oh, wow, it's really good!" says Jenny.

Tamara digs in with gusto.

"Yeah, I like it," Sabbi says. She licks the cream off her fork.

"Aren't you eating yours?" Luka asks. "Dude!"

"I tasted it. It's great," I say. And the people at the table take notice.

"Baby Tom—I mean, Tom—you're not eating it?" Jenny says. She looks horrified.

"I tried it!" I lie.

Tamara glares at me like she's out for blood.

"I'll eat yours!" Luka says and, in three bites, he's cleared my plate. Jerk.

Now the army of waiters is bringing around coffee and tea, pouring it into the cups already set at our places. I see there are some little pitchers of cream set around each table, but no sugar.

Then a waiter sets down a little sterling dish at the center of each table filled with packets of Solu. They are the trademarked shade of lavender.

The color was blended by an exclusive French color expert. It's supposed to be a shade that gives hope and comfort.

I know this because it's on my list of talking points, along with their motto, "Solu: Life's delicious."

Tamara picks up the dish and takes a packet. Then two.

She passes it to the next person.

The attention of everyone at the table is focused on that little silver dish and those slim lavender packets. It goes around the table and everyone, politely, takes two packets.

When it comes to me, I plan on passing, but I see Tamara glowering at me. I take two packets.

There were exactly two packets per person at the table. So that's that.

LAUREL

I AM STARING AT AN ÉCLAIR.

My stomach is seizing up sporadically. Clenching up to let me know that if I lay one fork tine on that slender little pastry, I'm gonna blow bile all over the beautiful linen tablecloth.

So, yeah, I'm still really seasick.

I'm *also* horribly underdressed.

Viv was right—my wardrobe is completely inadequate.

I don't know what I'm going to do. It's not like I can write home and ask my mom to send me a care package of better clothes (to a ship at sea!).

Apparently there's a boutique on board, but I'm quite certain the fifty dollars my parents gave me for an emergency won't buy me the evening dress I'm wishing I'd packed.

I am wearing, instead, a form-fitting black tank top and my very nicest black jeans.

Around my neck, I have a set of dog tags that actually were a free giveaway at the mall. (They say, ARMY OF RAD GIFTS AND NOVELTIES! but I'm hoping that no one looks at them closely.)

Viv is wearing a trendy little dress made of neon lace over navy-blue material and matching heels. It's maybe a twitch too tight on some of her more curvy aspects.

"Here it comes," Viv says. "My first taste of a new future!"

She digs into her dessert.

Around the table, everyone follows suit.

When we were first seated at the eight-top, I saw Viv's face fall when she saw who shared our table. I am a nice person but even I have to say—it's a table of losers.

Rich losers.

There's one family with two ninth-grade boy twins, and a fat couple who look like they're at retirement age. The two teenagers just look at their phones through the whole meal. I guess *their* parents aren't concerned with the exorbitant fees for data usage on board. The mom and dad look like they *wished* they were looking at their phones and the two old people just kept their heads down and ate everything that was put in front of them without saying a word.

There was not a celebrity in sight.

Well, I could *see* Tom Fiorelli. He was in my sight. Sort of. He was seated way in the center of the room, with good old Sabbi Ribiero and other people of his kind.

I flushed red with embarrassment, even just seeing him at a distance.

"There he is," Viv said, under her breath. "*El bebé* T. T."

"Obviously, I need to avoid him for the rest of the cruise," I said.

"I dunno. It's a pretty small ship," she noted.

Just then the waiters arrived at our table with our plates, and voilà, dinner was served.

"Oh," I said, as my stomach gave a decided and audible protest.

"Oh my Lord, look at the size of that steak!" the husband of the miserable family said.

"Yummy!" Viv chimed in.

The giant steaks were some kind of icebreaker and everyone started chatting. We all told about where we were from . . . and if it was our first cruise . . . that kind of thing.

I cut a bite. It was pink in the center and juicy, with a crust of herbs on the outside.

I put the bite in my mouth. It was both delicious and repellant at the same time.

I didn't want to waste it. It was probably the nicest steak I would ever be served in my whole life.

But I also could not have it in my mouth.

I tried a teeny tiny bite of the fluffy, buttery mashed potatoes and got some acid reflux up my gullet.

That was it. No more food for me.

Not even a historical éclair.

"Wow! It's delicious!" Viv exclaims.

"You'd never know it wasn't real sugar!" the mom agrees.

"I don't know," the dad says. "Tastes a little chalky to me."

"If it makes me lose weight, I'll eat straight chalk!" the retired man hollers. I think he is a bit deaf.

I set my fork down.

"What? You don't like it?" the mom asks me.

"I'm not feeling well," I say.

"Dude, look at her face," one of the ninth-grade twins snickers, pointing to me. "She's gonna hurl."

"No, she's not!" Viv says. "Are you?"

I shake my head no.

(But I may.)

I can keep it down. I think I can keep it down.

Viv flags over a waiter.

"Can you get my friend another ginger ale?" she asks.

The waiter returns a moment later with another soda and, glory be, a couple of heavy-plastic travel-sickness bags.

"Thanks," I whisper as I tuck the bags into my giant purse.

Viv pats my hand kindly.

"Sweetie," Vivvy says. "If you're not going to eat your dessert, do you mind?"

T O M

WE'RE AT THE CLUB CASSIOPEIA.

Sabbi hinted she'd be coming here after she changes outfits. Rich and Tamara insisted we come. I don't love being bossed around, but at least I get to dance. Get in a little cardio.

The truth is, I like dancing. I'm good at it and the same thing happens that happens when I run—after about twenty minutes, I get an endorphin release and I can forget about everything for a while.

Some girls dance up around me and try to engage. I dance with them. But I don't lock eyes.

I'm in it for the endorphins.

I see some people taking pictures of me with their phones.

I'm sure Rich and Tamara will be happy about that. They want me tweeted and Instagrammed and Snapchatted all over the Web. That's what Solu's paying me for, I guess.

I do like to dance.

When you're twelve or thirteen, I think most guys all decide that dancing's for girls, but when I was twelve and thirteen, I wasn't really around guys my age. I was getting tutored on set and hanging around with my mom. The only kids I hung out with were my "sisters" on the show.

In fact, when the producers figured out I actually liked to dance, they brought in an instructor to work with me.

All a part of that initial phase where they wanted me to lean down.

It was cute for me to be chubby as a little kid, but when I hit eleven, they decided it wasn't so adorable anymore.

Mari Ayn showed up and I started spending an hour a day on hip-hop lessons. It was fun. Yes, they were trying to control me and shape me up according to some plan they had, but it was fun.

After a year, Mari Ayn brought in B-Boy Derek and then it got interesting.

And now I can b-boy, or breakdance, as the old folks say. I have a little routine put together. I'm not that good, not enough to compete, for sure, but maybe someday.

At first I was just a twelve-year-old kid and Derek was just my b-boy coach, but then we became friends. Derek has since stopped focusing on dance and he has his own personal training business. He trains me and we talk, every day.

I hadn't focused on b-boy since that first year with Derek, but when I started seeing Bonnie Lee I got the idea to surprise her at her eighteenth birthday party.

Me and Derek worked on it in secret.

When she dumped me I almost spilled it.

Can you imagine: "But I *can* be fun. I'm gonna breakdance at your birthday party!"

TMZ would have had a field day.

Some kind of slow song comes on and a short but very pretty brunette tries to lock me in, but I back away.

"Gotta hydrate," I tell her with a wink.

Fake smile, fake wink. It's easier to dodge girls when you act like a jerk. So I do it sometimes.

Back at the table, Rich and Tamara are talking about the next day's shoot.

Rich starts applauding as I walk up.

"Now that is what an ambassador does! He gets the crowd moving!"

"Thank you." I laugh. I down a bottle of water. "I actually like to dance."

My mom keeps pressuring me to go on *Dancing with the Stars*.

But I don't know—that seems like a last resort.

I haven't given up hope on film.

"Tom, you are one intriguing fellow," Rich says. "You should be the new 'most interesting man in the world.' The teenage version."

"That's not a bad idea," Tamara says. "I'm going to text Molly."

"It's what I do, people," Rich says, twisting the ends of his mustache with a flourish.

Rich really is some kind of a publicity genius. His age is a secret, but he can't be more than twenty-two or twenty-three. He's known for big ideas and apparently only takes on one client a year. This year it's Solu.

I signal for more water.

"Wow. You are really sweating," Tamara observes.

I've soaked through my tux shirt. Even the bow tie hanging round my neck is drenched.

"Yeah," I say. "When you're in shape, you sweat a lot. That's what my trainer says."

"You have some serious moves," Rich tells me.

I do a little pop and lock. I grin.

"I can really work with this. I got some good shots," Rich says, showing me his phone.

Then it happens—the new single from Daft Punk blares out, blasting over the end of the slow song.

It's the song my routine is set to! And I'm feeling good. Endorphins, probably.

"You want some video?" I ask, giving Rich a crooked grin. "Something worth posting?"

"Hells yes, I do," he sings.

I toss back the rest of my water and throw the bottle on the ground.

I step out onto the dance floor, Rich close on my heels.

"Shoot it! Shoot it, y'all!" Rich calls out, recruiting others to take video.

On the floor, I dart back and forth, clearing a little space, top-rocking. Three bounds and I drop. Lots of handwork, a set of swipes, then windmills, working into my power moves, then I pop up onto my elbow.

Derek would be proud. I'll have to send him the footage.

I circle up on the tip of my elbow—I stole this move from him, with his blessing.

Everyone is screaming for me, hollering with surprise. Egging me on.

Rich is taping. I see him at the edge of the crowd.

I roll up into some footwork, now, a little break.

Then I knee-drop into some CCs. Up for some flares.

I feel good. I feel alive.

I wonder, for a second, if Sabbi's arrived yet.

I do a swipe to launch myself up onto my feet.

Only—SHOOT—the floor's too wet. My own darn sweat. I slip.

I fly forward, my feet coming out from under me, and I slam into a girl.

We go down.

THIS IS WHAT HAPPENS WHEN YOU LOSE CONTROL, I'm shouting at myself in my head. THIS IS WHAT HAPPENS WHEN YOU TRY TO HAVE FUN!

'Cause now *this* is what will run on YouTube—me trying to b-boy and then wiping out and taking this girl down.

Oh, man, I've flattened the poor girl.

"So sorry," I say. "I'm an a-hole."

And then I see who it is.

LAUREL

I AM COVERED WITH TOM FIORELLI'S SWEAT.

Actually, I am covered with Tom Fiorelli *and* his sweat.

I'm on the floor. It's cold against my back, and Tom's body is hot and slippery on top of me. His face is buried in my neck.

(I cannot describe how incredibly good this feels. Even though my head hurts and I can barely breathe.)

He's heavy and muscular and now he's pushing off me so I feel his weight shift over me.

He takes his hand out from behind my head.

He starts apologizing and cursing himself.

My hip hurts, I realize. I must have taken the fall on my hip.

"Are you okay?" he asks.

I realize that I have a handful of the wet, slick cotton fabric of the back of his shirt clutched in my hand. I let go.

People are pulling us up now. Together.

Tom's massaging his hand. I think he hurt it.

"Are you all right?" he asks. He's shaking off the people around him. Rich, my friend from the gangplank, is there.

"I'm okay," I squeak.

Rich is right close to us. "You okay, girl?"

"You sure?" Tom asks me.

I nod.

"Kiss her," Rich says, under his breath.

"What?" Tom asks.

"Trust me. Just kiss her."

Tom looks at me, a question in his eyes.

I blink.

Is a blink a yes? Because then Tom leans forward and takes my face in his hands and kisses me.

I feel shocks running through my body as if I've been touched by a live wire.

It's a very, very thorough kiss.

It's a whole-body kiss.

The people around us burst into huge CHEERS.

They are going nuts.

I realize my hands are holding Tom's back. The muscles under my hands are firm and rippling.

It's the best kiss in my life.

I'm flooded by feelings—and suddenly I realize under all of it I feel anger.

He's using me. This kiss is some kind of impromptu publicity stunt.

(And it's such a good kiss.)

But no.

I put my hands on his (sweaty, hard, cut) pecs and push away. The people around us are screaming and hollering in delight.

Tom releases me and the guys around him are slapping him on the shoulder.

"Epic!" one of them says. "You rule!"

The crowd surges around us. Mostly people surrounding him and I get pushed away from him.

Viv's in my face. "Oh my God, Laurel!!! I can't believe that just happened."

"I want to go," I say.

"But we can't go now!" she yells. "You just got, like, famous!"

"Vivika." I grab her and look hard into her eyes. "I'm leaving!"

I storm away and I hear someone ask Viv, "Who is that girl? Is she your friend?"

Viv stops to answer and I get out of there.

(Hooray for me) I make it back to the room without getting lost or throwing up.

I take a shower to get Tom Fiorelli's sweat off me.

My hip is red—there will be a bruise there.

I let the hot water pound me from three different fancy nozzles.

He kissed me because Rich told him to.

He kissed me.

He kissed me because he knocked me over and made a fool out of himself and the kiss would give people something else to think about. Make it look like a victory, or a plan, or something.

Tom Fiorelli kissed me.

And I hadn't liked the circumstances, but I sure as hell liked the kiss.

Rats.

I try to untangle my feelings about it as I get into our (whoa, the softest sheets ever) bed.

The shades have been drawn for us and the bed is turned down.

There's a chocolate on each of our pillows—a Solu chocolate, of course.

I put mine on Viv's pillow. I'm not going to take any chances of the nausea coming back.

It would have been easier to hate Tom if it hadn't been for one thing.

His hand.

He protected my head when we fell.

I remember him shaking his hand out—he hurt it when my head slammed down on it.

Somehow—in our jumbled bodies colliding with each other and then the floor—he had put his hand out so my head wouldn't hit the dance floor.

And in the dark, in the king-size bed in our luxury cabin, I smile.

It may be hard to stay mad at Tom Fiorelli.

TOM

"HEY, MAN!" COMES DEREK'S VOICE. "I was wondering when you'd call. How's the ship?"

It's good to hear his voice. Really good.

"All right," I say. "Pretty sweet, actually. You should see my room. And I did the set."

"What?! How'd it go? Wait, no. Give me your food first and then I want to hear all about it."

I tell him everything I ate during the day.

That's how we do it.

People wonder how celebrities stay in shape. We have trainers like Derek. He's my secret weapon.

"Sounds good, but watch the steak," he tells me. "When they serve you a giant slab of meat like that, it's easy to eat more than you need."

"Got it," I say.

"So, tell me about the set. I can't believe it! How did it go?"

"Terrible. I was sweating so much I slipped when I tried to flip onto my feet."

"Did you hurt anything?"

"I hurt my hand. Nothing major. But I sort of crushed this girl."

"Uh-oh."

"I could've really hurt her. I should never have tried it."

"Tell me about the girl."

"Oh . . . you know. Strawberry blond. Pretty. Curvy. Freckles. Really pretty, actually, but she might be a hippie."

"Huh."

"Don't," I tell him.

"Sounds special."

"You're the one who told me to lay off the girls," I remind him.

"Oh no. I told you to lay off the starlets. Big difference."

"Then you're not going to like hearing about Sabbi Ribiero."

"*Teens of New York* Sabbi Ribiero?" he asks.

"They've set us up for a thing."

"Tamara talk you into it?" Derek asks.

There's not a lot of love between Derek and Tamara. He thinks she's too mean and she doesn't like how much "influence" he has over me.

"You ready for something like that? Sabbi Ribiero is a force."

"Tell me about it!" I laugh. "I don't know. Not really."

There's only one person I feel comfortable talking to about this kind of stuff and Derek's it.

"Well, you can say no. Tamara is supposed to be working for you. She doesn't own you."

"Yeah, yeah, I know. But it's good publicity."

"Ahh, my ambitious friend. Yes. But that shit can take a toll on your heart, man."

This is sort of a theme between Derek and me. He tries to remind me about feelings and stuff. It's because when we first met back when I was twelve, I was still "eating my pain," as he called it.

He came by my dressing room early to pick me up to train and found me sitting on the couch, eating my lunch off the coffee table.

Eight hot dogs, a bag of Doritos, and a two-liter bottle of Pipop.

"What's this?" he said.

"What? It's my lunch," I said.

He watched me inhaling dogs for about a minute and stood up to leave.

"I can't do it," he said. "Sorry, little man. Catch you later."

"Wait! Where are you going?"

"Out of here."

"WAIT!" I cried. "Wait, what's wrong?"

He came back in and shut the door. Threw his duffel bag on the floor.

He stood there looking at me for a minute. I think I had a half-eaten bite of hot dog hanging out of my mouth.

He knelt down in front of me.

"You got dealt a shitty hand, Tom. All this pressure—all this fame— it's too much for you and you're stuffing your face to avoid the pain. You're eating your pain, and it's going to take you down."

"But I'm hungry," I said.

"Of course you are. You're a growing boy and you're not getting *any* nutrition. There's nothing you need in this crap. It makes you fat and, worse than that, it makes you *feel* fat. Know what I mean?"

I did. I felt lethargic and sad and useless, despite the antidepressants my doctor had put me on.

"You need protein and greens, son."

"Okay," I snuffled. I may have been crying.

"And you need to get some friends."

I nodded. Then I asked him to be my friend.

And he said yes.

"Well," Derek says. "I like the sound of Freckles, if you ask me."

"I'll figure it out," I say.

"You always do. Talk to you tomorrow," he says. "Lay off the steak."

I think about the girl, after I hang up with Derek.

I rub my hand. The meat between the thumb and pointer finger hurts. Real tender. I should probably ice it.

I left the club after the incident with the girl. Sabbi was probably pissed, but we have six days to play it up for the cameras.

I needed to get some sleep. I'm working the cruise.

The strawberry blonde.

I should find out her name.

That's probably a good place to start.

LAUREL

"**GOOD MORNING AND WELCOME** to the second day aboard the Solu Cruise to Lose! I don't know about you, but my waistband is already feeling a bit more comfy!"

I turned on the TV, and the cruise director, Lorna Krieger, is on the screen.

"Make her stop!" Viv moans from the bed.

"Today we will be docking at artsy, quirky, and beautiful Key West. Whether you're headed ashore for beach time, shopping on historic Duval Street, or jetting off for an excursion, you're sure to have a fabulous time. Maybe we'll catch sight of Luka Harris out surfing the waves at Lux Beach, the private beach owned by the operator of the *Extravagance*, Lux Cruise Lines! But please remember, do not take any Solu off the ship. Right now, Lux Lines has the exclusive right to offer you Solu, and we don't want to share!" She winks.

Viv throws her pillow at the screen.

I shut the TV off.

"Ugh," she says when I open our window shades. "How can she be so chirpy? What time is it?"

"Nine. She's chirpy because she didn't stay out all night partying."

"How you feeling?" Viv asks.

"Meh," I say.

I had hoped my seasickness was gone, but as soon as I set my feet on the floor, the lining of my stomach came up to say howdy to the bottom of my throat.

"I gotta get off this ship," I say.

"Nice," Viv says. "My dad would love to hear that."

"Because of the seasickness," I answer.

"You," Viv says, rolling onto her side and watching me get dressed, "are basically famous. Everyone kept asking me who you were and how do you know Baby Tom-Tom and was the whole thing planned. I need coffee."

"Settle for a Diet Pip?" I ask.

"Okay."

I hand her one. I see that whoever turned the bed down last night also refilled our mini-fridge.

I make a mental note to take a couple ginger ales when I go ashore. We might have to pay for stuff on the island and I'd better save my fifty.

Viv cracks the top on the soda, as I put on my navy one-piece and pull on my jeans shorts. Over this I wear a faded white jeans shirt.

"Are you really not going to tell me about it?" she finally says.

I shrug.

"You didn't like it?"

I sit on the floor to pull on a pair of hot-pink knee-high socks. There's a hole in one toe, of course.

"LAUREL! What was the kiss like?"

I sigh and lie back on the fluffy-soft carpet.

"It was amazing," I say.

Viv echoes my sigh.

"It looked amazing. So romantic."

We both sigh together. (Oh, brother.)

"No. Actually. That's the problem." I sit up. "There was noth-ing romantic about it! He didn't actually even *want* to kiss me. It was Mustache Rich, the publicity genius of the universe."

"What are you talking about?"

"After Tom crashed into me, Rich said, 'Kiss her!' It was just to distract everyone from the fact that Tom fell during his big show-off dance."

"That dance was awesome!" Viv objects.

"Viv, he kissed me to cover up for his goof. That's all. There's nothing between us."

"It didn't look like that," she says.

I pull on my cowboy boots. I feel like I need a sharp toe today.

"Really? Cowboy boots? We're in Key West. Have you never met a flip-flop?" she complains.

"I'm going to go to the buffet to get some fruit. Do you want anything?"

"Yeah—whatever they have with Solu. I swear, Laur, I'm los-ing weight already."

"You're beautiful already. You're perfect the way you are."

"Yeah, yeah, yeah. I didn't see any former child stars tack-ling *me* on the dance floor," she says, shooing me off.

"By accident," I add.

"By accident, by choice. You're lucky and you don't even care," she says.

"I'm so lucky I'm going to spend the rest of the cruise avoid-ing him."

Viv throws her second pillow at my head.

I read in the leather guidebook in our room that there's a buffet breakfast available on the pool deck each morning.

I'm alone, standing at the head of the buffet, and trying to decide if my stomach will allow me anything more substantial than honeydew melon, when I hear an argument coming from behind a swinging metal door. It must lead into some kind of small kitchen.

"You should put him ashore," a female voice says.

"Please! I did nothing! I did nothing!" a man pleads. "I'm just crabby in the morning. I just needed some coffee!"

"You threatened me with a knife!" the lady snipes.

I don't mean to eavesdrop, but a knife?!

The door has that one little window that waiters see through when coming and going, but I can't see anyone. I hear three voices, though.

"It was just in my hand! This was just a little kitchen tiff. It was nothing! I just need a cup of coffee to settle my nerves."

A waiter asks if I need anything. I shake my head and smile.

He goes in the service door and I get a glimpse of a skinny, scruffy man clutching a crumpled chef's hat and a plump, self-satisfied-looking female chef. They're both pleading with a ship's officer with his back to me.

The door swings shut again.

"Francois, when's the last time you ate?" the officer asks the male chef.

"I'm tasting food all day long."

"He's tasting the *desserts* all day long," the female chef says snarkily. "The ones with Solu. He tells the rest of us not to eat them, because Solu's too expensive. But then he eats them when we're not looking."

"This one," growls the man, "she wants to be the head pastry chef. That's what *she's* after!"

I take a bowl and pick out some strawberries, blueberries, and melon. I'm loitering. (I hope not *too* obviously.)

"The two of you, get yourselves together!" The officer raises his voice. The bickering chefs fall silent, abashed.

A couple of silver-haired passengers grab plates from next to me and start to take food.

I prod at some pineapple with the pincers, stalling.

"Solu is not for the staff!" the chef states.

"But lots of staff are having it!" Francois whines.

"Then you get them to stop!" the officer orders. "Francois, take the day off. Stay in your room. Rest. Don't have any Solu, for God's sake. Eat three square meals. I'm sure you'll be better tomorrow."

"Yes, sir, but can I—" Francois begs.

"Can you what?"

"Can I just get some coffee please? Just one packet of Solu? Please?!"

"Good morning, miss!" comes a cheerful voice.

I turn.

It's Jaideep.

"May I bring you something from the kitchen?" he asks.

I shake my head, but I can feel a blush creeping up my neck. That blush always gives me away.

One of the kitchen doors swings open and the officer looks out. He catches my eye. I can see him wonder how long I've been standing there.

Jaideep sees the officer and sort of straightens up.

"No, no," I say. "I actually—do you have any toast?"

"Of course, madam," Jaideep says, using a more formal tone. "Would you prefer white, whole wheat, sourdough, or rye?"

"Oh. Sourdough," I say.

"If you would like to have a seat, it will be my pleasure to bring it to you."

"Thank you," I say.

He gives me a wink.

I proceed down the buffet line and see at the end a special table with a lavender tablecloth—lavender's the official color of Solu, I guess. It's the color on the packets.

On the table is a tray with mini-muffins. A little sign says, SWEETENED WITH SOLU!

I take two for Viv.

They look really yummy. I pick one up and smell it. Cinnamon and nutmeg.

My mouth starts watering.

I guess I *am* ready to eat again.

But before I pop it into my mouth, I stop.

I don't know . . .

What do we know about this stuff, anyway?

I think I'll wait for my toast.

TOM

THE *EXTRAVAGANCE* HAS ITS OWN BEACH.

That's where we head to tape, after a brief waste of time on Key West's famous Duval Street.

The street was crowded with tourists from other ships who kept photo-bombing the hell out of me.

"Baby Tom-Tom!"

One after another.

I nearly strangled some fraternity wipe wearing a backward baseball cap who kept sneaking into the shot and pretending to jerk off.

This is more like it.

The ship has set up lounge chairs and striped umbrellas all along the beach.

Uniformed attendants are fetching drinks and snacks for the *Extravagance* passengers.

"Day Two on the Solu cruise and spirits are high!" I say.

As if on cue, the crowd behind me erupts into laughter.

"Last night, me and four hundred and ninety-nine of my closest friends had our first taste of Solu, the new sweetener that not only tastes delicious, just like sugar, but helps you lose weight.

"We're here on Key West at Lux Beach, the sunny, white-sand beaches owned by Lux Cruise Lines."

A middle-aged couple with deep tans crosses nearby. I wave them over.

"Scale of one to ten, what would you give the cruise so far?"

The woman flashes me a smile. With her mouth. The rest of her face? Not moving so much. Botox. No question.

"I have already lost two pounds," she says. "We've been on the cruise for one night. I'm floored!"

Then I see her! I see the girl from last night. My strawberry blonde. She's headed down the beach.

"Awesome," I tell the tan woman. "Enjoy the day!"

I hold my pose, waiting for Tamara to call cut.

The couple kind of look at each other, startled I've pulled the plug on the interview. After a moment, they wander away.

"Cut. What's wrong with you? They were good. They looked good," Tamara says.

"Give me five," I say.

"We just started!"

I head over to the girl. She and her friend are looking for chairs.

"Hey," I call. I up my walk to a jog, my flip-flops kind of slowing me down in the thick white sand.

I kick them off and scoop them into one hand.

"Hey!" I repeat, louder.

The girl puts her hand up to shade her eyes from the sun.

She's carrying something slung over her shoulder and I see now it's a pair of cowboy boots.

"Oh God," she says, when she sees it's me.

She fumbles her boots and drops them, then she sits on a lounge chair and then stands back up, all in the space of five seconds.

"Hi," I say.

"Yeah, hi," she answers.

We just stand there.

I'm about to ask her for her name when she interrupts me:

"Do you want to go first or do I have to go first?"

"Doing what?" I say. "Talking?"

"No. Apologizing." She exhales. "Okay. I'll go first. I'm sorry I threw up on your shoes."

"Hey, no problem. They were from wardrobe."

She cocks her head.

"They weren't mine," I clarify. "I don't own anything I wear when I'm on screen."

She lifts an eyebrow. Very delicate eyebrow, blond, almost not there at all.

I continue, "As for me, I'm really sorry I knocked you down."

She nods for me to continue.

"I can't believe I fell like that. I've been practicing that set for, well, for a really long time in private and for some reason I thought last night would be a good time to debut it. I felt like such a jerk. I'm really sorry."

Then she stands there, waiting for more.

Her friend has doubled back to us by now. She stands about five feet away, gawking at me.

I give her a little wave.

My strawberry blonde is wearing a blue bathing suit that's pretty conservative, but her body looks great. She has that kind of skin that's freckled on the top of her arms, but is creamy white on the undersides. She's very curvy.

She starts to blush. Maybe I'm being too obvious, checking her out.

I give her my lopsided grin. I'm surprised to find my heart's beating fast.

"Usually, before I crush a girl on the dance floor, I like to ask her name—" I say.

It feels good to flirt. Like actually flirt and mean it.

But she turns her back on me and starts to walk away.

"Hey!" I call. "Wait! What'd I do wrong?"

"If you don't know, I'm not telling you."

I stumble after her. Hit my shin on a stupid lounge chair.

"Ow! Wait. Please wait!" I call.

She stops and turns back to me. I hop toward her and she steps up close.

Her face is bright red. She's either blushing like crazy or has developed a sudden third-degree sunburn.

"You should apologize for kissing me," she whispers. She looks into my eyes. Hers are blue—light blue, almost gray. "It was embarrassing to me, to be kissed in a crowd like that. For a publicity stunt."

Honestly, my mouth falls open. I feel like a total moron.

"I'm sorry," I say. And I really am.

It never occurred to me that anyone wouldn't want to be kissed in public. It never occurred to me that any girl—any girl who was rich enough or famous enough or powerful enough to be on the *Extravagance*—would be shy.

I think this girl is shy.

I feel like I have never met a shy person in my entire life.

I fumble for an excuse—an explanation. "I did it . . . I did it on the spur of the moment and because Rich told me to, but you're right, it was a lousy thing to do."

She shrugs.

I have the idiotic urge to hug her.

"Okay," she says. "I accept your apology."

"TOM!" I hear Tamara shouting to me. "That five's turning into a twenty!"

"I have to go," I say.

I turn around. I think, the sooner I get away from this girl the better. She's making me act weird. I don't like it.

"I'm Laurel," she says, as I go.

I turn. Awkwardly stick out my hand. "Yeah, Tom. Tom Fiorelli."

She puts her hand in mine and my hand is a mitt compared to hers. Her hand is soft and fine with long fingers. The tips of her fingers are calloused.

I want to touch them, to figure out why they're like that.

"TOM!" Tamara hollers.

"Okay," I say. "Good."

Laurel and her friend are probably laughing their asses off as I walk back through the sand to where Tamara is waiting for me.

What the hell just happened?

Tamara takes a bottle of water from a bag, walks over, and hands it to me.

"Stay focused, Tom," Tamara says.

"Yeah, yeah," I say.

"I mean it," she insists. She slides her sunglasses down her nose and peers at me. "Remember how much we have riding on this. This is the gig that catapults you to a national spotlight. They're looking at you for *American Idol*, you know that."

"No one's gonna bump Seacrest out," I say.

She raises an eyebrow at me.

I look away. I haven't really told Tamara that I still want to do film.

After the disaster with *Double Fang*, my mom and I decided not to pursue any legit jobs for a while. But this hosting stuff—I don't like it. It feels fake. It *is* fake.

And I think Tamara has a hunch I feel this way.

"Let me put it another way, this is the gig that'll give you the freedom to start picking and choosing projects," she says.

She takes the bottle of water away from me.

"So can I get your A game now?"

"Yeah," I say. "Sorry."

LAUREL

TOM HEADS AWAY AND VIV GRABS MY ARM. Her fingers dig into my flesh hard.

"I cannot believe that just happened!" she says. "You just, like, leveled Baby Tom-Tom."

"Vivika, please."

"He was putting the moves on you and you just, like, did some kind of girl-judo on him. Laurel Willard emotional judo."

I sink down onto the nearest lounge chair.

"We need drinks! That's what we need!"

She starts waving at a server.

Viv was right, I do need a drink.

Viv orders two piña coladas and the server does not raise an eyebrow. I'm getting the feeling that while they won't stock our mini-fridge with liquor, no one on the staff is going to deny us anything we want from the bar.

I sip the piña colada carefully. It ain't a virgin.

"He's totally into you!" Viv keeps saying. She keeps talking about how awesome I was and how awkward he looked until I reach over and put my hand on her shoulder.

"Viv, can you please shut up?"

"Probably not," she says.

Then, happily, she's distracted because Sabbi and her posse of beautifuls are strolling toward us on the beach. Sabbi is wearing a tiny bikini and a giant hat (must have been in one of her hatboxes).

Tom is still taping, a little ways ahead of us.

I see Sabbi see him, but his back is to her.

Sabbi steps into the water and kicks water onto one of her friends.

The friend squeals and splashes her back.

Suddenly it's a big splash fight and Sabbi's white bathing suit cover-up gets all plastered to her body.

I see Tom's cameraman start to shoot her and her group frolicking in the waves.

"Think I'll go for a swim," Viv says.

"Go get 'em," I tell her.

She wants to hang out with Sabbi.

I don't really approve, but she knows that. Anyway, she doesn't need my approval.

Viv makes her way down the beach. She's not the only one. Some other young people from the boat are drawn to Sabbi's group, too.

Why wouldn't they want to be on TV, splashing around, having fun?

Why am I so different from them?

Another question—Why couldn't I have lied to Tom Fiorelli about the stupid kiss? Why couldn't I just have played it cool, like the kiss meant nothing? Like I wasn't upset?

Why, why, why do I always tell the truth in these situations?

You would think that someone who's sensitive would learn to hide her emotions. That would be smart. But my brain doesn't even fire in those situations—I'm all heart.

Ugh.

Sometimes I exhaust myself.

I see Viv, out dodging waves near Sabbi's crew.

One of the guys—muscular but really short—is talking to her. She splashes him; he does it back.

Good, let her have some fun.

I see Tom and the camera crew are packing up.

I guess they got what they needed.

I reach up and grab the umbrella, snugging it down in the sand so the shade covers me.

So sensitive to everything. Even the stupid sun.

Talking wakes me from my nap.

"It's thirty dollars each," I hear behind me.

Near the palm trees, I see one of the Indian crewman from the *Extravagance* talking to a couple of tourists.

They're not from our cruise. How do I know this? Tacky clothes. (She's wearing a tube top and spandex pedal pushers and he's wearing a giant T-shirt that says, "I rode a Princess," with a cartoon of a man humping a cruise ship.)

"Thirty each one? We will be able to buy them for three dollars a packet on Saturday at midnight!" the woman protests loudly.

"Shhhh! Hey, I'm not supposed to let anyone who's not on the cruise have these," the crewman says.

"We should just wait until midnight Saturday," the woman says. "Walgreens will be open."

"Does it really work?" the man asks.

"It does. The passengers are losing weight remarkably quickly."

"Why would we pay three hundred dollars for what we can buy at the store for thirty on Saturday?" the woman asks.

"To be a part of history," the crewman says. "Sir, you are the one who answered my post on Craigslist. Do you want them or not?"

For a second, I remember the two packets I have in the bottom of my purse.

I could use the money. I could stand up right now and say I'll sell them my two packets for twenty dollars.

It's wrong, but it doesn't seem wrong quite as much as it seems like taking advantage of stupid people. Are these people really that desperate?

Mmmmmmmmmm. I'm kind of tempted.

But Viv comes back, just then, a big smile on her face.

"That guy's funny," she tells me. "Trevor. He kept saying there were crabs biting him and going under and pinching my legs."

I look over the back of my seat, trying to see if the couple bought the Solu.

"Wanna go back to the ship for lunch?" Viv asks.

I look again. The couple is walking away and the crewman has disappeared.

"What are you looking at?"

"A crew member just sold some packets of Solu to people not on the ship, I think."

"Really? Are you kidding me? They can't wait a week?"

Viv towels off.

"Though really, Laurel, I think I'm already losing weight," she says.

"Totally," I say, without really looking.

"No, Laur, really," she says.

And I look at her.

And . . . she has. I can see her belly's a little less bellyish. Her thighs look leaner.

"Wow," I say. "I guess that stuff really works."

"When you're feeling better, you're taking it, right? I mean, you have to!"

I think about the chef I saw.

"Viv, it's safe, right? Solu. I mean, it's been, like, tested, right?"

"No, Laurel, they didn't test it at all. They just, like, mixed some chemicals in a vat and poured it into little purple packets and said, 'Try this!'" She rolls her eyes. "Of *course*, they tested it. I'm sure it's been through every trial known to man. The FDA would never approve it if it weren't safe. Come on!"

"Okay, okay," I say. "I just . . . "

"You just what?" She has her hands on her hips.

If I say anything bad about Solu, it'll hurt her feelings. Her dad paid for us both to come. She's counting on this cruise being a huge, life-transforming experience.

"Nothing," I say. "Hey, what are we doing tonight, anyway?"

"Besides stalking Baby Tom-Tom?" she teases.

"I am not going anywhere near him, Vivika. There's nothing there."

She starts to rib me some more, but I think she can see that I mean it.

"There's this thing called Movies Under the Stars," she tells me. "We watch a film up on that top deck that overlooks the pool."

I give her a grin.

"Sounds perfect!"

And it is.

It's the new romantic comedy with Emma Stone and Chris Helmsworth. It's silly and fun and exactly what I needed.

No Tom Fiorelli and no Sabbi Ribiero, either. At the beginning of the movie, Viv kept craning her neck, trying to see if they were among the eighty or so guests on the deck, but they were nowhere to be found.

The staff came around handing out soft fleece blankets and buckets of popcorn.

I saw Jaideep.

"Hey!" I waved.

"Ah, look at you, out enjoying the evening. I think you are feeling better," he said.

And I realized I did feel better.

At dinner I was actually able to eat some (unbelievably delicious) lobster. After the meal, I pocketed two packets of Solu, like everyone else, but again, I didn't eat the dessert. I think Viv can tell that I'm not so into it, but she didn't question me.

She was too happy to eat my flourless Solu-sweetened chocolate cake!

"This is my friend Viv," I told him. "Jaideep works in the kitchen. We met on the first day."

"Hi! Tell me, Jaideep," Viv said, in a mock-serious tone. "Is this film any good?"

"Sure!" Jaideep said without hesitation. "If you happen to be a girl."

We laughed. Jaideep handed us an extra popcorn and headed off.

"Enjoy the show, ladies!" he called.

And we really did.

T O M

I WORK OUT HARD when the day's shoot is wrapped.

I only have an hour and a half because Almstead's asked me to dine with him at his personal table and he eats at five thirty.

Why do old people eat so early?

I call Derek while I pick out what to wear.

"Tom-ass! How's it going?" he says.

I can hear the grin in his voice.

So it can be dangerous to make friends with the people you pay. I learned that the hard way. But Derek's different.

There were years when my mom would try to bribe kids to be my friends. Like the time she said to these three skateboarders at the park, who I didn't even know: "You know, all Tom's friends this year will be invited to our place for a gaming party—and everyone will go home with their very own Xbox!"

And there I was, ten years old, fat and miserable, standing off to the side, wanting to die.

"Come ride my board!" they called. "Dude, I love that show you're on!"

I made my mom take me home.

At least I had that much pride.

But things were always different with me and Derek.

"How was the day?" he asks me.

I tell him, recount my food.

"I'm eating in the steak house tonight," I tell him.

"They always serve grilled chicken in a steak house," he tells me. "And hey, dude, you have to call your mom. She called *me*, asking how you are."

"Sorry," I say.

"Please tell me you'll call her. ASAP."

I pull a sports coat out of the closet. It's just a Jack Spade—nothing fancy—but I really like the cut. I pick out a pair of dark jeans to go with.

"How's that girl?" he asks. "Freckles."

"I made such an ass out of myself," I say. "It's probably best if I never talk to her again."

"You definitely have to talk to her again."

"You know, I think she's shy. You know what I mean? She, like, doesn't want to be the center of attention."

"Rare breed," Derek says. "I like her more and more."

We hang up and I make the dreaded call.

"Really?" my mom says by way of answering. "I have to wait two days to hear about the cruise of the century? From my own son?"

"Hey," I say. "Sorry. It's been very hectic."

"I guess it's a rough life," she says.

My mom has a way of making everything, even something undeniably awesome, sound like a drag.

"I'm having dinner with the head of Pipop and Solu tonight," I tell her. "So things are going pretty well."

"Tell him I hate the new Diet Pip. They have to bring back the old one."

"I'll tell him."

"The coverage looks good, but I'm not crazy about your forehead."

"Thanks, Mom. I'm not crazy about yours, either."

"You know what I mean. It's greasy. Tell Tamara you need more powder."

"Will do."

I pick out a nice gray shirt to go with the jacket.

"Hey, I'm running late."

"All right. Well, Susanna called. MTV is jerking us around on *Spring Break*. They don't see their way to raising your fee and I told Susanna—"

I just uh-huh and okay my way through the rest of the conversation.

My mom can't seem to let go of control. We agreed that Tamara would come on as my manager, but my mom still insists all the calls from my agent go through her.

This is the year I tell my mom I don't want her to be involved in running my business anymore.

I've been telling myself that since I turned fourteen.

I think my problem is this image I get of her, sitting in the home office she had built into our big Brentwood house. She's got this large wooden desk and framed photos of me on different gigs, with different stars, on all the walls.

I see her there, with the phones dead, just sitting there. It's too sad.

The smell of steak is intense. How am I going to not eat a steak? Grilled chicken. Thanks, Derek.

I'm the first to arrive, but the waiter knows to lead me right to the best table. Crisp linen tablecloth, real silver flatware. Each table lit with a small, antique oil-burning lamp. The steak house is on Deck 11, with a view of the ocean.

This is a classy ship, no doubt about it.

Tamara clearly doesn't approve of my sports coat. I can see it in her face when she arrives with Rich, who is, of course, wearing a suit.

"Tom, I hear the day's shoot went really well," Rich exclaims. "Congratulations."

"It's all Tamara," I say. "She set it all up."

"Oh, shut up, the both of you," Tamara says. But there's a hint of a smile on her face. "Our goal in this meeting is to get to know Almstead better—and find out if there's anything he wants from us that we're not giving him."

"Lord, she's efficient, ain't she?" Rich says.

"Nothing but efficient. Literally," I joke.

Tamara narrows her eyes at me. "Wiseass. I need a martini," Tamara says, waving for a waiter. "Diet Pip for you, Tom?"

"I'll take a soda water with lime."

"Here he is," Rich says under his breath.

Mr. Almstead has entered the steak house, flanked by his burly assistant.

Darn it. Almstead's wearing a three-piece suit with a tie.

There are a bunch of other diners, even at this ungodly hour, and each of them stops Almstead to shake his hand and thank him as he makes his way over to us.

"So pleased you three could join me," Almstead chirps as he draws close.

"Good evening, sir," I say.

We all rise to greet him. Is it right for Tamara to rise? Maybe women are supposed to stay seated? The fine points of etiquette escape me sometimes. But Tamara's up and shaking his hand.

"Please, sit down. Don't make a fuss," he says.

The assistant holds Almstead's cane and helps Almstead by pulling back his chair.

Then the big brute just . . . stands there.

"Will your assistant be joining us?" Rich asks, nodding toward the monster.

"Oh no. Amos is built like a brick shithouse. He could stand there all night and not move an inch, isn't that right, Amos?"

"Yes, sir."

Almstead waggles his eyebrows.

"He used to say 'Sir, yes, sir.' We're not fooling anyone, are we?" he asks. "Amos is a former marine. I'm afraid my board of directors has strongly recommended I have a bodyguard. It makes me feel silly, but maybe you read about the attack."

I had.

"This deranged guy insisted that his obese wife's death was due to a soda-pop addiction and tried to take me out with a sawed-off shotgun."

"It was an outrage," Rich says.

"Very disturbing," Tamara agrees.

"I've said it a million times," Almstead says. "It's soda! If you don't want to be fat, don't drink it!"

A waiter hands us menus.

God, the steaks.

Twelve-ounce porterhouse. Eight-ounce filets. A twenty-ounce New York strip.

Grrr.

"Now more states are proposing those ridiculous regulations on the sizes of drinks stores can sell!" Tamara says.

"Oh, those bother the board, all right, but I don't pay them any mind. People want what they want, and they're willing to do just about anything to get it, most times. A man thirsty for twenty-four ounces of pop, why he'll just buy two sixteen-ounce bottles, drink the extra and be all the happier."

"Look at this!" the guy at the table next to us exclaims. The waiter is setting down a beautiful steak in front of the man. It's the twenty-ounce strip, has to be. It's sizzling hot. The smell of crackling butter radiates from it.

The waiter sets a seafood risotto in front of the man's wife.

My mouth waters.

Our waiter approaches and asks for our orders.

Derek would be so proud, I order a chicken breast and steamed vegetables.

Almstead looks at me with surprise.

"You can't be trying to reduce!" he exclaims. "You on a diet, Fiorelli?"

"No, sir," I say. "It's just . . . every morning I make a food plan and I stick to it."

Almstead starts clapping.

"That's the way! I can't tell you how much I respect that! Say there," he calls to the waiter. "Change my order. I'll have what he's having."

The waiter nods politely. "Very good, sir."

"I hate it when they don't write down the orders," Almstead says. "They think they're being fancy, but something always gets messed up."

"Mr. Almstead, Tom and I were wondering if there's any particular element to the story behind Solu that you'd like us to focus on in the next few days," Tamara says.

"You're doing great. We just want people to know it works and it's safe," Almstead says. "And they can see that from your footage. Seeing is believing!"

"We just wanted to make sure because . . . well . . . you may have seen the *New Yorker* article," Rich says delicately. "They focus on your involvement, putting forward the idea that you invested in Solu because of some kind of guilt about the role that Pipop has played in the obesity epidemic."

"Bull crap!" Almstead says. "I don't feel guilty about our pop. Never have. I invested in Solu because I know business!

"You know, when I was young, we had nicknames that didn't lie. They weren't 'ironic.' If you were short, they called you Shorty. If you were fat, they called you Fatty, or Piggie or Lardy or Oinkers. If you had a gimpy right arm they called you Lefty. If you had one eye you were Dead-Eye.

"You know what I was called?"

We shake our heads.

It occurs to me that we don't really have to talk at all at this meal. Almstead likes to grandstand. He just wants an audience.

Seems like lots of old people are like this.

"I was Oinkers. Yep, I know I don't look it now, but I was round as a pumpkin."

"I guess you and I have that in common, sir," I venture. "I had a little trouble with weight when I was a kid, too."

I give him a smile.

Almstead looks at me blankly for a second, then snaps his fingers. "That's right, you were a tubby little sucker, weren't you?"

I thought we'd bond about it, but the way he says "tubby little sucker" makes me feel kind of pissed.

"I bet I know what happened to you," he goes on. "Girls! You realized you'd never have a shot so you leaned down. Am I right?"

I shrug. "Sort of."

Here Almstead's eyes flash to the man at the table next to us. The man has cut off a piece of steak that's too big and is chewing with his mouth partly open.

Disgust flashes over Almstead's face.

"No, the Oinkers of the world need a solution. And Solu is the solution. Plain and simple."

Tamara raises her glass. "To Solu!"

We all toast.

"I'll tell you what, you can talk about this in your press releases and whatnot—Pipop started out as medicine. I bet you didn't know that. My grandfather, Thomas Almstead, was a druggist and a general-store owner. And he mixed up Pipop as a nerve tonic."

"That's so cool," I say.

"We can definitely use that," Tamara says.

"Pipop was *his* contribution; Solu is *my* contribution!" Almstead says.

Four waiters arrive in tandem, setting down our covered plates and removing the silver domes in unison.

As I look at my chicken, I guess I look a bit down in the mouth.

Almstead laughs at my expression.

"Cheer up, son!" he says. "There's always tomorrow."

I smile.

"Yeah," I say. "I think steak is on the meal plan for tomorrow."

"I'll drink to that!" Almstead hoots.

He's a funny guy.

I like him. Kind of.

LAUREL

IN THE MORNING, I tell Viv I *have* to practice my guitar, and it's true. She tells me she *has* to get more sleep. So I leave the room.

I'm working on a Bach prelude. It's impossibly hard and I'm horrible at it, but I'm hoping that practice will make (not perfect but) marginally acceptable.

I need that scholarship. Pensacola University has a pretty good program in classical guitar. Vivika thinks I should audition for Juilliard, but she doesn't know what she's talking about. (And it's, like, fifty thousand dollars a year. And it's really far away from home. And it's in New York City.)

The ship is designed so that there are little private areas dotted around the upper deck, at the back of the ship. I find one of these and plunk myself down.

I was worried that my playing might disturb the other passengers, but about a half hour ago, this girl came over near me and sat down. I know she's listening to me, but she's pretending like she's reading a *Teen Vogue*. She's just a kid and must weigh 350 pounds. (If Solu works for anyone, I hope it works for her.)

I sort of want to strike up a conversation and advise her to ditch the *Teen Vogue*. I mean, why's she torturing herself? Even a size 0 would feel depressed after reading that rag.

But the Bach. The Bach calls.

I'm working the piece backward, the way Mrs. Sandstrom wants me to.

There's this tripping little phrase.

I just work it. Repeat. Bee dee-dee-dee. Bee dee-dee-dee. Bee dee-dee-dee.

I should apologize to the girl listening, but I didn't ask her to sit near me. And I really want to nail it. Bee dee-dee-dee. Bee dee-dee-dee. Bee dee-dee-dee. I go for speed.

"Whoa!"

I look up.

It's Tom Fiorelli, and for some reason, he is holding a tray with a white teapot and a cup and saucer on it.

"That is some serious guitar playing."

He's grinning at me.

Damn blush. It spreads instantly. I can feel that my face and neck are turning beet red.

"It's Bach," I say. "I mean, it's just one phrase I'm having trouble with. From Bach."

"It sounds . . . well, it sounds insane, but I'm sure the rest of the piece is really awesome."

"It is!" says the girl. "And she plays it really good."

"Hi, oh, hey! We met yesterday, didn't we?" Tom says to the girl.

"You interviewed me! I'm Claire," she says. She's grinning broadly at Tom.

"I remember."

While he's not looking my way, it's easier to study him.

It takes some time to get used to seeing someone in person you've only ever seen on screen.

It's hard to explain how handsome this guy is.

It starts at the eyes, which are light hazel, and fringed by impossibly dark lashes. Thick eyebrows. His skin is tan, with a trace of stubble at the chin.

"I got a message from my friends. They totally saw me on TV! They said it was awesome," Claire says.

"Cool. Well, tell them I say hi," Tom says to the girl and turns back to me.

His hazel eyes are twinkly, glittery.

"So I made this for you," he says, setting down the tray on the small table next to my chair. "It's fresh ginger tea with honey and pepper. Whenever I'd get sick on set, they'd make me this in craft services. It really helps to settle your stomach. I thought it might help."

He made me tea?!

"That's really nice of you," I say.

I stand up and lift the lid of the teapot. The spicy smell of ginger comes wafting up.

We're standing pretty close. Almost too close, but it would be weird to sit down now.

Claire is peeking over the top of her lounge chair, like a little kid in a restaurant booth.

It makes me blush harder.

"How did you make it?" I ask. "Did you go in the kitchen?"

"No," he says. "I asked my room steward to bring me hot water and ginger with my breakfast."

"Oh," I say.

(I should say something besides *oh*.)

Why can't I think of anything to say?

"Well, it's really nice of you."

"Thanks," he says. He sticks his hands in his pockets.

(Think of something to say, Laurel!!!)

"Well, I hope you feel better," he says.

"Thanks," I say. "You're nice."

(I am an idiot! Be interesting! Say something real!)

"Thanks," he says.

He looks somewhat bemused.

I hear a digital lens click and see that Claire's taken a photo of us on her iPhone.

It seems that every embarrassing moment I have with Tom Fiorelli will be in the public eye.

Claire's probably about to tweet our conversation. #SoluGossip. #TomFiorelliAndSomeLoser. #SheCan'tHoldARegularConversationWithAGorgeousGuy.

Tom looks at my face and reads my expression.

"Hey, Claire, can I ask a favor?" he says, flashing her a smile. "Could you delete that picture? Laurel's not really into that social media stuff. Instead, let's take one of us together."

Claire beams at her idol. "Sure! Really? Okay!"

Tom crosses to her chair and takes the phone from her.

"I have longer arms!" he explains.

He holds his arm out, slightly above them, and takes a shot.

"You always want to shoot just slightly from above," he tells her. "This is something I've learned. Makes you look tough."

They're both relaxed and smiling.

"Nobody's tougher than us," Claire jokes.

"That's right. Tom and Claire, swaggin' and braggin'!"

They take another shot, trying to look tough.

Claire is giggling so hard she nearly drops the phone when Tom hands it back.

"My friends are going to die!"

Tom turns back to me.

"So, I hope you feel better," he says.

"Yes," I say. "I will."

"Cool," he says. "It's . . . it's okay I brought you the tea, right?"

"Okay? Yes. Super-yes. It's probably the nicest thing a guy has ever done for me."

"Well, that was too easy. I'll have to try to top myself next time."

Eep. Um. Blush. Tingles. (I am a mess.)

"Okay. Good."

Claire is just watching us like we're a movie or something.

"See you two!" he calls as he walks away.

"Thanks for the selfies!" Claire says.

Claire and I watch him walk around the side of the ship until he's gone.

"He is the most beautiful thing I have ever seen in my whole life." Claire sighs.

I sit down.

"Yeah," I say.

I feel like I'm a little bit high. And it's not from the ginger-scented steam rising from my teapot.

TOM

THAT'S MY A GAME.

Not that I'm playing the girl. But I like her. So if I like her, then I'm going to show up and let her know.

I have a feeling Derek would approve.

The day's interviews are weird.

Tamara has me changing clothes all day. I've literally worn four different shirts. I understand about getting coverage, but this is a little ridiculous.

Tamara's also lined up gorgeous people, almost exclusively.

"Don't we want to show some real body types?" I ask her. "I mean, these people all look like they don't even need Solu. Don't we want to see some transformation happening?"

"Almstead wants some segments with very pretty people saying that Solu works. I don't think that's unreasonable," Tamara says.

She grooms my hair, spraying some sea salt stuff in it and tousling it.

"What we need now is a generic open for a segment wrapping up Day Six," Tamara tells me.

"Day *Six*? Why?"

"During the fifth and sixth days, the ship will have limited satellite access. It will take a very long time to transmit the footage, so we're shooting some extra coverage. The editors are going to put it together as a fail-safe."

I catch Cubby's eye. He shrugs.

"Day Six? That just seems wrong," I say.

"Please, Tom. This is what our client wants."

"So I'm going to lie?"

"You're an actor," she says, as if I need reminding. "So act. Roll tape."

"I'm Tom Fiorelli, coming to you from the decks of the *Extravagance*. It's Day Six of the Solu cruise, and wow, we have seen some powerful transformations on board! Take a look."

My mouth feels oily.

I signal for them to cut.

"What will they go to?" I ask, thinking of the editors. "We don't know what people are going to look like on Day Six."

"They're going to do shots of skinny girls swimming in the pool, if they have to. We're just prerecording so they have backups. It's not a conspiracy, Tom. Lighten up."

"Okay, Tamara. It's just not good television."

"Sabbi Ribiero is fine with it."

"What do you mean?"

"We're interviewing her this afternoon and she's agreed to say it's Day Six."

I roll my eyes.

Sabbi Ribiero is probably getting paid a million dollars to be on board. She'll say whatever they want.

Me, I'm getting paid $250K for this whole gig.

And I guess I'll say whatever they want, too.

"Speaking of Sabbi, her people are wondering what the hell is going on. Sabbi was very upset you didn't join her for dinner last night."

"I was with you at dinner! We ate with Almstead."

"Her people are pissed. Are you doing this or not?"

I shrug.

"Well, I hope you make up your mind by five p.m. That's when we shoot her."

We do a set of poolside interviews and people are really wild, pushing one another in the pool behind me, and photo-bombing. I guess they're all drunk.

The partiers are not just the teenagers on the ship; I see a bunch of older people, too. Thirty-, forty-, fifty-year-old guys ogling the younger girls. Cougars on the prowl.

Everyone is in a great mood.

I'm talking to three middle-aged Australian women in bikinis. They're raving about Solu. We have to shout to be heard over the crowd.

"It's amazing!" a bleached blonde says, grabbing my mike.

"You wouldna believe how much weight I've lost!" another yells, reaching across me to get the mike. As she reaches, her bikini top straps slide off her shoulders. Momentarily topless, she screams. They all scream in delight.

The woman hauls the top back up.

"That's what I'm talking about!" she yells. "This fit me two days ago!"

"Wow!" I say. I laugh. "As you can see, Solu is working almost too well here on the pool deck of the *Extravagance*!"

The three women are hugging me and kissing me and screaming about Solu.

I hear "cut" and I mouth to Tamara, *Get me out of here!*

I get a break, which I need.

I go to the gym and work out hard.

Sometimes it's the only way to clear my head. Just lift until the endorphins cut in.

Like Derek says, you're going to be addicted to *something*. Might as well make it something that's good for you.

I should call him, but I need to relax.

No, that's not true.

I don't call him because he'd ask me about Sabbi.

And I still don't know what to do about her.

I keep thinking about Laurel, but hey, I just met the girl. And anyway, the Sabbi thing is just for the press.

After a shower, I dress for the interview.

Sabbi is one of the most beautiful girls in the world. I should be psyched.

I try to be.

They've set up a cabana on a balcony on a lower deck.

Sabbi's there already. She looks picture-perfect. She should, with her team of hair and makeup people.

I see one of the guys—I'm guessing he's gay—reach into her bathing suit to arrange her bust. Rich is talking to her and no one even bats an eye, while this wardrobe guy is getting her cleavage just so.

Gotta love this industry.

"Hey, Sabbi," I say, sitting down next to her. "How's it going?"

Sabbi's hair and makeup people and Rich all back away.

"Fine," Sabbi says. "Except I thought we were going to hang out." She bites her lip.

"Totally," I say. "Yes, I'm sorry. These guys keep me jumping all day. They've got me way too busy."

"Well, we've got plenty of time on the cruise, yes?"

She leans over and straightens my collar.

I see Rich snapping shots on his iPhone.

"I've always thought you were so cute, Tom," she says. "I'm really excited to get to know you."

Her giant brown eyes are looking up into mine and I find that I'm starting to relax. She seems genuine.

Tamara comes up.

"So, it's Day Six and everything's gone amazingly well," Tamara reminds me, and Sabbi, I guess. "We just want to hear about how great Solu is. You have to use your imagination a bit, but just go with the idea that Solu has delivered past everyone's wildest dreams."

Whatever.

Sabbi nods. "I can do that!"

"And . . . we're rolling," Tamara says. "Tom, whenever you're ready."

"Hey, everybody, Tom Fiorelli here on Day Six of the Solu Cruise to Lose on the *Extravagance*. Man, the time has *flown* by! It feels like just yesterday I was saying it's Day Two!"

That's for Tamara.

"I'm here with Sabbi Ribiero, one of the stars of *Teens of New York*. Sabbi, can you believe the cruise is almost drawing to a close?"

Sabbi wets her lips and gushes, "Tom, this cruise has been life-changing for me and so many others. We girls, you know, we worry so much about what we can eat. We have to watch our figures for you men!"

"Actually," I say. "I think you have that backward. We watch your figures for you!"

She swipes at me playfully.

"Well, what I'm trying to say is that all that worrying, all that obsessing about weight—we don't have to do it anymore thanks to Solu."

"We have seen some significant weight loss," I lie.

"Everybody is looking fantastic! I mean, I'm seeing fifty-year-old men and just a few days ago, they were looking pretty porky, and now I'm like, who is *that*?!"

Wow. She's amazingly good at this. She just sold all the men in America on Solu.

"Sabbi, what about the cruise itself? The service? The meals?"

"Oh, the food, the porters, everything. They've done an amazing job. I will never go on any cruise ship besides the Lux Line in my life ever."

The cruise people are going to love that.

"So what's your favorite thing about Solu?"

There's a gleam in her eye as she answers.

"It's funny, because I imagine you will think I'm going to say it's the weight loss. But you know what, it's not that. Solu makes you feel good. It makes you feel special and alive."

Sabbi gestures me close to her and leans in to the camera, tilting her body slightly so the camera gets more cleavage.

"I think there's something in the Solu itself, that makes you feel just a little, itsy, bitsy bit . . . "

She purses her lips, then releases them. She shivers.

"Excited."

Tamara gives me two thumbs way, way up and I know Sabbi just earned her million dollars.

And my respect.

She is a pro.

"It's really true, what they say," Sabbi continues, " 'Solu: Life's delicious.' "

And she worked their ad slogan in?! I'm blown away.

The thing is—I'm not into her.

I'm not.

I can't fake it.

I'm sitting here thinking about Laurel and that if she knew that I was contemplating this thing with Sabbi . . .

Well, it would hurt her feelings, for one.

And she'd probably think I was sleazy.

Because . . . because it *is* sleazy. It's fake to pretend you like someone so people will take your picture and help you stay famous.

Seems like something I should have figured out a good long while ago.

Sabbi looks at me as her wardrobe guy fishes the lav mic out of her bust.

"That was fun," she says.

I'm going to have to figure out how to tell Sabbi.

I think a call to Derek is in high order.

I smile at Sabbi.

"That was great!" I tell her. "You're amazing."

"Mmm, I was beginning to wonder when you'd figure that out!" she says with a wink.

I kiss her hand and get the hell out of there.

LAUREL

LAST NIGHT A LITTLE CARD was set on our (luxurious, fabulously plump) pillows along with the Solu chocolate. It was an appointment card informing us that our weigh-in time for today is 10:00 a.m.

Viv is super-excited about it.

I am not so excited. Of course, I haven't lost any weight, so why would I be? But Viv reminds me that getting weighed every other day is actually mandatory—we signed an agreement when her dad bought the tickets that we'd participate.

"Are you sure you don't want a little muffin?" she asked me at breakfast. They were giving each passenger two little Solu muffins each.

"I know it works fast, but I don't think it'll help me lose weight between now and ten a.m!" I said.

"You never know!" she said with a grin.

It's nice to see her so happy.

I wave off the muffins. Really, I'm just not into it.

I do have about ten packets of Solu squirreled away in an unused airsickness baggie.

(Just in case I overcome my morals and have the chance to sell them in Cozumel.)

I put them in the safe in our room. I didn't want Viv to see them. I think she's still a little mad that I'm not taking them.

And it was fun to program the safe.

I made "BOOTS" the code.

They've made a treatment room in the (world-class) spa into a weigh-in center.

It reminds me of a fancy version of Weight Watchers. (Viv made me go with her for two months in seventh grade.)

The same scale from the gangplank is set up here.

"Good morning!" A sixty-something woman with maroon-colored hair greets us. (Hello, Clairol.) "How are y'all feeling today?"

"I feel fantastic!" Viv gushes. "I'm so happy!"

"That's what we like to hear!"

Maroon-Hair Lady swipes Vivika's ID card and then motions for Viv to step onto the scale.

"Oh my goodness. Can you step off and step on again, dear?"

Viv darts a questioning look at me, steps off the scale and back on.

"Hun, you have lost thirteen pounds!" the lady says.

Viv's mouth drops open.

"Oh my God!!!" she squeals. She pulls me into a crushing hug.

"Thirteen pounds! I can't believe it!"

Maroon-Hair Lady beams. "Hun, body-percentage wise—this is one of the biggest losses we've seen!"

Viv is hugging herself, jumping up and down.

"Before I came on board I thought, 'If I lose five pounds, I'll be happy!' Thirteen pounds! I have to call my dad!"

"Now, I have to ask you—have you been eating more than the recommended three to five servings a day?"

Viv looks at me.

Of course she has.

She has two Solu pastries at breakfast, a Solu dessert at both lunch and dinner *and* they give us two packets at every meal *and* there's that chocolate on our pillows at night.

"Maybe," Viv says. "I'm not sure."

"Well, you know, this is an exciting loss, but I think you're going to want to restrain yourself now. Three to five servings is right for a young woman like yourself. I'd play it safe."

Viv is nodding, nodding, agreeing.

I'm going to have to remind her of what the lady is saying. I can tell Viv is hardly listening.

"Okay, sweetie," the lady says to me. "Why don't you step up here and let's see what Solu's done for you!"

I step on.

(Cue a comic wah-wah-wah.)

"Well now, huh," she says. "It must be the boots. Remove your shoes, honey."

"But I was wearing them when I got weighed the first time," I point out.

"Is that right?" The lady looks bereaved. "Well, I'm stumped. This is not at all what I expected."

She looks at me, like she's a doctor giving news of a fatal illness. "Sweet girl, you have lost seven ounces so far."

"That's what I expected," I say, but she rushes on.

"Tell me about your experience with Solu. Have you been taking the recommended dosage?"

"My friend was really seasick," Viv butts in. "And she hasn't been able to take her doses yet. But she's feeling better, right, Laurel?"

"I guess so—"

"Oh! That's a relief!" Maroon-Hair Lady gushes. "I haven't had anyone fail yet this morning. I don't want you to be the first one."

Fail? That seems a little harsh.

"She's going to take it at lunch, right, Laurel?"

"I don't know—"

"You could up the doses, just a bit," the lady says.

She pats me on the butt.

"You've got some tub to lose."

She wrinkles her nose.

"Solu will just nip away the extra, you'll see."

Viv bundles me out into the hall.

"Thirteen pounds!" she marvels.

"'Nip away the extra,'" I say. "I hate that woman. She called me tubby."

"Laur! Thirteen pounds."

"I'm a failure because I didn't drop a bunch of weight?"

"She just wants you to get to feel what everyone's feeling!" Viv says.

"Maybe I'm happy the way I am! Maybe I don't want to feel what everyone's feeling," I grump.

"Laurel!"

"Well, I don't!"

"No, of course, why would you?" Viv says.

She crosses her arms.

"Laurel Willard is not like anyone else. She's different."

I do not like the tone her voice is taking.

"She has to practice her classical guitar. She always wears boots even when it's not appropriate. The cutest guy ever invented wants to get to know her, but she won't have him. No, she's above it all. She's soooo superior."

"You're being a jerk," I tell my best friend.

"Ditto," she says. "Maybe you hold yourself apart like you do because you're a big, fat chicken. No, I correct myself, a perfect-the-way-she-is chicken, who doesn't even want to lose weight."

"You're just mad because I don't want to try Solu," I say.

Two women in the hall look at me with shock, not because I'm yelling, I don't think. It's because I don't want to try Solu!

"No," she yells back. "I'm mad because you weren't even excited for me. Not even a little!"

"I don't think you're fat, Viv. I don't think either of us is fat. I think that we look perfectly normal. Why do we have to be thinner, thinner, thinner all the time?"

"Because when people see this," Viv says, grabbing her belly, "they see weakness. And I don't want to be seen as weak."

"That's not true!" I tell her. "That's not what I think when I see someone's belly—"

"Well, it's what *I* think," Viv says. And I see her eyes flash to my gut.

That hurts.

This is an area we don't venture into—it's an unspoken agreement in our friendship. I allow her to obsess about her extra fifteen pounds, and we never mention mine.

"Well, I don't care how people see me," I say, my eyes prickling with tears.

"I don't believe that for a second," my best friend hisses at me. "All your weirdo choices are designed to make people see you as an outsider. You're scared to fit in."

I go back to our room. I practice the Bach until my fingertips are screaming.

All the while I'm thinking about Viv and what she said.

At first, I'm just mad. How dare she blah blah blah.

But the thing about Viv is, she knows me.

And as I run the piece, I realize maybe she's right about me. About some of it, anyway.

I really don't mind my extra weight. I really think I look just fine.

But the stuff about dressing weird and not fitting in . . .

Around five the PA comes on. I'm expecting a message from Lorna Krieger about shuffleboard or something, but it's not.

"Good afternoon, guests. This is Captain Hammonds. I'm pleased to announce that Dr. Zhang has just informed the bridge that as of three fifty-five p.m. this afternoon, the ship as a whole has met its first weight-loss goal. The passengers of the famous Solu Cruise to Lose have lost a combined average of five percent of their body weight. We had expected to meet this goal on the fifth day of the voyage, not the third! To celebrate, we will hold a ball tonight in the Aurora Restaurant. Black tie is requested. Congratulations to all."

Maybe forty-five seconds later Viv comes charging into the room.

"A ball! A ball!"

I stand up.

We apologize at the same time and just cut it all short with a hug.

"I don't know why I was so mean," Vivvy says. "You were right about the weight. Neither of us is fat."

"You were right about my stupid boots," I tell her. She tucks a wisp of hair behind my ear.

"You're the best and I love everything about you and I was being stupid and selfish," she says.

"Well, me, too."

We hug again.

This is the thing about Viv and I. We're both only children so we feel like sisters. Always have.

Our fights never last long.

"Viv, I've been thinking. Tonight . . . will you dress me up?"

Viv looks at me—an Are-you-for-real look.

"I mean it."

"I have dreamed of this day!" she says. "Oh my word. I am going to make you look so hot."

Vivika grabs my hand and pulls me into our closet.

There's a long purple cocktail dress, a tight black-and-white-striped minidress, a skirt made out of silver sequins.

"I think that this might work best with your combat boots," she says, taking the cocktail dress off the rack. "It would give you a kind of a punk glamour thing."

"No," I say.

She's not looking at me, instead she's rummaging through her drawers.

"You have to keep an open mind," she chastises me. "I want you to promise you'll try on anything I say."

"I meant, no, I'm not wearing my combat boots."

Viv looks up.

"I want to borrow some of your heels."

"Whoa," she says. "Are you sure?"

"I am," I tell her.

And I mean it.

Because, truth be told, Viv was right about me. I hide behind my alternative, weirdo choices. I need to take some risks, and for me, that means dressing mainstream and wearing heels.

She brings out a pair of stacked stilettos, like eight feet tall.

"Oh, please," I say. "I'm not suicidal!"

"I just wanted to make sure the real Laurel was still in there."

"It's me. I promise."

Viv squeezes my hand.

"I told you this cruise would change everything."

TOM

THEY REALLY KNOW how to do over the top on this boat.

The vibe in the ballroom is ecstatic. Women in sparkly gowns, men in black tie. Champagne flutes chiming. Candlelight glimmering in the chandeliers.

The big band is playing some old-school jazz. Uptempo. And the belle of the ball is the old man Timothy Almstead. He's surrounded by a constant cluster of people thanking him and wishing him well.

A uniformed waiter passes by with a tray of these little perfectly crispy lamb chops. It's unreal, how delicious they are. Lamb is lean enough. I have three and ask him to find me when he comes out again.

After a good long talk with Derek, I e-mailed Rich and Tamara. I was really careful to tell them that I know what a great opportunity this is, but that I've met a girl and it wouldn't be right to investigate a relationship with Sabbi when my heart's elsewhere.

Yeah, it was a bit of a leap on that respect. I mean, me and Laurel hardly even know each other, but it was the best way to get out of the Sabbi thing.

Rich sidles up, taking me by the elbow.

"Good evening, Mr. Fiorelli," he says, suave as ever.

"Same to you, Rich."

He looks sharp. Black shirt, charcoal-gray tie, neon-green pocket square.

"Rich, you really know how to wear black tie," I tell him.

"Thank you, my pretty," he says. He straightens my tie.

"I got your e-mail," he says.

"Did you tell her people?"

"Not. Just. Yet," he says. "Have I told you how happy we all are with the coverage? Solu could not be more thrilled, especially with the Sabbi interview."

"She's a pro," I say.

"Of course she is." His gaze goes out over the crowd.

"Look at them all. On the adventure of a lifetime. They will all tell their grandkids—they were the first."

"If it works," I say.

"Of course it works. Look at them all. Those people are thinner."

"Yeah. For a while, anyway. Maybe."

"Buzzkill!" He laughs, elbowing me in the ribs. "You haven't tried it? I would, but I'm working."

"Same here. And anyway, my trainer insists I eat real food, in the right amount."

"You're like a little Puritan, aren't you? Like an Amish person. Or a monk."

"Yes," I say. "I'm the first Amish television host."

"So, listen, I think you're wrong about Sabbi. I'd like to tell you why—"

I brace myself for some seducing from him when Tamara strides right between us.

"You're a jerk!" Tamara hisses. "I can't believe you're blowing this."

"Look, I just like this other girl, okay?"

"Who? Boots?! There's nothing there. She's a nothing."

"You don't even know her."

"Neither do you! You're just being a coward," Tamara says.

She grabs my arm, hard, digging her fingernails into my skin.

"Hey—" I protest.

"You got burned by Bonnie Loo and you're scared."

"Bonnie Lee, and she has nothing to do with this. I'm just not into Sabbi."

"Well, get into her. Get into her right now, because here she comes and she's got a photographer," Tamara growls.

She points with her chin, and sure enough, Sabbi is slinking over, a photographer on her heels.

Sabbi's wearing a satin gown with a slit up to her hip and has a white fur stole draped over one shoulder.

Tamara moves away from me. Rich moves away.

"Tomazino," Sabbi purrs, her arm out to me.

She wraps one arm through mine and leans up to whisper in my ear.

I . . .

I . . .

I smile and lean in.

It's the polite thing to do. It's what I'm supposed to do.

I *am* a coward. Tamara was right.

The photographer flashes away.

This is the shot on the cover of *People*. It's happening.

"You look delicious in that tuxedo," Sabbi whispers.

Then she nibbles on my earlobe.

And it's hot. But it's also not what I want. And I don't know what to do.

And then,

OF COURSE,

I see Laurel.

She's standing twenty feet away. Her friend is just behind her. They're both holding champagne flutes and Laurel looks amazing.

She's wearing a sequined silver skirt and a black silk camisole. Long silver earrings kind of pour down through her hair onto her neck.

The skirt is clinging to her curves and shimmering with light bouncing from the chandeliers.

She's not wearing boots but she still looks beautiful.

Sabbi reaches up and touches my face, to bring my attention back to her.

"Tom Fiorelli," she sings. "Tomazino. Take a nice picture with me, sweetheart."

Passengers around us are taking our picture on their phones now.

Laurel's eyes meet mine and it's like I can see her thought process.

I see her register the way Sabbi is pressing her body into my side, the fact that my arm is around her. And she's looking right into my eyes and I try to tell her it's not a real thing, but her eyes fall away.

Her lips are drawn tight and she's starting to blush.

She's thinking that she's a fool and I want to jump back in time and have played the whole thing differently, but I can't.

Laurel turns away from me—from me and Sabbi.

One of her ankles bends awkwardly. She's not so steady on the heels.

"Laurel!" I say. "Wait!"

Sabbi stands on her tiptoes, deliberately blocking my view of Laurel.

She makes a tut-tut sound with her teeth.

"Focus, Tomazino."

Laurel kicks off the heels and runs.

Her friend shoots me a dirty look, snatches up the shoes, and goes after Laurel.

Sabbi squeezes my arm.

"Give me a kiss, then you can go after her," Sabbi says.

I look at her.

Big brown eyes. Lashes thick. She's beautiful. The woman is undeniably beautiful. Millions of guys fantasize about having her in their arms.

I see now that she's very, very in control of this situation.

"Come on, baby. Make it a good one."

My eyes dart to Rich and Tamara, who are watching us and pretending not to watch us at the same time.

I'm mad, mad at myself. I hate myself, so I grab Sabbi Ribiero and I kiss her hard.

I'm giving them what they want.

I'm acting like a child. I know I am.

And I'm so angry I don't care.

I gather Sabbi to me and her head drops back and I pull her in tighter, my hands dig into her hair. I kiss her.

Click-click-click, the photographer's shooting as fast as he can. I hate the photographer.

Then I drop Sabbi onto her feet.

I look at Tamara.

"Can I go now?" I ask her. And Sabbi. And Rich.

Tamara nods. Rich looks sad for me.

Good.

I turn to go and realize Sabbi has hold of my hand.

"Tomazino," she says as she squeezes. "Try to have some fun."

"WHO CARES?" I SAY.

"Yup. Who cares," Viv echoes.

She signals to the bartender. We're at the upper deck lounge, which is deserted.

"He can cuddle up to whoever he wants!"

"Of course he can!" she says to me. Then to the barkeep, "Two mango daiquiris, please."

The bartender doesn't miss a beat. He's certainly not asking for IDs.

"I don't even know him."

"Nope," she says.

"Tom Fiorelli is a jerk."

"Totally," she agrees.

The drinks come.

"Mango? Really?" I ask.

"Totally," she tells me.

She's right. It's delicious.

"You can go back to the party," I tell her. "I think I'm going to go to bed."

"Drink up," my best friend tells me. "And I'll tell you what we're going to do. We're going to go back to that ball. And we're going to eat a bunch of delicious food. And we're going to walk around and look gorgeous and have fun."

"I don't know—"

"And we're going to get out on the dance floor and dance. We're not going to be looking for Tom Fiorelli or for anyone cute or famous or even interesting. You and me are going to have a good time. Nobody's gonna take that away from us."

I close my eyes and breathe deeply. The sea air is fresh and warm. It wafts through my hair.

"Okay," I say. "You're right. I'm not going to freak out because Tom Fiorelli is who he is. He's just that guy. He's the guy who has famous girls biting his earlobe while people take his picture."

"Sucky, but true," Viv says.

"I'm in charge of who I am," I declare.

"Yes!" Viv says.

"And tonight I am a girl who goes to a fancy ball on a fancy cruise and gets drunk."

"Okay," Viv says. "I can work with that."

So, you can't chug a daiquiri, because they're thick and frozen. (But we sip quickly.)

Tom's not at the ball when we go back.

Which is great, I tell myself.

I do notice that Sabbi is there. So they're not somewhere hooking up. Which is none of my business, I know that.

Viv was right to insist I come back to the ball.

We laugh and dance, spinning each other around. Some guys come and try to dance with us and that's okay, but really, the night's about Viv and me, being best friends.

This is a kind of relationship I know how to handle!

At midnight they wheel out a round table heaped with a huge statue of cream puffs in the shape of an S. The cream puffs are held together by thin strands of caramel.

"Ooooh," a lady in a black evening gown says to her husband. "Darling, look at the croquembouche. Isn't that clever?"

(That's how I learn the name for this fancy dessert.)

The people draw close to the platform where the huge S stands. Rich helps Dr. Zhang onto the platform. She's handed a microphone.

She's wearing a rumpled cobalt-blue satin evening dress with her big tortoiseshell glasses. To tell the truth, she looks like someone's least favorite bridesmaid (or worse, a *brides-matron*).

The people draw closer and closer to the platform. They're surrounding it and cheering—clapping like crazy.

"Ladies and gentlemen," Zhang says. "I just wanted to thank you all. This dessert has been created in honor of Solu—but I dedicate it to all of you—"

It's kind of hard to hear her voice over the cheering.

The people are getting so close to the little stage that it gets jostled.

Dr. Zhang loses her place.

"On behalf of Almstead and myself—"

And then a man reaches out and grabs a handful of the cream puffs.

He shouts with joy.

"Wait," Dr. Zhang says. "Hold on."

But the man's grab is followed by another and another and people swarm up onto the platform.

"So much enthusiasm!" she tries to rally. "All right—enjoy!"

Dr. Zhang actually loses her footing and I see Rich helping her down.

Men and women in their elegant clothes are edging forward, grabbing cream puffs. There's a lot of laughter and whooping, good-natured elbowing, stuff like that. But there's a feeling of fakery to me. Like they're pretending to be playful, when what they really want is to get as many pastries as they can.

I look to my side and see Viv, staring hard at the pastries.

"They're trying to act so dignified," I say.

And I see her swallow.

She looks at me and laughs.

"Solu," she says. "It tastes good."

She steps forward. One step, two steps.

I put my hand on her arm.

"Viv."

She shakes her head, smiles at me.

"Let's get more champagne," I say. I've had . . . okay, a lot of drinks, but I've also eaten a lot. Now that my appetite's back, I've been making up for lost time.

Viv, on the other hand, has eaten hardly anything. "Or maybe a Pipop?"

"Yeah," Viv says. "Okay."

Then she looks back at the table.

"But it just looks like people are taking more than their share. And I haven't had a dose since lunch. So . . . "

She heads toward the table.

Everyone, I realize, is heading toward the table.

I'm like a rock in a river. They all flow around me, toward the table.

Huh.

Maybe it's just me, but it seems like after the passengers have their Solu, the party seems to get wilder.

People call for the music to be turned up. The band stopped playing after dinner and now it's a DJ.

"Louder!" a guy shouts. He gets up on the table and everyone's cheering for him. "Louder!"

They turn it up.

The dancing gets very, well, dirty, with lots of grinding and grappling.

Viv is totally spaced out, dancing with her eyes closed.

"Okay," I say. "I'm done here. This is too much for me!"

She opens her eyes and she has trouble focusing on me for a second.

"Viv!" I shout. "We need to go!"

She nods and keeps dancing.

I grab her by the arm.

"Are you okay?" I ask.

She drapes her arms around me.

"I got a little drunk," she says.

"I know. Me, too."

She kisses me on the cheek.

"Did you have fun, Laurey?"

"So much fun!" I say. It's hard to help her walk when I'm in these stupid heels. We kind of careen out of the banquet hall.

"I want us to have the best time," she says.

"We are!" I promise her. "We really are."

Well, we *were*.

Before the stupid dessert.

TOM

UPPER DECK, LOWER DECK. I couldn't find Laurel anywhere.

The concierge wouldn't give me her suite number, he said it's the ship's policy, but he did connect me with her room phone.

I left only two messages—any more would have been pathetic. Given my history with messages, leaving just one was colossally stupid, but I was obviously on a stupid jag.

Then I called Derek.

He didn't pick up.

"Man!" I said to his voice mail. "I really wish you'd pick up. I need to hear . . . I need a friendly voice. Argggh. Okay. Call me. Whatever."

Then I went to the gym and exercised until I threw up.

Which is what I should have done *before* the stupid ball.

If I don't work out twice a day, I don't get rid of all my . . . whatever, emotion.

I should have known better.

At breakfast, Rich came and found me.

Doing damage control. Checking in on me. Seeing how I was.

Would I still be acting like a jerk or would I be rational?

I could see him sussing me out as he walked over.

"Good morning, Tom," he said. "I wanted to apologize for last night. I never meant for you to be put on the spot that way."

"Whatever, Rich," I say.

"The coverage, you should know, is really great."

He has an iPad under his arm.

He sees my eyes dart to it.

"Do you want to see? It's everywhere. *TMZ, HuffPost Celebrity*, it's even on RyanSeacrest.com."

"No," I say. "I don't want to see."

"Well, listen, if the thing with Sabbi is making you feel bad, we'll can it. We need you focused and happy so you can keep on doing your thing—making sure everyone knows how wonderful Solu is, et cetera. If you spend not another moment with Sabbi, it's fine with me. I'll smooth things over for you."

"Thanks. That's really generous of you."

"Oooh," he says, waving the air away. "The sarcasm in here is overpowering. I said I'm sorry. I don't know what else to say."

He's honest. I have to give him that.

"I'm just . . . I'm tired of my personal life being something that's just for show," I tell him.

"That's heavy, man. I feel you," he says.

Tamara appears, carrying a plate of oatmeal with berries and cream. Did they plan to double-team me again or is this a coincidence?

"Rich," she says. "I noticed something you might want to look into."

She doesn't even address me, just sits down next to me like everything's fine.

She takes his iPad and loads his Twitter feed, entering the hashtag #Solu.

I scan down the list, reading along with Rich.

Luxury, whatever. I want more #Solu.

Hungry! Where's my #Solu?

Who gives a f*#% about shuttle board. GIVE ME MORE
#SOLU

#Solu #GottaHaveitNOW!!!!!!

This cruise sucks. All I want is MORE #SOLU

Parties are awesome but they need to give us more #SOLU.

Imma kill someone if I don't get my dose LOL! #Solu

"People seem angry," I say.

"Hmmm," Rich says. "Will you two excuse me?"

Rich slips away. Tamara opens a packet of Solu and sprinkles it over her oatmeal.

"How you liking that Solu?" I ask. If she wants to pretend like the thing with Sabbi didn't happen it's fine with me.

She shrugs.

"It seems to be working," she answers. "On me and on everyone else."

She nods toward the rest of the dining hall.

I take a look, a real look, at the passengers chowing down.

They look thinner. No question. There's a general bagginess to the clothes of almost all the people in the dining hall.

The other thing is that people look crabby. Dour around the mouth.

Maybe everyone's hungover after the ball.

There's a small crowd of passengers near the maître d's stand.

"They didn't make the muffins," Tamara says, commenting on the direction I'm looking. "They're saying each passenger can have two packets of Solu—nothing else. People are pretty grumpy about it. May be a tough day of shooting, I think."

She takes out her phone and brings up an image.

It's a shot of me kissing Sabbi on PerezHilton.com. The slugline reads: SABBI GETS POUNDED BY BABY TOM-TOM! WHO'S BANGING WHO ON THE SOLU LAUNCH?

"You know, it's just business," Tamara says, sipping her coffee.

"Not to the girl I like," I respond.

"Who? Boots? She's a big girl. She'll understand."

"I doubt it," I say.

"Since when do you care about the commoners?"

"What's that supposed to mean?"

"You haven't dated a regular, mortal girl in . . . ever," she says.

She looks at me. Her eyes are silver. The color of a scalpel.

"Laurel's the first real girl I've ever had the chance to talk to, if you want to know the truth," I tell her.

"You set with questions for the Zhang interview?"

Classic Tamara. She ignores what I've said, as if we're done with the topic.

"Yeah," I say.

I'm thinking about what a drag it's going to be working, when all I want to do is find Laurel and explain. Try to explain.

Tamara snaps her fingers in my face.

"Stay with me, Tom. It's Day Four. We're more than halfway done with this effin' gig."

I'm surprised. Gruff as she may be, it's not like her to curse. Especially not about a paying job.

Tamara licks her finger and inserts it into the empty packet of Solu.

"What?" she says, catching me studying her.

LAUREL

"COME ON, SWEETIE." I try to coax Viv. "We're in Mexico. Mexico! It's going to be so fun. This is the excursion you were the most excited about!"

I read from our tickets: "Snorkeling and gourmet lunch on a catamaran! See the colorful sights on one of the most pristine coral reefs in the west Caribbean. Enjoy a feast of authentic local delicacies prepared and served on a luxury catamaran."

"Stop talking," she growls from under her pillow.

"If you won't listen to me, listen to Lorna!"

I turn up the volume on the TV.

"Another beautiful day at sea as we begin Day Four of this beautiful journey. Friends, I don't know about you, but I'm down a size! Thank you, Solu!

"I saw Luka Harris out by the pool yesterday and his swim trunks nearly fell off. Again I say, thank you, Solu."

She winks at the camera. (Ew.)

"We'll be disembarking in beautiful Cozumel in one half hour. Please meet up in the Celestial Lounge if you are headed out on an excursion."

"Ugh," Viv groans. "Just go already and let me die."

I shut off the TV as Lorna launches into a list of the shipboard activities for the day.

"Are you sure you don't want to come?" I ask Viv. "You were looking forward to the snorkeling so much."

"If you put a mouthpiece in my mouth, I will fill it with vomit, I promise you. Just go."

"You're sure?"

"A million percent. Just set me some Pips on the night table. I'll see you at dinner."

I grab my purse and slide my feet into my prairie boots.

"Hey, Viv," I say. "Do me a favor and don't have Solu today? You've lost so much weight already. Maybe just lay off for the day?"

"Yes," she says. "I know. I've been overdoing it. Honestly, I'm going to lie here and watch movies and just veg out. Now, go!"

Under the sea, there is no Tom Fiorelli.

There is no cruise. No weird new sweetener that makes people act like drug addicts. No audition for Pensacola U hanging over my head.

There is only the gentle rhythm of the sweet, warm water and colors dancing in sunlit ripples on the white ocean floor.

I was a little scared at first. They gave us masks, fins, a flotation device designed to make snorkeling more comfortable and a little speech about how to clear your snorkel. (Okay, it's not rocket science, you blow.) But jumping off the boat out into the middle of the ocean was kind of intense. And my breathing sounded super loud, like I was in a horror movie.

But then I saw fish.

Amazing fish. All different colors—from neon through the rainbow, to sneaky camouflage browns and grays. And the different kinds of fish have these personalities. The yellow-and-gray ones have long pointy noses and they edge away from me, real suspicious, and there are some little round blue guys that come right up to me and try to nibble my hair. The prettiest, I think, are the swarms of silver fish, shining and rippling as a mass, like they are made up of sunlight.

Even though I'm surrounded by other snorkeling passengers, and the boat is only a hundred feet away, I feel like I'm alone in this precious new world. It makes me want to play some music.

It makes me feel at peace, for the first time since I came aboard the *Extravagance*.

Screw Tom Fiorelli.

Lunch is really fun, too. I so wish Viv were with me.

We sit at a table set in the middle of the boat, where there's shade from the roof.

The waiters set down giant pitchers of sangria, lemonade, and iced tea on the table. And a bowl with Solu packs.

Almost everyone besides me takes two packets (you can tell some people want to take more, but they're civil about it.)

They sweeten their iced tea and *clink!* Everyone cheers!

I'm drinking the lemonade, which is already really sweet and crisp. (Nothing wrong with good old-fashioned sugar.)

I'm *so glad* my nausea has finally gone away.

The waiters pass big platters of *chicharrónes* (fried chicken chunks), rice and beans, and fried sweet *plátanos*.

It's not gourmet, but it's *delicious*.

"Mmmm, now that's good!" says the woman next to me. Her name is Peggy; she and her husband, Hal, are from New York.

"And you can eat as much as you want, my dear," says Hal. "Your diet days are over!"

"I'll drink to that!" booms a guy from Milwaukee from across the table.

"Can you imagine?" Peggy says to me, a huge grin on her face. "We can eat whatever we want! Solu will take the weight right off."

All the passengers are laughing and eating with gusto. Maybe I'm wrong about Solu. It does seem to work. And it's making these people really happy.

I feel so great when I head back on board at the end of the day. I have that delicious, beachy, sunburned kind of tiredness. And I'm really excited to have a great time with Viv. Whatever she wants to do, I'm going to do it.

Viv's not in the room.

She's left a note: "Got too hungry. Went to dinner. Alone." With a sad face.

I shower quickly and dress for dinner.

I wear the black-and-white-striped minidress Viv offered me the night before, with a pair of her sandals.

I'm betting she'll get a kick out of me wearing her stuff.

I enter the Aurora and see . . . Well, the first thing I see is Tom seated with another big table full of VIPs. One of whom, of course, is Sabbi. But I see that they're not next to each other, which is weird. Whatever. I'm not going to notice (okay, I already did).

I'm not going to *care*.

Viv is sitting with the family from our first night on the boat and it looks like they've already eaten their main courses.

When she sees me, she jumps to her feet.

"Where have you been?" she says. "I was worried."

"I'm sorry," I say. "It was so beautiful out there. I just got swept up in it all."

She does *not* look well.

Her face looks gaunt, with dark circles under her eyes.

"Are you okay?" I ask.

She waves my concern away.

"I will be," she says.

"It's not right," says the mom. "You shouldn't make your friend worry like that." I guess Viv's been complaining about me to them.

The freshmen twins look like they're enjoying my discomfort.

"Are you going to sit down or what?" Viv snaps.

"Viv, what's wrong?" I ask.

"You don't show up for dinner. You're gone all day. I've been really worried!"

"I didn't realize the time," I say.

The mom huffs aloud, like I'm a big jerk.

A waiter comes by.

"Excuse me," I say. "Is it possible for me to put in an order? I was late. So sorry."

"Of course, madam," he says.

"I love it when they call me 'madam,'" I say to Viv.

She won't even look at me.

One of the twins is bouncing his leg so hard the table's moving. And what's weirder is that no one notices but me. The silverware's jangling and the water in the glasses is jumping and all the people are just looking around in the room.

"When's it coming, Mom?" the other twin asks.

"Soon, baby, soon."

Suddenly I get it.

It's the Solu. They're all waiting for the Solu to come out. The hairs on my arms prickle in a wave.

"Viv," I say. "We need to talk. I think we need to talk about Solu."

She grabs my wrist, hard, and hisses.

"Don't say one word about it. You don't understand. You're not taking it. You don't get what it's like."

"You're hurting me," I say.

Another waiter passes by.

"Where's our dessert?" the father of the teens demands. "We're all waiting!"

"Yeah!" people at our table and other tables chime in.

"It will be out momentarily," the waiter assures them all.

When it comes out, there's lots of complaining. The dessert is a small sliver of key lime pie—the portion is pretty meager.

"This isn't enough!" I hear a woman complaining. "Not nearly enough!"

Then when they bring out the packets, there's only one packet per person.

"With all the money we're paying to be here? This is an outrage!" the dad huffs.

People are pissed, but they dig in to their desserts quickly. They basically inhale them.

My mind flashes to the ten packs of Solu I have in our hotel safe. I bet I could sell each packet for fifty dollars to these people. Maybe more.

My roast chicken comes just as people are finishing their pie. The waiter has set my slice of pie in front of me and I realize that everyone at the table is staring at it.

"Can I have it?" Viv asks.

"I don't think you should, Viv. I really don't. The Solu is making people act weird," I say.

"I'll eat it if you don't want it!" one of the twins says.

"No—" I say, but before I can, he reaches across the table and takes it.

"You jack-hole!" his brother yells and tries to grab some of the pie for himself.

Everyone at the table starts yelling at the boys, but Viv turns to me.

"I can't believe you!" she shouts. "You're supposed to be my best friend!"

She looks pale, really pale and then, to my horror, her eyes roll up in her head and she slides off her chair.

I stand up.

The twins are still fighting over my pie crumbs.

I try to pull Viv up, but no one helps me.

The waiters around the room are being accosted by irate passengers.

I stand up and yell for the only person I can think of. "Tom!"

He's standing in a heartbeat. He scans around the room, looking for me.

I see him see me, and (Oh, thank you, God) his face lights up.

"I need help!" I shout.

He makes his way through the dining hall.

"What's wrong?" he asks. "Are you okay?"

Then he sees Vivika.

"My friend Vivika collapsed," I say. "I don't know what's going on! Everyone's acting crazy."

He bends and gently slides his hands under Viv.

When he lifts her up, the shoulder of her dress slides down. She's, like, floating in that dress.

"I got her," he says. "It's okay."

"This way," I tell him, and I edge my way through the people. I see the waiters rapidly distributing even slimmer second slices of pie all around.

Sabbi comes up to us. She's wearing a red leather vest that squishes her cleavage up like two balloons.

"Where are you going?" she asks Tom. "I thought we were going to hang out later."

"No, I'm afraid not," Tom says. His eyes dart to mine. "That whole thing is not gonna happen."

We start to move out the door.

She follows us into the hall.

"What do you mean, 'is not going to happen'? It already is happening. It's all over the place."

"This isn't a good time, Sabbi. We can talk later."

"He is *carrying* a person," I chip in.

"Carrying a person or not, arrangements have been made. Should we meet at the club?"

"Sabbi, I'm sorry. But I'm not into it," Tom says.

"But the photographer is expecting us."

"I don't want to do it. Us," Tom says. "I don't want to do us."

Sabbi's mouth is slightly ajar. Her eyes are wide. Her head cocked to the side. She reminds me of a little bird.

It takes her a full count of three Mississippi to realize what he is saying.

"Oh," she says.

This is definitely the first time she has been turned down.

I should not, should not, should not enjoy it. (However, I do.)

"But . . . if they just have photos of us together from one event, it looks like a one-night stand. That's not what we're going for," she says.

"I'm sorry, Sabbi, but this girl is in trouble," Tom says. "We need to go."

She looks at him, at Viv, whose head is lolling back in the air, and at me.

"I will be calling your people," she says in a voice like stone.

"Which way to your room?" Tom asks me.

TOM

"OH MY GOD," Vivika moans. She looks up at me. "Baby Tom-Tom is carrying me."

"You passed out," Laurel says. She's rumbling with her room key, having trouble getting the door unlocked.

"You can put me down," the girl tells me.

"Viv, you fainted right in the dining hall," Laurel says.

I set Viv onto her feet. She's pretty wobbly.

Laurel gets the door open and Viv teeters in.

Their room is the mirror image of mine, except it's really messy. Clothes are draped everywhere. There's shoes and boots strewn around, and magazines.

I see the last issue of *US Weekly*. I know there's a picture of me in the "Stars Are Just Like Us" section. I'm shirtless and drinking a Jamba Juice. Jamba paid me to take that shot.

Viv sits on the couch.

"Nu-uh," Laurel says, pointing. "Get in bed."

Viv slumps her way over to the bed.

"Tell me, what did you eat today while I was gone. Anything?"

Viv shakes her head, miserable. She starts to cry.

"I'm sorry I was so mean. I just feel horrible. I have this monster headache and it won't go away."

Laurel gives her a hug.

"I should go," I say.

"No," they both say at the same time.

"Please don't go," Laurel says.

She reaches out and puts her hand on my arm.

Her touch, which is very gentle, sends a jolt through my body. An electric jolt.

I can't tell if she feels it, too, because she turns back to her friend.

I'm not going anywhere. Not yet.

Laurel hands her friend an apple and a handful of walnuts from the fruit basket and gives her a bottle of milk from their mini-fridge.

"I didn't know the fridges had milk," I comment.

Laurel blushes.

"Huh," she says. "Well, ours does."

"Because we're underage," Viv adds.

"Oh! I'm only nineteen, but mine is stocked with beer and liquor. Weird."

"You're a VIP," Viv says.

"Hey, um, just how underage are you guys?" I ask.

They both laugh and I realize I'm the one blushing now.

"We're both seventeen," Viv says. Then, "Phew, right?"

I laugh out loud.

"Right. I guess."

I push some of the clothes to the side and sit on the couch.

"Sorry it's so messy," Laurel says. "I was in a rush."

"She was late," Viv adds.

Laurel starts tidying up while Viv munches her apple.

"I went snorkeling. Have you ever been snorkeling?" Laurel asks me.

"No," I say.

"It's so beautiful."

"If it's so beautiful, why is it called snorkeling?" Viv says. "That has to be the ugliest word ever! Snooorkel."

Laurel laughs.

She's so pretty when she laughs. I can't help but grin.

"It sounds like a villain from *Game of Thrones*," Laurel says. "I am Snorkel. Bow to me!"

"I used to get the word *snorkel* confused with yodel," I confess. "When I was around seven we did a couple episodes in Hawaii and I kept trying to get my tutors to go yodel with me."

Both the girls laugh.

"I remember those episodes. You ate some poi and did this funny gagging thing," Viv says.

Laurel's done hanging up the clothes and starts tossing the shoes into the closet.

"That was vanilla pudding. The real poi almost made me throw up for real."

Laurel comes out of the closet now and there's nowhere for her to sit but next to me on the couch.

But she looks to me, then away, and goes to sort of perch next to Viv on the bed.

Yeah. Shy.

"Laur, play something for us," Viv says.

"No." Laurel shakes her head. "No."

"Yeah! Do," I say. "Play that crazy fast thing from the deck."

She's got that "modesty" look on her face—like she wants to play and is happy to have been asked, but doesn't want to look like a show-off.

"Really, Laur. Please? It will help me to feel better," Viv pleads.

"Okay," she says.

Laurel rises and gets her guitar from the closet.

"Here, sit here," I say. I slide off the couch and sit on the floor.

She takes the guitar out of the case and tunes it for a good, long while.

"Mind if I have an apple?" I ask.

"Yeah, go ahead," Viv says. "Our fruit basket is your fruit basket."

Laurel looks up, "This is 'Lágrima,' by Francisco Tárrega."

It's this light, little dancing melody. I'm transfixed by her fingers, darting all over the strings.

She hits some wrong note only she can hear and grimaces.

There's a center section to the song that's more sad, and then it comes back around to the first phrases again.

She finishes.

"I've got a long way to go," she says.

"It's beautiful," I tell her.

"I need to work on that last transition."

"No, it sounded great."

"Ugh, my fingers are so slow. You should hear someone really good do it—"

"Hey, listen to me, when someone likes your work, just say thank you. When you apologize, it takes something away from them. If you don't mind my saying so."

Laurel gives a single nod. Viv nods enthusiastically. "That's what I've been telling her for years!"

Viv pulls the covers up. She yawns. "Play me my favorite, please, sweetie?"

"Okay."

I lean back and stretch my legs out so I'm lying on the floor, raised on my forearms.

Laurel shakes out her hands and sits up straight. She sweeps her hair over her shoulder, getting it out of the way, and begins to play.

This one I know. I've heard it played at weddings—very slow and pretty.

I lie down, resting my head on my elbow, and I watch her.

There's a wall sconce behind her and it's picking up a halo of blond flyaways.

She's not the best guitar player in the world, but it feels really special somehow, to be in a room with someone who can make music.

It's weird that her playing this beautiful music makes me want to grab her and make out. Do all guys have this same urge to, like, tackle delicate things?

She finishes and there's a moment of silence, broken only by the sound of Viv's heavy sleep-breathing.

"Beautiful."

She takes a beat, then says, "Thank you."

Laurel sets the guitar next to her on the couch and I rise, on my knees.

I put one hand next to her on the couch.

She looks at me, our eyes connecting in the dim light.

I move toward her, just a bit, and she moves away. I'd better do this right.

"Laurel," I whisper. "Can I kiss you?"

She gulps, and her eyes dart to her sleeping roommate.

She takes my hand and rises.

I get to my feet and Laurel leads me . . .

Into the closet.

There's shoes everywhere—the ones Laurel threw in earlier—and we stumble a bit. She pulls the doors closed behind us and the light goes out.

I can't see a thing.

She is *really* shy.

I graze my fingers up her arm, tracing them along her neck.

Go slow, I tell myself.

I put one hand on either side of her face and I bring my mouth to hers.

Her lips part. Her mouth is soft.

She has her hands up, touching my hair.

I move my hands to her back.

She's not all skin and bones, which I like. I like it too much.

Slowly now, I tell myself.

I lean into her, just a little, and we sway. She steps back to steady herself.

"Ow!" she says.

"Sorry!"

"No, it's good. I stepped on a hanger, that's all," she says.

"I think I'm standing on a boot," I confess.

"That's probably true. I like boots."

I can feel her breath on my neck.

"Do you want to go up on deck?" I ask. I'm thinking about starlight. Should be romantic. Moonlight on the waves. That kind of thing.

"Can I tell you the truth?" she asks.

"Sure," I say. "Why not?"

"No."

LAUREL

"OKAY," HE SAYS, drawing back a bit.

He's got his hands on my hips. Mine are resting on his (hugely muscular) forearms.

I know he's nineteen, but he smells like a full-grown-*man* man. Like a lumberjack. Leather, soap, spice—everything you ever thought they'd put into the best cologne in the world.

He smells so good I feel faint in the knees.

That's the problem.

He's so *everything* that my brain feels *flooded*.

How am I going to explain this to him?

"Is it . . . because of people with cameras?" he asks.

"No!" I exclaim. "That's not it."

I put my hand on his shoulder and pull him back to me.

My heart is hammering so hard.

"The thing is, about you, is that you are very, very handsome."

I'm so glad he can't see my face right now.

"And when I'm around you, I get a little overwhelmed. So if we stay in the dark for a while, I thought maybe it would help me . . . get used to you."

And now I feel like I can hear him smiling.

"Okay," he says.

His breath is sweet, like nutmeg.

He moves and pushes some boots or shoes with his feet.

"It would be easier if there was less stuff around," he says.

It is pretty cluttered in this closet.

"Wait," I say. I bend down and feel around on the floor, moving all the shoes up onto one of the built-in dressers. I'm basically on my hands and knees, rooting around his legs.

"This is a new one, for me," he says.

A laugh bursts out of me.

"This is what we do in Fort Lauderdale, on dates," I say. "We get boys into dark places and then we clean around their feet."

"It's pretty kinky."

I try to get up, but it's awkward, then he finds my elbows and hoists me up.

"You're really strong," I say.

"I'm pretty strong," he says. He puts his mouth on my neck and kisses me.

"And you can breakdance."

"We call it b-boy," he says. "I don't know why it's called that, but it is."

His hands are so strong. Everywhere he touches me lights up with this warm, electric longing.

"Tom?"

"Yes?"

"What's it like?"

"What's what like?"

"Being famous," I say.

He pulls away and exhales. I feel him run his hand through his hair.

"Dumb question. I'm sorry," I apologize.

"No, it's okay."

He leans away from me, onto the bureau behind him.

"I don't know," he begins. "It's fun. And it's a pain in the ass. You feel like you never have enough. And sometimes you wish you were just a regular guy . . . but not for very long." He sighs and my heart wrenches in my chest.

"You get used to it," he says.

"Can I ask you one other thing?" I say.

The darkness is helping me feel brave. I know I'd never ask him this, not in a million years, in the light of day.

"Do you wish I was thinner?"

"No!" he says immediately with a gentle scoff in his voice. "No."

"Because I know I don't look like girls in Hollywood and I don't even want to be like them, to tell you the truth—"

"Your body is . . . it's . . . it's luscious and soft and, I don't know, real."

I am experiencing a whole-body blush.

"And reality's okay?" I ask.

"Reality's . . . hot," he says.

His hands slide around my hips and up my back.

"Reality is hot," I say.

I put my hands on his neck. I run them up, over his stubbly jaw, over the cleft in his chin. He makes a low sound in his throat that makes me weak in the knees.

I touch his cheeks, his eyebrows, his ears.

"I really like reality," he says.

His thumbs rub down my hipbones. Right near my belly and I don't draw back.

I lean up and kiss him on the mouth, pressing my mouth into his. Pressing my body into his.

"When you touch me I feel like . . . uhm, like I've never felt this way before. Not with any other girl."

"Not even that famous one?"

"Nope. What we had . . . I think I get it now. She was right. It was no fun. There was no juice. No spark."

I kiss him and he kisses me back.

(There's a spark, all right.)

"Okay," I say after a while. "We can leave the closet."

"It is getting a little hot in here," he says.

"Steamy," I add.

He laughs and I push open the doors.

We step out of the closet, out of the room, and into the hall.

It's really, really weird to be out in the light. We're both squint-

ing and I shield my eyes against the light.

"I liked it better in the closet," he says. "Do you want to go get a drink or something? Some milk?"

"No. I think I'd better go to bed," I say.

It's a lot to take in, frankly.

And I don't want to rush anything. It would be easy, very, deliciously easy, to go too far with this guy. I don't want to do that. (I like him too much.)

"We're in Belize tomorrow," I say. "Any chance you can get free to do some yodeling with me?"

He smiles.

"I doubt it. Tamara's got me working all day. But I have my night free."

"Okay," I say.

He pulls out his iPhone. "I should get your phone number. I'll text you when I'm free."

I'm about to explain that I'm not allowed to use my phone on board—that it's too expensive, when he frowns. "This is weird. I have no bars at all. I had five just before dinner."

"The ship has its own hotspot thing, doesn't it?" I ask.

"Tamara told me we'd probably lose connectivity," he says. "I guess she was right."

He frowns at his phone, trying to refresh the screen.

It's still easier to look at him when he's not looking right at me. I can't help it.

He looks like he did when he was a boy, as he's working the phone. It's something about the way he is concentrating.

It's weird that I know what he looked like as a boy.

And also weird that his real personality is nothing like the goofy rascal he played on *The Magnificent Andersons*. He's more restrained and serious.

Maybe more ambitious. I get the feeling he doesn't goof around, much. Focused is a better word.

"What?" he says, looking up and seeing my expression.

"I was just thinking how much better you are in person," I say.

He pulls me into an embrace.

"You're a real surprise, Laurel Willard," he tells me.

"You, too, Tom Fiorelli . . . Hey, how'd you know my last name?" I ask.

"I made the concierge give it to me. Didn't you get my messages last night?"

I shake my head.

"Well, do yourself a favor and erase them!" he says.

"Are you kidding? I'm going to listen to them right now."

"Oh, jeez. That's just . . . whatever."

He's grinning and embarrassed. He's beautiful.

"Good night," I say.

"Good night."

"Laurel, hi, this is Tom Fiorelli. Look, the thing with Sabbi. I don't know if you even care, but listen, that's something our

publicists cooked up. It's not real. I don't like her at all. Please. My suite is number 1041. Just call me back if you get this, okay?"

"Hi there, it's Tom Fiorelli again. Well, I really hope this is the right room. Laurel, I looked everywhere for you and I realized on the last message I left that I didn't say sorry. Well, I am sorry. Sometimes I'm a jerk. That's the truth. But that doesn't mean that you shouldn't give me another chance because everyone acts like a jerk sometimes. Right? I mean, I think they do. Anyway I did and I'm sorry and I'd better hang up now before I say something even more stupid . . . God, please don't sell this to TMZ, okay? My publicist would kill me. I hope I get to talk to you again soon. Find me, okay?"

I am grinning and spinning with joy as I lie on the bed next to my konked-out best friend and listen to Tom Fiorelli's sweet run-on apologies.

My Tom Fiorelli, who feels for me what I feel for him.

Viv was right—this cruise is changing everything! It *has* changed everything.

TOM

I'M DRESSING in the day's wardrobe—fresh from my workout. It felt great to hit the gym hard. Exercising when you're pissed feels good 'cause you can work it out. But exercising when you're actually excited about something in your life—it's like going to church.

The only thing I feel bad about is that I didn't get to talk to Derek yesterday and now there's no signal. The message I left him was pretty crabby.

He'll probably figure out that we are out of range when he calls me back and it goes straight to voice mail.

I want to tell him that everything's okay now.

Better than okay.

Laurel's amazing. She's unlike anyone I've ever met. She's so surprising. I have no idea what she'll do next, and when she does it, it's thrilling and odd and so frickin' charming.

I can't wait to see her again.

Before I start taping, I'm going to see if I can buy some flowers to send her somehow. That's exactly what I'm going to do.

I have the idea to get some for Viv, too. A get-well kind of thing.

Or I guess I could order them some room service. That would be pretty cool.

There's a knock at the door.

My heart actually jumps—like it might be Laurel.

But it's just Tamara, who barges in without even a greeting. Par for the course. But she looks horrible. Stressed and strung out.

"Just spoke to the captain. Internet, phone, everything's down. Aren't you glad we prerecorded all those segments?!"

"Hey," I say. "Good morning."

Her face is gaunt and her suit is hanging off her. Even her shoes look too big. She starts to pace and I honestly think she's going to lose a loafer.

She's toying with the clippy thing on the top of her clipboard and she won't meet my eyes.

"I'm going to give you the morning off. We'll do some more recording in the afternoon and just stockpile it until we get back into a service area. But I think it would be really good for you to go find Sabbi and make nice to her."

"Tamara—"

"You don't need to kiss her like a madman, like you did the other night, just be polite to her. Her people are very, very upset."

"Tamara!"

"What?!" she snaps.

She stops and I see her hands are shaking.

"Are you okay?" I ask.

"Yes! I'm fine, for God's sake. That Solu makes you a little jittery, I think. At least, it makes me jittery."

"You need to stop taking it."

"Oh, I could stop if I wanted to. But you know, it's free on board and back when it's released stateside, it's going for seventy-five dollars a box! For twenty packets. I mean, it's a huge story. Rich is ecstatic. The demand is so high they're actually raising prices before the launch. Not that we'll be talking about that in our segments, of course."

She's talking so fast I have trouble making out all of her words.

"So, listen, call time is pushed to one p.m. I'm going to go ashore and contact the production office. We may do the afternoon segments on the mainland, where we'll have service. In the meantime, talk to Sabbi, be sweet. Let Rich take some photos. We have to follow up the big kiss with some other stuff so it looks like you're boyfriend/girlfriend, not just a one-night thing. She doesn't want that. If you're going to go onshore this morning, just leave a message on my room phone. Those phones are still working at least!"

She's headed toward the door.

"Tamara, wait! Hold on!"

And as psyched as I am to have the morning off, I am really worried.

"Can we talk for a moment?"

"Sure, yes, what?"

"I want to talk about Sabbi but, also, I think we need to rethink how we're covering this cruise."

"Oh? Really? In what way?"

She's literally tapping her foot with impatience.

I take a big breath.

"Solu is addictive," I say. "People are acting really weird. To me, it looks like people are losing too much weight, too fast."

"Great! I'm so glad to hear your expert opinion," she snips.

"I think we should be exploring some of the downsides to the drug in our coverage," I say.

"It's not a drug, it's a supplement," she snaps.

"Whatever. It's addictive."

Her arms are crossed.

"You think we should 'blow the cover' on this?" she asks.

"These are some major side effects," I say.

"You think you should do, like, an undercover reporter thing?"

The sarcasm is so overstated it brings up bile in the back of my throat.

"Solu is seriously addictive. You don't see it because you're taking the stuff yourself!" I say. "Look at yourself, you're acting like a classic junkie!"

"Oooh, investigative reporter Baby Tom-Tom!" she snaps. "He's so desperate to be taken seriously that he will tank the best gig he's had in years, just to shoot himself in the foot!"

"That's not fair!"

She grabs me by the front of my shirt.

Her eyes are bloodshot and wild.

I am, just for a second, actually scared by my forty-five-year-old, female, hundred-twenty-pound producer.

"Do your job, you effin' clown," she spits.

LAUREL

LORNA KRIEGER'S VOICE wakes me up: "Good morning, passengers, please excuse the interruption. Code Ingrid, suite 910, Code Ingrid, suite 910."

I wake up, and oh my God, it wasn't a dream. The stuff with Tom.

My mind is flooded with pure happiness—it wasn't a dream.

Viv is not in bed with me.

"Viv?" I say. "I have to tell you—"

Vivika's wearing the size-6 dress she was so excited about, over her smallest bikini. She's sitting against the wall, near the window, and she's sobbing as she eats her bag of Oreos.

"Sweetie, what are you doing?"

She's got tears running down her face and she's jamming one cookie after another into her mouth.

"I snuck these in, in my luggage, did you know that? I brought two bags of Oreos because I wasn't sure I could get them on board and I knew I'd never make it without them."

I walk over and slide down the wall to sit next to her.

"And then, for days, I didn't even think about them."

She offers the bag to me and I take one.

"When I eat Oreos, I feel better. I eat a whole bag, this whole bag, and then, by the end I feel full. I feel numb. I feel disgusted with myself. I feel comforted."

She throws the bag at the wall and the black crumbs go every-where, skittering over the plush carpet.

Housekeeping will not be pleased.

"They're not working. They don't make me feel *anything* now. I can't even get a rush."

I put my arms around her and she cries into my hair.

"All I want is Solu."

I hold her and she's so thin in my arms. It feels like I'm hug-ging some other person. Not even my Viv.

"I think that I've been getting high on sugar my whole life, trying to make myself feel better. And now, now that sugar doesn't work anymore, I can see how stupid it is."

"You're being too hard on yourself, Vivvy," I say, smoothing down her hair. Her skin is kind of waxy. Her face shiny with tears.

"No, I'm just telling the truth. I'm a binge eater and I've never told anyone and somehow I thought I could hide it my whole life, but I want you to know."

"Okay, now I know," I say. "And I love you just the same."

She buries her head in her hands.

"Solu is bad, Laurel," she says. "You were right. It's really bad. And I still want it."

"Let's get you in the shower. We'll go ashore in Belize. Maybe we should call your dad." It kills me to even suggest this, but Viv's well-being has to trump my romance. "Maybe he should send us some tickets home."

She nods her head. Tears drop from her bowed head.

Voices come then, from out in the hall. They're excited and there're the sounds of yelling and fists hitting against the hall-way walls.

Viv and I look out of our doorway at the passengers.

"Let's see what's going on," I suggest.

She nods and we follow the flood of people up onto the pool deck.

The captain, Mr. Almstead, and Dr. Zhang are standing up on a little raised deck near the pool, and passengers are crowded around, yelling at them. But the passengers aren't getting too close, because there are three guards standing at the foot of the platform.

I see the one hugely muscle-y guy with the crew cut. His two buddies are nearly as gigantic. (It's like he cloned lesser copies of himself.) The three of them are standing, arms crossed, in front of the platform, wearing steel-gray security uniforms.

They have guns! I see shoulder holster-y type things under their arms!

It's eighty-five degrees and as balmy as bathwater, but I break out in a cold sweat.

Viv starts to push forward, into the crowd. I follow her, as best I can, but people are much more aggressive than your usual crowd. (It's not like they're gathering around a street performer.)

This is . . . it's an angry mob, I realize. I am standing in an angry mob.

"Look, folks, what can I say? We made a mistake. We should have realized we needed to start you all on a small dosage and go from there," Mr. Almstead says as loudly as he can.

I feel bad for him. He's just this little old man.

Suddenly I'm glad he has armed guards. He might actually need their protection.

And I am really glad to be wearing my motorcycle boots right now. They make me feel safe.

"We are surprised by the symptoms you are experiencing and we're very sorry," Dr. Zhang adds. Her younger, stronger voice carries farther into the crowd. "And by decreasing your doses gradually, over the remainder of the cruise, we will gently ease you away from the stress you are experiencing now—"

"It's not bloody stress," a British man shouts. "It's excruciating!"

People holler their agreement.

"It's clear to us we're going to need to make adjustments in the formulation," Dr. Zhang says.

"Hey, it's a great product, but it needs to be tweaked. That's life," Almstead, maybe not so helpfully, adds.

"When do we get our doses?" a woman demands.

"Yeah!" a man echoes. "We paid for Solu and we want Solu!"

"We've decided to distribute one packet of Solu for each passenger at each meal," Dr. Zhang says.

The crowd boos and hisses.

Looking around, I see all these wealthy people—all the minor celebrities, and their faces are drawn and lined and angry.

Clothes are draping off them.

They look like extras in some bizarre modern-day luxury-cruise production of Les Miserables.

I feel someone's eyes on me from behind. I turn and see Sabbi and her clique. They're standing up on the observation deck above, where the hot tub is, looking down at the whole scene.

I can't hear what they're saying, but I see Sabbi say something and the rest of them laugh. They're looking down on the angry crowd.

Good. I mean, good for them. Really. At least someone has the sense to stay out of this insane scene.

Sabbi sees me looking at her and gestures to me, waving me up to join them.

I elbow Viv and nod toward Sabbi.

Viv looks up.

Sabbi signals again, mouthing the words, *Come here.*

"Oh my God," Viv says. "We've been summoned. Let's go."

I'm not sure what to do, so I follow Viv as she fights through the crowd.

Up on the observation deck, Sabbi's got two bottles of champagne chilling on ice and a tray overflowing with cheese, grapes, and nuts.

The people in her clique look just as unnaturally skinny as everyone else on board. One of the girls is wearing a bikini that looks like it's made of yarn and postage stamps.

They have music playing off someone's iPhone and everyone is bopping, moving to the beat. Some of them don't even look like they realize they're moving, but they're twitching, bouncing their feet. Edgy.

One of the bronzed, minor-deity-looking guys is rubbing Sabbi's back. I realize I know him. He's an actor. He's known for his shaggy blond hair.

Luke someone. The one Lorna Krieger keeps going on about in her morning messages.

Sabbi is thinner, but still mind-numbingly gorgeous. She looks like the famished twin of her more voluptuous self.

I bet there are fan protest sites going up about how much weight she's lost off her butt. (Though I guess the most recent shots won't be getting out there since the Internet is down.)

"*Bom dia,*" she says. "You're the girl Tom likes, right? Laura?"

"Laurel," I correct her.

"Have some champagne. You ever had Cristal? It really is better than the rest. It's not just marketing."

"I've never tried it," Viv says.

"You'll love it," Sabbi purrs. "What's your name?"

"Vivika."

"I love that dress. Stella McCartney?"

Viv nods. I'm glad to see her pepping up a bit.

"I have it in green," Sabbi says. "Trevor, we need Cristal."

A short guy in a pair of really baggy green trunks comes over.

"Hey, I know you," he says to Viv.

"We met at Key West," Viv says. "On the beach."

"Yeah, totally." Trevor checks her out. "Looking good, baby."

Viv rolls her eyes, but laughs.

He pours her a glass of champagne and she tastes it.

"Wow, it is really good," she says.

"You know what makes it better? Drink it in the hot tub."

Viv laughs.

"You think I'm kidding, but I'm serious!" He's smiling, bouncing on the soles of his feet.

Viv gives me a look and I shrug. She can go in the hot tub if she wants.

Trevor puts his hand on Viv's shoulder and leads her over to it. More of Sabbi's people are in there, lounging and splashing and, yes, drinking Cristal.

"Luka, my sweet, would you mind if I talked to Laurel alone?"

"Sure thing, Sabbi. I'll go soak."

He walks over to the tub. His suit is riding perilously low on his hips. (Lorna would freak out.)

"We're gonna be a thing. Me and Luka," Sabbi tells me, watching Luka. "In the papers. Tom's not going to come out looking so good."

"Oh," I say. "Did you want me to tell him or something?"

Sabbi looks at me, those famous brown eyes taking my stock.

"Who are you, anyway?" she asks.

"Just Laurel Willard, from Fort Lauderdale."

"What do you do?"

"Well . . . I play the guitar."

"Are you in a band?" she asks.

"No. I'm just a high school senior. I play the guitar. I go to school."

"I see. So it's a plain-Jane kind of a thing," she says with a kind of sad, pitying smirk on her (gorgeous, famous) face.

"Yep," I say. I lean in. "Maybe he even likes me because I'm plain. Maybe he's freaky like that."

I turn to leave.

"Wait, stay, hang out with me. I want to know you."

"We're going ashore," I tell her. Not that it's any of her business.

"No, you're not."

"What do you mean?" I say, turning back to face her.

"You're not going anywhere today."

"Aren't we docking in Belize?"

She shakes her head.

"They canceled it. We're staying at sea. Didn't you watch the morning announcement lady?" I shake my head.

"They canceled going ashore?" I ask, my voice rising. This is not good. "But . . . we need to go."

"People were selling Solu on shore," a lanky girl with bleached out hair over by the cheese tray says. "That's why we're not going to dock."

"Shut up, Maggie," Sabbi says. "You don't know what you're talking about, as usual. They canceled docking in Belize because of this," Sabbi gestures out to the crowd of now-dispersing but still-angry passengers. "Bad publicity. It's the same reason they shut off our Internet service."

"You think they did that on purpose?" I ask.

"Tsk. You, my friend, are very innocent."

A waiter comes up with a covered tray.

"Miss Ribiero, Mr. Almstead gave us permission to honor your request. He asks that you use discretion, so as to not upset the other passengers."

Sabbi smiles and winks at the waiter.

"Of course, absolutely!" she says.

She reaches down to a little silver pouch in her straw hand-bag and takes out a hundred dollar bill. She presses it into the waiter's hand.

"*Obrigada*," she says.

He's wearing a big smile as he removes the silver cover from the platter and places it down on an empty side table.

Splayed out in a fan are maybe thirty packets of Solu.

"Everyone! Snack is here," Sabbi calls.

All of Sabbi's crew immediately come out of the hot tub and draw around, dripping wet.

"Yes!"

"Awesome!"

Sabbi takes three-packets for herself and the others dig in.

She looks at me and smiles.

"Go ahead," she says.

"No, thanks."

"Are you sure?" she says. She runs her eyes up my figure.

"Yes. Quite," I reply.

Viv is standing just outside the group. I see her staring at the remaining packets.

"Come on, Viv," I say. "Let's go . . . Let's go . . . "

She's transfixed by those packets.

Viv looks at me and looks away.

She starts to shake.

"Let's go and have a swim!" I say. "Or Jet Ski! Let's go find the captain and demand he puts us ashore. Come on, Viv."

I cross to her. I'm going to drag her away, but as I'm moving she flashes her hand out, too, and grabs two packets.

"Don't!" I say. "Don't have any more."

"Hey!" Sabbi says loudly. "Vivika is welcome to party with us. More than welcome. And I think you should leave her be to make her own decisions."

"Yeah," Trevor says. "We're all grown-ups here."

"Viv, please!" I tell her and I try to take the packets from her.

"You should go," Viv says. "You should go, Laurel."

I see that Luka is now chopping up a pack of Solu on a glass table. With a razor blade.

Dear God, they're going to sniff it like cocaine.

"Please, Vivika." Tears are falling down my face. "Don't do any more of this stuff."

But she turns away from me, and stuffs the two packets in her mouth.

"Viv, DON'T!"

She chews, then swallows the packets, paper and all.

"Oh," she moans. She brings her hands up to her head. "Oh God, it feels so good."

Sabbi's crowd cheers and Trevor pulls Viv to him and kisses her on the mouth.

I stumble down the stairs.

I need Tom.

TOM

I'M PUSHING MY WAY through the crowd on the pool deck. People look scary thin.

Almstead has just made some kind of announcement, but I missed it.

Laurel and Viv must be here somewhere. First I see Cubby.

"Cubby!" I shout.

He pushes his way over to me.

"Have you seen Tamara?" he asks.

"She came by my room earlier," I tell him. "She gave me the morning off. You, too?"

"Yeah," he says.

Studded between the angry, muttering, stick-skinny, Solu-taking passengers I see a few other people who look robust and healthy. Regular, non-addicted people.

They look as dazed and scared as Cubby and I must look.

"Hey, aren't you glad you didn't take the stuff?"

"God, yeah!" I answer. "These people are sick."

"Me, too," he says. "I knew it was too good to be true."

The addicts don't seem to know where to go. They're buzzing and griping, milling around.

"Tom!" I hear Laurel's voice.

I step up onto a lounge chair so I can try to find her.

I see her waving to me from near the stairway. She looks upset.

I push my way to her. Cubby follows.

"Watch it!" someone growls. I'm surprised to see it's one of the staff—a Filipino waiter, gaunt and scowling, circulating a tray of cappuccinos and espressos, which no one seems to want.

"Sorry," I mutter.

Laurel crashes into my arms.

"Are you okay?"

"Not really," she says.

"Oh, Cubby," I say, remembering Laurel. "This is Laurel."

"I remember you," Cubby says. "Good to see you looking . . . not really skinny."

"Same to you," Laurel says. It would be funny—we're all happy to see one another with some body fat. Except that it's not.

Laurel grips my arm.

"Tom, Viv is up with Sabbi and they all took—" She stops midsentence, looking at the passengers around her in sudden fear.

She leans up to whisper in my ear.

"They all took extra doses of Solu. A waiter brought them their own tray."

I'm listening to what she says, but I can't help but enjoy the sensation of her breath in my ear—her mouth so close to my neck. I am a guy, after all.

"We have to get her off the boat," Laurel says. "But I heard the captain canceled our stop in Belize."

"What?" I say. This is news to me.

"They're keeping us all on board."

I look around at the milling, angry passengers. Cubby and I exchange a glance. This is not good.

"Come on," I say, taking her hand.

"Where are we going?"

"To talk to Almstead."

"You guys do that," Cubby says. "I'm going to work on something else."

"Tamara said to meet at one," I say.

"I'll find you before then," Cubby says.

There's a bodyguard at the door of Almstead's suite. Irate passengers are demanding entrance.

"It's no use." Laurel sighs. "Look at this crowd."

"Let's give it a shot. Maybe I can get through."

We're holding hands and she keeps close to me as I elbow through the group.

Over the PA, Lorna Krieger announces, "Pardon the interruption, Code Ingrid, suite 633. Also, Code Ingrid, suite 1100." Whatever that means.

I get to the bodyguard. He's built and he's armed, which seems like overkill to me, frankly. A Semper Fi tattoo stretches around his forearm.

"Hey," I say. "Tom Fiorelli. Mr. Almstead wants to talk to us about coverage. You know, how to handle all this." I indicate the crowd with my shoulder.

"Oh. Okay," he says, chewing gum. "Baby Tom-Tom."

I nod.

He lets Laurel and me through.

Almstead's suite is luxurious just under the point of being obnoxious. Like the hallway, it's filled with irate passengers, but these are a cut above. These are the celebrities on the cruise. The famous chef Tony LoPrima—who used to be jolly and chunky and now looks wrinkled and haggard. The billionaire tycoon and his bleached-blond, heavily "augmented" Russian wife. Her silicon implants are drooping dangerously low. Jenny Palmer and her husband, what's his face. The Grub Guy.

"This is not what we signed up for!" LoPrima says.

Almstead is standing near a table. Standing just behind him is his bodyguard, Amos, the one from the restaurant.

Amos looks stone-faced. I feel bad for the guy. He probably thought he was going to have a cushy gig on a cruise ship—now he's in the middle of a big mess.

"I know it. I know it." Almstead sighs. "This has not gone at all the way it should have."

"When we regain Internet service, the first call I'm making is to my lawyer!" the billionaire announces. "And I invite you all to join in a civil lawsuit with me!"

There are nods and murmurs of agreement.

"I don't blame you," Almstead says. "Honestly, I'm furious myself. As an investor, I put seventy-eight million dollars into this. And they gave me every assurance it was ready to go. Years of testing."

"Well, what went wrong?" the Grub Guy asks.

Almstead looks at him sadly.

"We think it's the diluting agent—it's calcium phosphate—supposed to be the safest stuff in the world. Zhang thinks there may be some kind of a reaction. Or that maybe the manufacturer has altered the formulation somehow. There's no way to test it here, on the ship, but we're trying to get to the bottom of it. I don't know, but I'm just . . . ruined. We're gonna have to delay the launch. We're pulling product from all over the country. It's a massive recall. The publicity is killing us."

That seems to strike a chord in the crowd—they can all relate to a PR meltdown, I guess.

Laurel snuggles against my hip and her body seems to relax. It is a relief to know that Almstead's on it—and to hear some straight talk.

"There's nothing wrong with Solu in my opinion," says the Bachelorette Jenny Palmer. "I mean, if you ask me, I finally look how I've wanted to feel my whole life. I love it! I think it's a great product!"

The billionaire's wife nods in agreement.

"I'm upset now to hear you, Mr. Almstead," she says in a thick Russian accent. "Now you going to change and ruin it. I want more Solu and I want it now."

"Yeah!" shouts Jenny Palmer.

Almstead holds up his hands.

"You promised us we have very much Solu!" the Russian woman complains.

"Code Ingrid, suite 1010. Code Matthew, Celestial Lounge."

Laurel gasps. "That means someone died!" she whispers.

"What?" I ask.

"Matthew. Someone died." She looks pale. "This guy from the crew I'm friends with told me about the codes."

I pull her close.

Almstead goes on.

"Look," Almstead says. "When we get the formula worked out, if you want to have it, I'll give you a lifetime supply of Solu. For each of you."

A wave of greed glimmers over the faces of the assembled passengers.

"Everyone in this room—but you all only. I'm not doing it for the whole ship."

I roll my eyes at Laurel. One minute they're suing him because the product is faulty, the next they're signing up for a lifetime supply.

"What about the passengers who need help?" Laurel asks, her voice shaky, but strong. "What's the plan for the ship? My friend needs medical attention."

A couple of people turn and look at her. I can see them wondering who she is.

She pulls back a bit and I squeeze her hand.

"Well, miss, that's the issue. Right now, we're turning around and going to haul butt back to the States. The medical treatment we can get there is just vastly superior to what we could get in Mexico or Belize."

"There's nothing wrong with Solu!" the Bachelorette screeches.

Laurel holds her ground.

"How long until we get there?"

"We should be back in eighteen hours. The captain has assured me of that. In the meantime, if everyone maintains a dose of three packets a day, they'll be all right."

I'd like to ask him about what Tamara and I should do in terms of the broadcasts, but Almstead holds up his hands as more questions are launched.

"Guys, you need to give me a break, now. I gotta get on the phone to the mainland. We got a whole lotta mess to figure out."

"You have a phone?" someone asks.

"It's one of those satellite jobs," Almstead replies. That creates a new round of complaints and threats. The bodyguards start ushering us toward the door.

Out in the hall, the celebrities go their separate ways.

Laurel's holding my hand.

"Will you help me try to talk some sense into Viv?" she asks me.

"Of course," I tell her.

"I feel . . . I feel so relieved," Laurel says. "Now that we know the plan and we'll be back home soon."

"I know."

"Tom!" I hear my voice called.

It's Cubby. He's carrying a stack of yellow legal-notebook pages. Each has a message written in Sharpie.

He tapes one up on the wall with Scotch tape.

"Me and some other AA old-timers are holding a meeting. Can you two come?"

The handmade flyer reads: *GOT ADDICTION? Come to the Starlight Lounge at 11 a.m. We can help!*

"Sure, if you think it would help."

"I think the more people who are clean who come, the better. You two find out anything?" Cubby asks.

"Almstead says they're recalling it all over the country. Something went wrong in the production. Maybe the filler they used, or maybe the formula got tweaked," I say.

"Well, at least now we know what happened."

"They're turning the ship around and hauling ass to the States," I tell him. "I can tell you more later, but right now we need to find Laurel's friend Viv."

"She's hooked. Really bad," Laurel says.

"Try to get her to the meeting," Cubby says. "It could help."

Laurel leads me back up to the hot-tub area. I can hear some Brazilian pop song blasting out of an iPod and some portable speakers.

It's a mess up there. There's fruit and cheese all over the deck and they've overturned some of the lounge chairs. There are three naked girls in the hot tub splashing around and a guy and a girl are making out on the deck, half on and half off a cushion from the lounge chairs.

Sabbi and that a-hole Luka Harris are laughing and throwing money on them, like it's a strip club.

It's a party scene right out of a nightmare.

Sabbi turns and sees me. A line of blood trickles down from her nose.

"Tomazino!" she yells. "You came!"

She reaches for me and I step back, but she lurches forward and grabs me.

"Stop it, Sabbi!"

She's trying to kiss me on the mouth.

I push her away from me and she slips and falls.

She laughs and the rest of the group howls.

They are way, way high on Solu.

"Viv! Vivika Hallerton!" Laurel's shouting.

I realize that the girl making out is Viv.

The d-bag has got her top off and she's oblivious.

"That's enough," I say. I step forward and pull the creep off Vivika. His eyes are glassy and the skin around his mouth is red and wet. Disgusting.

"Get off her, you jerk," I say. "She's high. You can see that!"

He tries to take a swing at me, but he's much littler than me and I heave him up and throw him off toward the rail.

He curses at me.

Laurel sweeps in and gathers Vivika to her feet.

"Leaveme'lone!" Viv is slurring. "I like him! I really like tha'guy!"

"You're wasted, Viv. Really wasted," Laurel hisses.

I grab a towel from a pyramid by the tub and wrap it around Viv. She throws the towel off.

"You can't tell me what to do! I'm not a baby!"

The guy I threw has a wicked rug-burn down his side from skidding across the deck. He comes back, trying to tackle me.

I get clear of Laurel and Viv and punch the guy in the face. Blood spurts from his nose.

He curses at me some more.

"Dude!" I yell, "I'm much bigger than you. Just leave me alone! We're taking the girl away!"

And we do.

We drag Viv away from them.

Once we're on the pool deck I take off my shirt and put it on Viv.

Her head is hanging down and she looks like she's about to faint.

"Wanna sleep," she says.

"No," Laurel tells her. "We're going to a meeting."

LAUREL

THE BAR IS FILLED WITH PASSENGERS—some look skeptical, some look desperate, most look way too thin.

The atmosphere in the room is tense. There's a lot of angry talk. The Solu seems to amp people up. I've never seen anyone on cocaine, but I have to imagine this is what it looks like.

We went by Tom's room and he grabbed a shirt to wear.

We got here a few minutes ago and were able to get seats in the front. I found Viv a Pipop and a bowl of honey-roasted bar-peanuts, but she wouldn't touch any of it.

Now she seems to be half asleep.

Tom's on the other side of her. He has his arm over the back of Viv's chair, with his hand resting on my shoulder. The weight of his hand feels wonderful. It feels like there's warmth and comfort coming right out of his palm into my body.

"I was thinking. After this, maybe we should take Viv back to our room and just hole up there. Order room service," I say.

"Good idea. She can rest."

"Would you . . . you'll stay with us, right?"

He brushes my cheek with the back of his hand.

"All I want to do is stay with you, Laurel."

And I know he's telling the truth because my heart rings like a bell.

Who falls in love during a creepy drug disaster?

(I do. No, we do—me and Tom.)

Over the PA, Lorna Krieger keeps coming on and announcing codes. Ingrid, Frieda, another Matthew, and an Oscar—man overboard!

"What a nightmare," I say.

"I know."

Three men and two women make their way to the raised area near the bar. Cubby's one of them. He gives us a little wave.

The five of them are all regular-size—that is, some are thin and some are fat but none of them look like bone-skinny addicts.

A gray-haired lady rings a spoon on a water glass to try to get everyone to quiet down.

"Attention—attention, everyone! I am Patricia and I'm an alcoholic."

"Hi, Patricia," the other four chorus.

"Oh, this is just rich," a skinny crone in the front row cackles.

"Would all who care to, please join me in the serenity prayer?" Patricia continues.

She and the others close their eyes and hold hands.

I bow my head. I don't know the words, but I try to go along with them: "God, grant me the serenity to accept the things I cannot change, the courage to change—"

"Go to hell!" someone yells.

They continue on with the prayer and someone throws a handful of peanuts at them.

"Excuse me!" the lady says. "We are here to help you! Please give us the respect we deserve!"

A guy in the back makes a raspberry sound.

"We are here to help you. We know what it's like to be at the mercy of addiction and we're doing our best to try to share with you our experience."

"Our only *problem* is that they've cut us off!" a lady shouts.

There's a chorus of yeahs.

Lorna announces more codes over the PA.

"Viv, wake up," I tell her. I give her a little shake.

"We paid a lot of money for this cruise," the lady screeches on.

"Would you shut up? I want to hear what they have to say!" another woman yells. I recognize her! It's the mom from our dinner table. I don't see her husband or kids anywhere. Jeez, I hope they're okay.

"I've been in AA for twenty-seven years," Patricia continues. "When I was drinking, all I thought about every day was when I could get my next drink. My entire day was consumed by thoughts of when I could get to a bar or to one of the bottles I hid around my house."

"That's because you're a frickin' drunk!" a guy heckles from the back.

"Hey!" one of the other AA guys interrupts. This one is short and muscular, like a fire plug. "Watch your mouth! We're here to share our experience, strength, and hope! AA meetings are a safe space!"

I trade a look with Tom. No way is this a safe space.

Cubby steps forward.

"Hi, I'm Cubby and I'm a grateful, recovering alcoholic and narcotics addict." He doesn't wait for anyone to say hi.

"We are here to tell you that there is a higher power you can turn to for help when you are powerless over a substance."

"Viv," I say, shaking her a bit. "Wake up!"

"The first step in AA is saying I am powerless over alcohol and

I must rely on a power higher than myself for guidance. Narcotics addicts like myself say we're powerless over drugs and compulsive eaters say they're powerless over food."

More than one person is shouting now, but Cubby soldiers on, speaking louder.

"You all have a problem with Solu, which seems to be more addictive than booze, or sugar or heroin, from what I can see. You're in deep shit! So say it with me: I am powerless over Solu, and I must turn to a power greater than myself for help!"

Someone throws a drink (whiskey?) at Cubby and the liquor splashes all over his face. He brushes it away with the back of his arm.

"Say it! I AM POWERLESS OVER SOLU!" he shouts.

There are some men at the back of the room who boil forward, trying to get to Cubby, to make him shut up.

"We gotta get out of here," Tom says.

"Viv!" I say. "WAKE UP!"

And suddenly she does.

Her eyes open. Wide-open. Bloodshot.

At that moment everyone in the room freezes.

Viv sits up straight.

And she sniffs.

All the addicts' heads go up. They smell the air.

And then they lurch up, scrambling, moving fast.

Viv breaks away from us, climbing over the back of her chair.

They all head for the door, for the door, for the door.

Howling, bellowing, screaming.

Their sounds—they make my flesh crawl.

They crawl over one another, all of them headed for the large stairway that leads down to the dining hall.

"Solu," Tom says. "It's gotta be."

We watch as the addicts stream down the stairs. They move forward in one giant, reaching, screeching mass. And fast.

The AA people step toward us.

"We'd better see what's going on," Patricia says.

I don't want to.

I want to go back to my suite and get in bed and not come out until we dock in Fort Lauderdale.

But Tom holds my arm and we wind through the overturned leather club chairs and toppled coffee tables.

The grand staircase sweeps down into the Aurora Restaurant.

As we come down the stairs we hear crashing and squabbling. Glass smashing.

Most of the activity is down at the galley end of the giant room.

Steel food-prep tables have been dragged out from the kitchen and there's blood on the doors and walls!

"There's bodies!" I scream. "On the ground!"

Addicts are trampling over people on the ground. They're swarming into the galley, at the far end of the restaurant. We can hear the sounds of them ripping it apart.

"Jesus, we have to help!" Tom shouts. He surges forward but Patricia pulls him back.

"You go down there, you're getting killed!" she says.

A man shouts in victory. He comes out of the galley holding a sack over his head, and everyone screams and cheers.

He rips it open and the powder falls and wafts out in a cloud and it's insanity. People diving and shoveling it into their mouths and licking the floor and scraping it out of the carpet with their fingernails.

A bone-thin woman with dark circles under her eyes and

greasy hair comes racing to Tom and Cubby and pushes a padded duffel bag into Cubby's arms.

I remember her, she's Tom's producer.

"We need to get this," she tells them. "Screw Almstead. You were right, Tom . . . "

She clutches Tom's wrists desperately. It's like she's afraid to let go.

"Tamara, we need to get you out of here!"

"You were right. Get the footage."

"Tamara, let's go back to your room," Tom tells her. She releases his wrists and backs away. Tom darts forward and grabs her hand.

"Come on!" Tom says. "I'm taking you to your room!"

Cubby has taken the camera from the duffel bag and is recording the chaos. He walks away from us and gets up on a table toward the middle of the room.

"Tamara, listen to me. It's not too late for you," Tom says.

She's straining at him.

"Let me go. Let me go!"

Two bone-skinny women come out trying to hide a crate of packets between them and they're tackled by other addicts. Some of the people coming out of the kitchen are brandishing knives. Butcher knives!

The packets go everywhere and people fly and skid over one another, trying to grab them up.

Then I see Vivika. My sweet Vivika, and she's in the melee, snatching packets as fast as she can.

People are jamming the packets into their mouths, and I see Viv do the same.

Her eyes shut in ecstasy as the Solu hits her mouth, but then they pop open again. She wants more.

She turns and pulls someone out of her way and dives down into a clutch of fighting bodies.

I lose sight of her.

"Viv!" I shout. "Vivika!!!"

Tom's still struggling with Tamara. I head for the crowd. I can't let Vivvy get hurt. She could be trampled or stabbed or worse.

But I feel Tom's hands on me. And I see Tamara shoot past.

He let her go to keep me back.

"It's Viv," I sob. "She's over there."

Tom lifts me up as easily as you would a child and puts me on the table with Cubby.

"Stay here," he says. "I'll go for her."

TOM

I'M FULLY ADRENALIZED and entirely terrified.

The addicts are all over one another. There's Solu everywhere and they're desperate to get it in their mouths.

People on the floor are snorting and licking. Other people step on them, kicking their bodies, their heads, as they scramble up and over, and the ones on the ground don't even care.

"Gimme that," I hear one guy say. He's holding a knife on another guy, who has a fistful of packets and is trying to steal away. "Don't make me hurt you. I don't want to hurt you!"

I see Viv. She's under a serving table, scraping at some Solu on the floor with her fingernails.

"Vivika!" I yell. "Come over here!"

There are probably thirty people between me and her, and all of them are on the warpath. They're scratching one another, stabbing, biting, clawing.

My only advantage is that I'm not going after the same thing they are.

I push and fight my way to her.

"Vivika!" I shout.

She's sucking the carpet now. I grab her leg and pull.

She screeches, trying to hold on to the carpet.

"Laurel wants you!" I shout.

Her eyes are blank. There's no recognition. None.

She twists and squirms, trying to get away.

"You have to come!" I shout. I have my hands on her thighs now and I'm pulling her toward my body.

She slaps my face and kicks free of me, crawling back into the snarl of addicts.

Then I hear a blast from a megaphone.

"Attention! Everyone is to report to their cabin RIGHT NOW!"

It's a security officer with ten other crewmen. They're all carrying batons.

"BREAK IT UP!" he shouts.

The crewmen start wading into the fight, pulling people apart and propelling them toward the exits.

The lead security officer shouts into the megaphone: "Dr. Zhang has pinpointed the cause of the reaction you are all having and if you will just get to your rooms, Dr. Zhang can reverse it—"

As the addicts realize who is being spoken of, a collective growl of anger and hatred seethes up.

A man grabs the security officer. He fights back, but the other addicts pile on—kicking and punching the officer.

His body goes down in the center of the mob and I hear his scream, but only for an anguished, bloody moment.

I turn from the sight.

It's maybe fifty feet away from me and the stench of blood and bowels and guts hits me.

Thank God Zhang isn't here. Or Almstead. Not even his armed bodyguards could fight this mob.

I look at Cubby on his table and he's taping. Even as people brush and bang against the table, he's taping.

But Laurel's not by his side, where I put her.

And my heart freezes.

Then I feel her arms around me from behind. She's come up be-hind me.

She's shaking, her eyes dilated in terror.

She clings to me.

I gather her up and just start plowing through the addicts.

Screw Viv. And Laurel can be mad at me, but I'm just one guy.

I have her in my arms and we're getting the hell out of there.

I can't get an addict away from Solu. It can't be done.

It cannot be done.

And that scares me.

LAUREL

I'M SHAKING AND CRYING and who even cares?

Tom carries me out of the dining hall.

"Jesus, Tom," I say. "That was . . . that was . . . "

He goes to set me down, but I'm all tangled up with him and we crumple down onto the floor in the hallway.

"Unreal," he says. "Terrifying. Are you okay?"

"I'm fine. I'm fine! I mean, nothing happened to me, not like . . . ! Did you see those—" I gulp.

"Those people crushed by the kitchen doors and that security guy—"

We're kneeling together, clutching each other.

I kiss him. His mouth and then his face, his cheeks, his forehead. I'm desperate to kiss him, suddenly. And I'm crying all over him.

"We're okay," he tells me.

He takes my hands in his.

"When the Solu's gone, that's when we're gonna go get Viv. And we'll lock her in your room until we dock. But before we do that, we've got to get the word out. To the mainland. We've got to warn people about Solu."

"But Almstead said they're recalling it," I stutter.

"Yeah, but the fact that it makes people kill?! It's huge. People have to know."

"You're right," I say. "Of course you are."

Tom stands up and hauls me up with him like I weigh nothing at all.

Maybe it sounds silly, but I'm very, very happy that I've suddenly found myself with a strong boyfriend. What would have been a superficial issue (his strength) is now really, really important. Like, to my survival.

"Cubby's got the camera," he says. "I've got to go back in there. You wait here."

"No way," I say. "I'm staying with you."

As we go in, people come careening out, some of them with Solu packets stashed in their pockets or clutched in their hands. They couldn't guard the packets more zealously if they were carrying thousand-dollar bills.

Just inside the door we pass Maroon-Hair Lady who weighed me at the clinic. She's sitting on the floor, licking her hands, her legs splayed out straight, like a toddler.

"There he is!" I shout. Cubby is lying on the floor near the table.

"Cubby! Are you okay?" Tom shouts.

We help him sit up, then stand. There's blood soaking the side of Cubby's shirt.

"Grab the camera," Tom tells me. "And the kit."

I see the camera, lying where Cubby dropped it. I guess the kit is the duffel bag. I take them both.

Tom is supporting Cubby's weight. I brace myself under Cubby's other side. It's the bloody side and I feel wet warmth seep into my T-shirt.

"I'm okay," he says. "I'm okay."

(He's totally not okay.)

Out on the deck, Cubby insists on taping Tom before he goes to the medical center.

He waves me away. "It's a flesh wound. It's a flesh wound."

Tom stands at the side of the deck. The sky behind him is cloudless.

(How can the day be so beautiful—the sky be so aqua-cobalt blue—when there's such evil and violence happening on the boat? It seems like there should be a typhoon or a hurricane outside.)

Tom runs his hand through his hair. Then laughs in self-deprecation.

"How's my hair?" he mocks himself.

"Perfect," I tell him.

"Rolling," Cubby says.

"I'm Tom Fiorelli, reporting from the deck of the *Extravagance* where we are witnessing one of the most horrifying catastrophes imaginable. The sweetener Solu is highly, highly addictive and is causing the passengers on this ship to behave like vicious, violent animals."

A small crowd of addicts is gathering near Tom as he speaks.

I can't help but flash back to the pleased, giggly groups of fans surrounding him the first day of the cruise.

Now they look like wild, dirty zombies—only zombies that think and act and scheme. Zombies—only *real*.

"A riot has just taken place in the dining hall and the chief security officer of the *Extravagance* was murdered before my own eyes."

Here a skeletal man stalks into the shot, photo-bombing it.

"You don't know what you're talking about!" the man shouts. "You're judging us and you don't know what it's like!"

The rest of the crowd chimes in.

Cubby reaches forward and hauls the guy roughly out of the frame.

"Solu is a dangerous drug that causes psychotic violent behavior. DO NOT USE IT under any circumstances," Tom says. "We are going to do our best to get this tape broadcast immediately. I don't know what is going to happen here on the *Extravagance*. We need rescue."

The heckler dodges into the shot again. He starts miming like he's humping Tom.

Tom turns around and coldcocks him.

The photo-bomber goes down hard.

Tom just looks down at him, shaking out his hand.

"I've always wanted to do that."

The crowd screeches and laughs and skitters away.

Cubby has to stop shooting. He hands the camera to Tom. He's having a hard time drawing breath. He sits down, leaning against the rail.

"Go . . . ," he gasps. "Take it to the bridge. They can broadcast directly from the camera. Use the Firewire Eight Hundred port to go to satellite."

He pushes the duffel bag forward with his foot and I pick it up.

"Cubby!" I take his hand. "We have to get you to the medical center. I know where it is."

He's pale, too pale. He waves me off.

"I'll find it myself. Go."

He's not going to find it himself. Cubby's not going anywhere.

His hand is pressed into his wound and blood is coursing through his fingers. It's pooling on the deck under him.

I kneel at his side and lay my hand against his forehead. His skin is damp and cold.

"Cubby," I begin, but I don't know what to say.

"I'm putting the serenity prayer to use right now," he says, giving me a pained smile. "And this gut wound is something I can't change. Go."

He closes his eyes.

Tom puts a hand on my shoulder.

"I'm sorry, Cubby," he says.

"Go" is the last word Cubby says.

TOM

CUBBY GAVE HIS LIFE to get the footage on this camera. We're going to get it to the bridge. It's across the pool deck—you enter it from inside the ship, near the most-expensive staterooms. I remember from my tour.

We just gotta get across the pool deck.

The addicts keep staggering out onto the pool deck. Angry and wild, before, they're now angry, wild, *and* high.

Some of them are grabbing one another and making out. Others are pushing and shoving, looking for a fight.

Age has nothing to do with it. Inhibitions are gone. It seems like all social contracts are gone. This is an ugly, anything-goes crowd.

We have to push our way through. The passengers are highly reactive. Three different guys try to pick a fight with me, and one terrifying old woman. Not old, I realize suddenly—she's one of the blond Australians from Day 3.

"Baby Tom-Tom!" one scrawny Latino guy cackles. "Come dance with me!" He grabs his crotch.

A tall and ropy older guy shoves my shoulder. "Think you're better than us. You do. I can tell! I know exactly what you're thinking!"

This guy was probably a lawyer or an investment banker. Now he's a burned-out addict and I pity him.

Is that what he's reading in my eyes?

"Give me a break," I say, trying to push past him.

"Looking down on us. But if you tried it, you'd be just like me."

"I'm sure that's right," I tell him.

"You're sure. You're sure," the man taunts. "You know everything."

Laurel tugs at my arm, leading me away from him.

The hallway outside the bridge is glutted with addicts, pushing and jock-eying for position in line.

"Coming through," I say. Laurel is close to me, right behind my back, and I have her hand in mine. No way I'm letting go of her.

I raise the camera above my head.

"We're waiting, too!" a woman screeches.

"You can't just CUT IN LINE!" another guy yells.

"We have urgent business with the captain!" I shout.

A guy my age puts both hands on my chest and shoves me hard.

"We have to keep going," Laurel yells to me.

Then we see a miracle coming down the hall.

It's Rich!

"Make way, make way, people!" he shouts. A bodyguard is shoving people out of his way.

Then he sees us.

"Tom! Tom Fiorelli! I have never been so glad to see anyone in my life!"

The bodyguard elbows people aside and Rich staggers to me. He clutches my arms.

His eyes are red. He's clearly been crying.

"Are you okay?" I ask.

He nods.

"You two?" he asks.

"We're fine," Laurel says. "But we need your help."

"I've got a tape," I say. "We've got to get it to the captain!"

"Come," Rich says. "Talk to me."

He draws Laurel and me away from the crowd. The bodyguard follows. We go down the hall to where the crystal chandelier hangs in the atrium with the elevators. From here we can hear the sounds of people below us partying, fighting, and screaming.

"This is hell on earth. Listen to them," Rich says.

"Look," I say. "We just came from the dining hall. I don't know if you know what happened, but kitchen workers were killed, and the chief security officer was ripped apart by the mob."

"Oh my Lord," Rich says. His face goes ashen.

"The passengers broke into the kitchen and took all the Solu," Laurel adds. "That's why they're . . . like this."

"Tamara is on the stuff. I tried to keep her from eating more, but I couldn't do it." I tell him.

Rich looks at me, and I see his eyes dart to the bodyguard he's with. He swallows.

"Rich, are you okay?" I ask.

"I'm . . . I'm a little scared right now. A little terrified. That's all."

"We are, too. But we have to warn the world, Rich. We have footage of the riot on this camera," I say. "We need to get it to the bridge."

"But it's not going to do anything," Rich blurts out. "I mean . . ."

He takes a breath. I can see him telling himself to get it together.

"What I mean to say is that everyone on the mainland is already aware of the problem. The captain has sent out a distress signal. Help is on the way."

He looks away from us, his eyes scanning the hallways below.

"Thank God!" Laurel exclaims. "They're on the way?"

"That's what I've been told. The coast guard. In full force."

"Nevertheless, I have to talk to the captain. He needs to send this tape through the satellite—"

"This is hardly the time to be thinking about your exclusive," Rich snaps.

"What?! Don't be insane! I don't care about that!"

"The public needs to know about Solu, Rich," Laurel butts in. "They need to know how dangerous it is."

"I'm sorry. I guess . . . I guess I don't really want the bad news to get out. But of course, it should. It has to. I'm sorry. I've been up for days. This is the greatest disaster of my or anyone else's career. Ever."

He's crying now.

"Hey," I say. "No one's going to remember a goddamn thing about who did the publicity for this. It's a nightmare. It's a tragedy. But it has nothing to do with you."

"I know. I know," he says.

"Can you get us up to see the captain?" I ask.

"No! No. You two should hole up and stay safe. I'll take the camera and the tape back to the bridge. They're expecting me back."

"I'd really like to talk to him—"

"No!" Rich says. "Trust me. It's awful up there. So many people and everyone's shouting. They probably won't even let you in."

He takes the camera and the kit from me.

"Cubby said there's a way to plug it directly into the communications system—"

"I'll get it done. Just promise me . . . "

"What?" I ask.

"Promise me you'll get hidden and stay safe."

"We'll stay safe."

We shake hands, then I pull him in and hug him. He's really a good guy.

"We'll come through this, Rich," I tell him.

He nods, looking at the deck, and wipes his eyes with the back of his hand.

Laurel puts her arms around him and hugs him, too.

"I was right about you two, you know that, right?" he says. "I'm the one who told you to kiss."

Laurel blushes.

She pecks him on the cheek.

"You were totally right. You stay safe, too," she tells him.

"I'm trying," he answers.

Rich leaves to take the camera up to the captain. I see Laurel looking into the small boutique that is up here. It's been ransacked.

"Maybe they have some snacks?" she says.

Some of the clothes are now hanging off the hangers and the rest are scattered on the floor. A jewelry case has been smashed, but it doesn't look like anyone has taken anything.

They destroyed the store with rage. Not greed.

I stick my hand into the case and pick out a pair of gold hoops, each hung with a little diamond.

"These would be nice on you," I say.

"Oh yeah?" she asks. "Because I thought *these* would be nice on you."

She holds up a pair of men's argyle socks.

I laugh.

We're alone in a trashed boutique and this is the first moment since the day began that I feel I can relax.

"I don't see any snacks," I say.

I pick through the stuff in the store. It's just sunglasses and jewelry and belts and handbags and makeup.

"Tom?"

"Yeah?"

"I'm really, really glad we met," Laurel says. She's still holding the socks and says it so straight, I burst out laughing.

"I mean it. I mean, I think if we hadn't met, I might be dead by now."

It's a funny thing to say, but she's not trying to be funny.

I step to her, over the broken glass and a scattered collection of trampled evening gowns. I collect her to me, pulling her in, and we kiss.

It's a hungry kiss, a life-affirming kiss.

I've never experienced one like it before. We're telling each other, somehow, that we are in a scary, horrible situation and that we're so damn glad for each other. It's a whole conversation in kissing and it's desperate and joyful at the same time.

Then her stomach growls.

I laugh, just a little. She rolls her eyes.

"Physical needs!" she scoffs. "So irritating."

"We need food," I say. "We should go find food and then go back to my room."

Laurel raises an eyebrow at me.

"Believe me, I'm not just trying to pick you up."

"We can't forget Viv," Laurel says.

"Right." To tell the truth, I had forgotten.

"I think we go get her and we put her in your room so she can sleep it off safely," I say. Laurel nods.

"Maybe if she's away from the others, she'll be able to rest," she says.

I look at her for a second. I really like her freckles.

"What?" she asks.

"Nothing," I answer. "You're pretty."

She elbows me, but I see her smile.

LAUREL

DOWN BELOW DECK, the halls are almost empty. We come across a bone-skinny man trying and failing to get into his room and I realize I know him. It's Hal! Hal from my snorkeling excursion.

"Hal!" I say. "It's me, Laurel, from Cozumel? We met on the catamaran."

"Oh yeah?"

There's no warmth on his face, only suspicion.

"Where's Peggy?" I ask.

"Who knows!" he roars. "She went off with someone and maybe they're inside! The door is locked! My key won't work! They locked me out! LET ME IN!" He pounds on the door.

"Okay," Tom says. "We'll help. But calm down."

Hal shoves his key card at us.

"It won't work. I'm trying it and trying it and I can't get in."

"What's your room number?" I ask.

"Room 6207, of course. 6207. 6207!"

Tom looks at me. Without saying anything, he steps to the next suite. (Hal was trying 6205.)

Tom double-taps the key card to the lock.

It opens.

"Ugkk," Hal spits. "Of course."

He storms into the room and suddenly turns.

His eyes narrow, becoming wary.

Hal tries to slam the door, but all the doors are designed to shut slowly and gracefully, so he ends up leaning on it, trying to make it close faster.

He eyes us all the way, like we're going to push past him and steal the Solu he obviously has inside. It's surreal.

"A friend of yours?" Tom asks.

"Two days ago he was the nicest man I ever met," I say.

"One guess as to what he's got hidden in that room," Tom says.

"How could they have gone so wrong in the formulation?" I ask. "I mean, what about the testing? Don't they have to do a bunch of testing?"

"In the packet I read to prepare for the gig, it said they did extensive research. So, who knows?"

We go down a flight of stairs and approach the curving stairway that leads down to the Aurora Restaurant.

"We have to move the bodies out of the way," a man raves. "So we can get at it. You people over there, you're not listening!"

We edge up to the doorway.

There are unconscious, maybe dead bodies lying on the floor and around fifty addicts scavenging. Some are walking, some are on their hands and knees. They're sniffing, licking, sucking.

The one who's yelling at everyone is trying to get people to help him move some of the fallen bodies out of the way so he can look for Solu under them.

I make a sound of disgust and Tom squeezes my hand.

We step into the room and cross to the area where I saw Viv last.

Tom starts hauling unconscious bodies out of the way. They're all intertwined. There's blood on everyone, but I can't tell who it's from. It's horrible. It's a battlefield.

Some of the fallen have their eyes open and are clearly high. Others are sleeping it off. Some might be dead and I don't even know how to tell!

"Thank GOD," the raving man says. "Finally some HELP! I kept telling everyone we need to organize. We need to move these dead or comatose people out of the way so we can do a PROPER search. No one listens!"

Tom and I share a look and keep working.

"Good! Good!" the man praises us. "Pile the bodies over there!"

I see my best friend's hand. I recognize her aqua manicure.

"Viv!" I say. "There she is. Viv!"

Viv is lying under a table, with two other people collapsed over her. Tom tries to pull her out, but the other people are too heavy. He has to get down on his hands and knees and try to shove his way under the table.

Finally he can get his hands under Viv and lift her out of the ghastly dog pile.

"Jesus," he says. "She's like a doll. She weighs nothing. I mean, I carried her not two days ago and she was a decent weight."

"But she's breathing? She's breathing?" I say.

Tom nods. We go to my room.

Tom lays Viv on the bed.

"Is she going to be okay?" I ask him. I know it's a stupid question. I'm kneading my hands together in worry. I can't seem to stop.

"I . . . I don't know, Laurel. There's nothing broken. She's just . . . she's knocked out."

"I know. Of course you don't know. Okay, get it together, Laurel," I say out loud to myself. "Washcloth!"

I walk to the bathroom and get one of the fancy washcloths and soak it with cold water.

Then I come back in and lay it tenderly on Viv's face.

Then my sweet friend Viv opens her eyes and starts talking.

"You slippery little *skank*! Why did you take me away? I was having such a GOOD TIME?!"

"Viv, what do you mean?"

"I finally have a boyfriend and you go and take me away?! Do you think you're my mother? Because you're acting just like her. Did she tell you to watch me? Did she tell you not to let me have any FUN—"

Viv pulls herself to standing and starts walking, shakily, toward me and I don't know what to do.

I just start to back up.

Her breath is awful. Like roadkill.

"Stop, please, Viv. You know I'm your friend. I only want the best for you."

"Sometimes I think they love you more than me! Laurel's so CREATIVE and so TALENTED—"

"Viv! Stop!" I yell. "Please! Look, we're going to leave you here. You need rest. Please go to bed, okay?"

"Did you know we call you the church-mouse at my house? And we LAUGH at you! We LAUGH at your boots and the way you say HERmeees instead of Hermès. You want to be so cultured but you're just TRASH, just trash."

Tom is pulling me toward the door. Viv is spitting in my face.

My hands are raised up in front of me. For protection.

"Please stop," I cry. "Vivika!"

"We're leaving," Tom says. "She's not herself."

"'She's not herself. She's not herself,'" Viv mocks. "Says the musclebound oaf—"

Tom pulls me out of the room and shuts the door in Viv's face.

I bury my face in my hands.

I sob against his shirt.

"It's a break. A schizoid break," Tom tells me.

He leans over, tipping my head up so I will meet his eyes.

"Laurel, listen, I did a guest star on *Criminal Minds*. I played the brother of a character who acted like that. It's called a schizoid break. I researched it. That's not what she really thinks. None of it."

My sweet Vivika. Saying those awful things.

"Forget everything she said. Just put it out of your mind."

I can hear Viv raving inside the room. Talking to herself.

He puts his strong hands on my shoulders and rubs them. "Erase everything she just said. She didn't mean a word of it."

"I know," I say. "But some of it must be true! Don't you think?"

"No, I don't. I really don't. Let's go to my room," Tom says. "I don't think . . . I don't think she's going anywhere. She seems so out of it. I don't even know if she could figure out how to open the door."

I nod.

I'm starting to feel weak. It must be two or three in the afternoon by now. I haven't eaten anything but an Oreo, eight lifetimes ago.

"But first we should find some food," I say.

"Thatta girl," Tom says. He hugs me.

Vivika is still talking, behind the door to our suite.

"Oh God," I say. "My guitar's in there."

Tom looks at me.

"I don't think it's worth going in there for it," he says. "But it's your call."

I exhale.

"You're right. Let's go."

Call me a coward, but I don't want to face her again.

TOM

LAUREL AND I head to the Club Cassiopeia. It's a club at night, but it serves a seated breakfast to people who don't want to go to the buffet on the pool deck. They have an omelet bar. It's where I've been getting my 6:00 a.m. egg whites.

We push the doors open and can hear a momentary sound of people talking and then the talking stops immediately.

"Who's there?" comes a nervous voice, just as another voice shushes it.

I exchange a look with Laurel.

"It's Tom Fiorelli. I'm—we're clean. Just looking for food."

My eyes adjust to the darkness.

Club Cassiopeia has a dance floor at one end, near where we've entered, and lounge seating going up in tiers around the stage. The room is dimly lit by strands of lights set into the floor edging around the tiers and steps.

At the back of the space, raised up by the gradual incline of the room, is the bar with two kitchen doors behind it.

"Hello?" I say. "Who are you?"

"We are just some of the crew members," comes a voice. This one's got an Indian accent. "Just looking for food ourselves."

"Jaideep?!" Laurel bursts out.

"Yes. It is I. Who's asking?"

A thin Indian waiter carrying two bags of hamburger buns steps out into the light.

"It's me, Laurel. The seasick girl."

"Laurel!" he says. "You're safe. I am so glad!"

She strides up the aisle and hugs the guy, then holds him by the shoulders, and hugs him again. "I'm so glad to see you," she says.

"And I you, Laurel!"

I step up behind Laurel and put my hand on her lower back.

Yeah. I'm showing that she's mine. That's how you do it. I know the guy's just a skinny waiter, but it's the code.

"My friend Viv, she's gone crazy," Laurel tells him.

"I am not surprised," Jaideep says. "Everyone who has taken Solu seems to have gone mad. You should see the crew quarters. Though we were prohibited from taking Solu, many, many people seem to have broken the rules."

I'm just standing there, forgotten, so I clear my throat.

"Tom, this is Jaideep. I met him on the first day. He helped me when I was really seasick."

"Hello, Mr. Fiorelli. My mother is one of your biggest fans. It is a pleasure to meet you. And I will introduce you to my friends," he says. "Guys, come here."

Four people come out from the kitchen. There's a short Filipino girl who looks way too young to be working on a ship, a chubby blond guy, an Indian man who's the oldest of all of us and has a bandage on his head, and a black girl carrying a bag full of oranges.

Jaideep names them: "This is Anna, Milo, Vihaan, and Kiniana."

"We're a walking United Nations, by the look of us," Jaideep says.

We all shake hands.

Milo makes a joke: "It's the end of the world, pleased to meet you." He's got a South African accent.

"What are you guys doing?" Laurel asks.

"We're fending for ourselves, that's what we're doing," Vihaan snaps.

"Whoa, whoa, Laurel's all right. She's not like the others," Jaideep says. He explains to us, "The passengers have been attacking us. Wanting us to get them Solu."

"A woman threw a bottle at my head," Vihaan says.

"And we can't stay in the crew quarters," Kiniana adds. Her accent is . . . Creole? Haitian? "The first mate is tossing all the rooms. He's on Solu and he's got the master key."

"And below deck, people are almost as bad as the people upstairs. They'd kill for Solu," Milo says.

"They have!" Jaideep says. "My friend Gede was stabbed for two packs!"

They all start talking at the same time.

"Help is on the way," I say. "That's the good news."

"Yeah, the coast guard is coming," Laurel adds.

"Our friend Rich told us to just get somewhere safe and hole up," I say. "But help is coming. It really is."

"We are concerned because we have stopped hearing instructions from the bridge," Jaideep tells us. "In a situation like this, we should be hearing codes and being told what to do."

I realize it has been a long time since we heard that annoying woman's voice.

"Well, maybe the PA system is down," I say.

"It could happen, I suppose," Jaideep says. He looks to Vihaan.

"Well, I think staying here in the lounge is our best shot," Milo interrupts. "We've food. We can . . . well, we can't lock the doors, but maybe we can block them with furniture."

"Most of the cleaning staff have barricaded themselves in the rec room. But they won't let anyone else in," Anna tells us.

"We should do the same right here," Milo insists.

"This room has four entrances, not counting the one in the back of the kitchen," Kiniana protests. "We can't block them all. We should go back to the crew deck and hide in someone's room."

"But Golan has the master key!" Anna protests.

"We'll hide in a room he's already searched!" Kiniana says.

"No. I've got a better idea," I say. "We'll all go back to my room. We can lock the door, and we've got a window and a balcony so we can see when the rescue ships come."

Laurel slides her hand into mine.

"It's a good idea," she says. "I think we're safer if we all stay together."

"Sounds good to me," Milo says. "Let's go crash at Casa Baby Tom-Tom."

Jaideep looks to Vihaan again and Vihaan nods.

"I think it's our best option," Jaideep says. "If you truly don't mind."

An hour later, you'd think we were having the best after-party ever.

The coffee table bears the remnants of our bizarre feast. We'd eaten what we could find in the club—all non-refrigerated breakfast foods they had on hand. The cold stuff was kept in the kitchen, Jaideep told us. It meant a feast of jelly sandwiches, dry cereal, raisins, nuts, and oranges.

Now Kiniana is sprawled out on the bed, trying to sleep, or maybe crying. Jaideep, Vihaan, and Anna are out watching for the coast guard on my tiny balcony and Milo is methodically working his way through the minibar.

"D'you guys want any scotch?" he asks.

"We're all right, man. But . . . "

"What?"

"You maybe . . . you maybe want to slow down," I tell him. "You're kind of drunk already."

"Yesss, and I plan on getting fully, righteously drunk by the time I'm through."

"I'll take a scotch," Laurel says. She elbows me.

"Yeah, me, too . . . I guess," I add.

Laurel rises and goes over to Milo.

He hands her two of the four tiny bottles of Dewars with broadly visible regret on his puffy, pinkish face.

Laurel comes back to me and she pretends to drink. Then she shoves the scotch down into the couch cushions. She's goofy. But her heart's in the right place. Me? I drink the Dewars.

Jaideep and the others come in from the balcony.

"No sign of the coast guard," Jaideep shrugs. "I don't know what we are supposed to do."

Milo shrugs. "There's no drill for ship overrun by zombie cokeheads."

"You said the coast guard was coming," Vihaan says, turning to me. "Which one?"

"What do you mean?"

"If it was the Mexican or Belizean Coast Guard, it should have arrived already," he explains.

"I have no idea."

"They should have been here already."

I scratch my head.

"Couldn't you see Almstead sending all the way back to the States?" Laurel asks us. "Like, a pride thing. He'd want to be rescued by Americans?"

That would be exactly his style.

Vihaan nods, too. "I agree. If that is the case, it could be hours before they arrive. Have you noticed that we've changed course?" Vihaan asks Jaideep.

"Have we?" Jaideep asks.

Vihaan nods again.

"We're headed back to the States, I'm certain of it."

"I feel powerless," Jaideep says. "We should be doing something."

"No," Vihaan says. "This is the right thing to do. We need to think of ourselves now. Screw the passengers. We're staying safe."

"I agree," says Anna. "Nothing against the passengers, but this is a different kind of emergency. They are the threat to us, now. We need to stay here, together."

Kiniana joins us from the other room, eyes red.

"I wish I were home," she says.

"Me, too," Laurel agrees.

"I haven't been home in four years," Anna tells us.

"Four years?!" I exclaim. "They don't let you go home?"

"I'm saving so much money," she tells us. "When I go, I'll be able to live off this money for a long time. My parents, too."

"To home," Milo says, raising a bottle of Absolut. Those of us with drinks clink them.

Milo rises unsteadily and begins to sing.

"Nkosi sikelel' iAfrika!"

In his drunken, wavering voice, he sings the South African national anthem.

Anna sings next, she rises and sings, tears streaming down her face: *"Bayang magiliw, Perlas ng Silanganan, Alab ng puso, Sa dibdib mo'y buhay."*

The language and the tune are so foreign-sounding. I've never heard anything like it in my life.

One by one, they stand and sing the anthems of their home countries.

It comes to Laurel and me.

"Do you guys really want to hear our anthem?" Laurel asks. "I mean, don't you sort of hate America at this point?"

But Kiniana puts her hand on Laurels and says, "We are singing

these songs as a prayer. A prayer to get to go home. That's what I think.
So you should sing, too."

Laurel stands up and, ugh, I join her.

I'm not a good singer.

I'm actually verifiably horrible.

I'm the guy they have to voice-over in post if there's a singing scene.

Laurel starts in, her voice sweet and round, just like you'd think it
would be.

"O say can you see, by the dawn's early light, what so proudly we hail—"

All eyes are on me. They're waiting for me to chime in.

I try just nodding along, like I'm so digging Laurel's singing that
I've decided just to listen.

"Sing!" Milo shouts. "Sing, Baby Tom-Tom!"

"Sing! Sing!" they chant.

"And the rocket's red glare . . . ," I start as quietly as I can.

"Louder!" Jaideep demands.

Fine. Let them have it.

"The bombs bursting in air . . . "

They all look at me, eyes round. I see Milo's chin start to quiver.

"Gave proof through the night . . . "

He breaks into a guffaw.

"That our flag was still there . . . "

All the others laugh, too.

"Oh my Lord, you sound like a whale singing," Jaideep says.

"A tone-deaf whale," Kiniana adds.

"A dying, tone-deaf whale," Milo corrects.

Laurel stops singing. She puts a hand over her mouth.

"You like it, huh?" I say to her. I nudge her under the arm. She
giggles. "You haven't even heard me do Katy Perry."

Half of them are begging me to sing Katy Perry, the other half are
covering their ears and protesting.

"Roar! Roar! Roar, roaaaaaaar! I got the eye of the tiger, a fighter, a mover, a shaker."

I can't quite remember the words, but I keep singing "roar" and I start b-boying. Pop and lock. *"Roar!"* Pop and lock. *"Roar!"* Pop and lock. *"Roar!"*

"My ears! My ears!" Jaideep wails.

Kiniana and Anna are screaming with laughter.

Laurel throws herself on the bed and puts a pillow over her head.

"Oh no, you don't!" I say and I dive next to her, prying the pillow out of her hands.

"You're completely tone-deaf," she says.

"Now you know my secret," I say.

I pull her to me. I see her eyes flicker to the others. I know she won't kiss me, not with all these people around, but I'm still hoping maybe—

When there's a pounding on the door.

"Who the hell is in there making all that racket?! Come out! Come out now and share what you have! Everyone has to share! You guys have a stash and that's not fair. No fair!"

The person pounds, one-two, on the door. One-two. One-two.

Other voices join, fists beating the door, demanding we share.

Laurel and I are frozen. Everyone is frozen.

We look to the door.

Anna puts a finger up to her lips. Her eyes are wide, scared.

"Shhh!" she tells us.

LAUREL

ANNA SEPARATED TOM'S KING BED into two twins. (She knew how, because she's from housekeeping.) She also made up the pull-out couch. So now, Kiniana and Anna are asleep on one of the two twin beds and Vihaan is sleeping on the couch. Milo crawled off to sleep in the closet a while back.

Which leaves one twin bed for me and Tom.

I've only ever slept in a bed with a guy two times, not counting my cousin Zach, who I used to bunk with when we were little.

Number one was Toby Brennan, my boyfriend in sophomore year. His parents went out of town and we all ended up crashing at his house. (Toby has since come out to me, which explains why we did a whole lot of talking that night and not much of anything else.)

The second time was at a major party at Letitia Leblanc's step-father's beachfront condo. I slept in a bed with Keith Steele along with Vivika and another girl named Bree. I woke up in the middle of the night with Keith's hands moving under my shirt and spent the rest of the night on the floor, furious and somehow ashamed. (But that's another story.)

This is completely, celestially different.

Sleeping in Tom's arms.

Well, not sleeping in them. Lying in them. Actually, laying my head on one of them.

It's wonderful.

There's this feeling of safety and comfort that radiates out from him. When he touches me it's like my body is hearing the bottom tones of a cello—soothing, calming, low and reassuring.

I'm a jerk to feel this happiness. I am the scum of the earth. I know it. I mean, my best friend is in terrible danger. I'm in the midst of a catastrophe unlike any other in recorded history (that I'm aware of). But I've never felt like this before.

Tom Fiorelli was some face on a magazine cover and now he's realer than real. I'm looking at his face now, in the moonlight, in a room where people are snoring and breathing deeply. He's mine alone right now.

He's flat on his back. My head is lying on his arm and my body is curled a little. My knees touch him. My neck, where it lies on his arm. My left foot is on top of his left shin.

His eyes are closed and I'm just looking at him. At how beautiful he is.

There's no way I can sleep.

I touch his hair. Just a little. It's shiny and thick. I like how the waves feel under the tips of my fingers.

"Laurel," he whispers without opening his eyes, "go to sleep."

(His breath still smells like nutmeg. How does he do that?)

"I'm trying," I say. "It's not that easy."

"Do you want me to sing you a lullaby?"

I stifle a giggle.

"Please, anything but that."

I close my eyes, but it's no good. His body is just too electric. I'm distinctly aware of every inch of my body that is touching his.

I turn my face slightly down and quietly (I hope) I inhale. I love how he smells.

How can someone smell like warmth itself?

"Are you smelling me?" he whispers.

Thank God it's so dark in the cabin. My blush would stand out like a flare.

"Maybe," I say softly.

"You're making it very, very hard for me to sleep," he tells me.

"Same to you," I answer.

"We should sleep because we might . . . who knows what will happen when the rescue ships come. It could get ugly."

"I know."

"Should I sleep on the floor?" he asks. "Maybe that would be best."

"No, don't," I say. I put my hand on his arm. "I like this too much. I'll go to sleep."

I turn my back to him.

Now my butt is pressed against his leg.

This is much worse.

His body is long. His weight makes a dip in the mattress and my body just naturally rolls into his. Feels like magnetism, but I know it's just gravity.

I stretch my leg out, so it's pressed against his.

His body is delicious. Long, lean muscles. The bulk of him. He's so frickin' manly. There's no other word for it.

He's a man.

"Remember when you fell on top of me on the dance floor?" I say quietly.

"How could I forget? I was mortified," he says. I can hear the smile in his voice.

I whisper, "I liked it."

There's a beat. Then Tom lets out a little groan and shifts toward me, gathering me to his body. He rolls me toward him, face-to-face, and he kisses me.

Which is what I wanted him to do.

He kisses me with urgency. His body slightly on top of mine.

Oh. There are other people in the room. I won't let us go too far. That would be tacky and gross, and oh God, his mouth on mine is so heavenly sweet.

A sudden rustling sound from the living room area makes us both freeze.

Milo stumbles out of the closet and blunders toward the bathroom.

Then I hear a splashy heave as he pukes in the toilet.

My heart is hammering. Stopping is the very last thing I want to do, but—

"Laurel, you know I'm crazy about you, right?" Tom says. His voice is husky and low.

"I think so," I say.

He slides out of bed.

"I gotta sleep on the floor."

I wake up in the early morning, not sure of why I'm awake. Everything is quiet. Peach-colored light is chasing away the blue of night. I look at Tom, curled up on the floor next to the bed on an extra comforter, sleeping on his forearm.

I don't realize it at the time, but what has awakened me is the stillness. The boat has stopped moving in the night.

I guess I fall asleep again.

The second time I wake up it's because voices are arguing.

"Why, why, why would they shut off the engine this way?" Vihaan is saying. "And where are the backup generators?"

There is no engine sound. I didn't realize how used to its hum I had gotten until now—it's gone. We are not moving in the water at all.

I see that everyone looks as weary and gross as I feel.

"We should get back to the crew deck," Anna says. "Maybe there is word down there . . . "

"What do you think's happening up on the bridge?" Tom asks.

"I worry they've been overrun with crazed passengers," Jaideep says.

"No, they have security doors. They have protocols!" Kiniana says.

"But why aren't we getting messages from the captain!" Jaideep moans. "What has happened to Captain Hammonds?"

"What has happened to the coast guard?" Vihaan asks. "That's the question!"

"We've got to get to the bridge and find out what's going on," Tom says. "We have to know that the mainland has been warned about Solu. And we have to know if rescue is coming—"

"And if it's not," I interrupt, "we have to rescue ourselves."

Tom looks up at me and smiles. As tired as I am and as scared as I feel, his grin makes my heart beat double-time.

"Exactly," Tom says.

"All right," Jaideep says as he takes the floor. "There's a satellite phone in the crew quarters. Steward Jim told me about it once. It's in the first mate's cabin. We should go find it."

"No," Kiniana says. "We should go to the bridge. We have to try that first."

As they argue, Milo groans, emerging from the closet. His hair looks like he combed it with a salad spinner and he's got some brown dribble on his white button-down shirt. (Upchuck, I suspect.)

"What's happening, my people?" he asks.

"That's what we're about to find out," Kiniana answers.

I'm terrified, but I try not to look like it. I try to look brave.

TOM

LAUREL LOOKS AS SCARED AS I feel, but she's trying not to show it so I try not to even feel it.

Jaideep and Vihaan are going to try to find the phone. It makes sense for them to go—they're fast and strong and will have an easier time getting in and out if it's only the two of them.

The rest of us are headed to the bridge.

But, honestly, as I see it, my job at this point is just to try to get Laurel and me off this ship alive. That seems doable.

Yes, we're going to find out what's happening on the ship. And, yes, we're going to make sure that our country's been warned about Solu.

But if we can't get onto the bridge, if we can't find out what's going on, I'm just going to evacuate the two of us in a lifeboat. Period.

Jaideep told me some of them are just rafts but some are motorized so we could actually take off and try to make it to Honduras or wherever the hell we are.

Obviously that's a last resort. I know nothing about navigating a lifeboat. But it's an option.

There's a smell of sewage in the hallway. And we can hear a woman screeching in the distance, and someone laughing.

It's eerie, with the engine dead quiet like this.

"It stinks out here," Milo says.

"Toilets backing up," Kiniana notes. "Do we know how long the engine's been cut for?"

"No," I tell her. "It was out when we all woke up."

Me, Laurel, Kiniana, Milo, and Anna. Not much of a team, here. Milo is built solidly, but he's still losing his fight with a hangover. Kiniana is strong and angry. That's good. Anna is a little hummingbird of a thing. Laurel is . . . tough. Tougher than I thought. And I wouldn't care if she was weak, anyway.

Laurel is my girl and I'm going to keep her safe.

Milo, ahead of us, groans and squats down unsteadily.

"Come on, Milo," Kiniana snaps. "We don't have time for this nonsense."

"I need a toilet," he says.

"Aaugh!" Kiniana grumbles.

"Hey," I say to Laurel. "Do you want to go check on Viv?"

"God, yes!" Laurel says. "That would make me feel so much better."

I walk up to Kiniana and Anna. I press my key card into Kiniana's hand.

"Would you two take Milo back to my room? Laurel and I are going to check on her friend and we'll meet you up on Deck Eleven."

"Fine," Kiniana says. She nudges Milo's thigh with her sneaker. "Come on, party boy."

"Milo, you should drink a Pipop," Laurel says. "My friend Viv swears by them for hangovers."

We head quickly to Laurel and Viv's room. We haven't seen anyone yet, any addicts, and it's starting to freak me out.

There's some weird stuff in the hallway—suitcases dragged out into the hall. A torn and bloodied tuxedo shirt. A brass plaque that seems to have been ripped off a wall. A lady's shoe with a gold stiletto heel that's got a crust of dried blood on it. Creepy.

"Oh NO!" Laurel exclaims when we get to her hall. She rushes forward.

The door to their room is open, propped ajar by one of Laurel's motorcycle boots.

The room has been tossed and trashed.

"Viv!" Laurel shouts. But Viv's not there.

Laurel checks the bathroom, the balcony, the closet.

She stops in the closet.

"What is it?" I ask. "Did you find—"

Laurel's staring at their wall safe.

The drywall around it has been chipped away frantically. The face of the safe has been battered, but not very effectively.

There's blood there, on the keypad.

On the floor is the body of Laurel's guitar. It's been smashed to hell. Probably against the wall safe.

"Oh, Laurel, I'm so sorry," I say. "We should have gone back for the guitar."

She turns to me.

"There are ten packs of Solu in that safe. *Inside* a sealed airsickness bag."

She swallows.

"Do you think . . . do you think Viv smelled it through the *wall*? Through the *metal*?"

"I don't know," I say.

But we both know the answer is yes.

As we're leaving, Laurel stops.

She unlaces her boots and steps into the motorcycle boot at the door. She hop-steps into the closet and finds the other.

"I need these boots," she says as an explanation, but I don't need one.

I take her hand in mine as we go back into the hall. I squeeze her hand and she gives it a weak pulse back.

In the middle of the staircase leading to the upper decks, there's a woman. She's seated and she's digging around in her mouth with bony fingers.

She is so thin I can make out her skeleton. Her eyes are like giant marbles in their sockets, the skin drawn tightly away. She is wearing an orange sequined evening gown. It hangs off one shoulder.

The woman sees us. She holds out two spitty, bloody fingers. On the fingers sits one of her molars.

She grunts at us. Her expression is one of grief and loss and confusion.

"I'm sorry," Laurel says. "I'm so sorry."

I hug Laurel against me and we skirt around the woman.

I'm ready for her to lunge at us. I'm ready for anything. But she just sits there as we pass by, and I'm careful not to step on the small pile of teeth she's collecting.

"It's okay. It's okay," I tell Laurel.

Inside, I'm thinking—if all the addicts are like this woman—quiet and comatose—we'll be all right. But I know that's not how this is going to play out.

Because we can hear them up top. Voices harsh and low. Agitated and morose.

We step up onto the deck.

To get to the hallway outside the bridge, we need to cross the pool deck.

I pull Laurel into the shadows next to the stairwell. The less we're noticed, the better. At least until we see what they're like.

There's no sign of Milo, Kiniana, or any of the others.

There are people milling around. There are people lying on the deck, scuttled up to the wall that borders the deck like blown debris. There are people arguing and people whaling on one another and people chattering and screaming at no one.

These people are revoltingly thin.

Their heads are big. Eyes protruding. Cheeks sunken so you can make out the structure of their molars underneath.

Some of them wear clothes, looking like walking hangers—the clothes just draped over shoulders. Belts drawn to the smallest hole or just tied off to hold up baggy pants.

Some are naked and that seems fine. Maybe because they look like cadavers. They look medical, somehow. Inhuman and surreal—why should they bother with clothes?

A small group has surrounded a man and they are screaming at him: "You were the last one to see it, Paul. You tell us where it is or else!"

"I lost it, I lost the packet," he cries. "I swear it."

"Bullshit!" one of them hollers and they push him onto his knees.

A skeletal woman with great folds of drooping skin blocks my eye line. She slowly draws close to a man lying in the fetal position on a lounge chair right in front of Laurel and me.

He's asleep or unconscious and doesn't notice the woman sniffing him. Stalking him with her nose.

She lowers herself onto all fours next to him. And starts licking the back of his neck.

"Tom, what's she doing?" Laurel asks, a tremor in her voice.

The man raises a sleepy hand and tries to shoo her away, like she's a housefly disturbing his nap.

The woman licks his neck, his collarbone, the hair at his neckline.

"I think . . . I think she smells Solu in his sweat," I say.

We have to get off this boat.

Something swaying catches my eye and I look up.

My grasp on Laurel's shoulders must tighten because she says, "What?"

I don't want her to see, but she follows my eye line.

There's a body hanging down from the observation deck.

Laurel staggers forward.

"It's . . . It's . . . " She gasps.

I know who it is. Elise Zhang.

She's wearing her Day 1 suit. Her glasses are off and her face is purple.

Her small body rotates, banging against the rail.

Laurel and I are clutching each other in horror.

She turns her face and buries it against my shoulder.

"We have to get across the deck," I say. "Stay calm. We're just walking across."

"Tom, I see Viv," Laurel says. Her voice comes out a dry whisper.

She nods with her head, and I see Viv, up on the observation deck. The deck must be Sabbi's territory, in the new, psychotic world order of the ship.

I see Sabbi up there, talking to her followers, who are clustered around her.

Viv is standing at Sabbi's side, transfixed by her words.

Laurel starts for them.

"Wait!" I say. "We have to go meet the others, Laurel."

"She's my best friend!" Laurel says. "I have to see if she's okay."

But we know she's not, I want to shout. I'm not sure Laurel understands the kind of danger we're in.

As we cross the deck, a man wearing a Yankees baseball cap sidles up next to me. "This is your fault," he hisses. "You! Baby Tom-Tom!"

He gets in front of me, blocking my way.

"Leave me alone," I tell him.

"You did this! You were a part of this! You stood there, taping your pieces, 'I'm Tom Fiorelli, jerking off on the deck of the *Extravagance*, poisoning all of America with my evil SWEETENER!'"

"I had nothing to do with it, man!" I yell.

Laurel squeezes my hand, telling me to let it go.

But the guy won't get out of my face and his breath smells like the slop in a port-a-potty.

"YOU DID THIS TO ME!" he screams. He pokes me in the chest. He's stronger than I thought he'd be.

"BACK OFF!" I shout and I push him off me. He tumbles over a lounge chair and clatters to the deck.

He looks at me like he hates me and I guess he does.

"Come on," Laurel says, pulling me toward Viv, Sabbi, and the upper deck.

LAUREL

"VIVIKA," I SAY stumbling up the stairs. "Sweetie, are you okay?"

Vivvy turns and looks at me.

Her face is blank for a moment, and then it hardens. Like I'm an old enemy of hers she wasn't expecting to see again.

She is still wearing Tom's T-shirt and her bikini bottoms. The T-shirt has blood on it, looks almost like some wayward pseudo-rough design. (Only it's real blood. Real rough.)

Viv looks like the other people.

Sick. Near dead of thinness.

And Sabbi does, too.

Like all the *Teens of New York,* there's a Barbie version of Sabbi Ribiero. I remember there was a fuss made over it because it featured a plump rear end, something not done in the world of plastic dolls before.

There's a Prom Sabbi and an Executive Sabbi and even a Veterinarian Sabbi, which they came out with after she announced on one episode that she always wanted to work with animals.

Well, this is Deathbed Sabbi.

The famous ass is gone.

She's wearing a bikini made of gold metal mesh. And the material on the seat of the bottoms is saggy and empty. Her butt is flat. It was the last deposit of fat and it's all gone.

She has the behind of a ninety-year-old woman.

I feel bad for her. But then I tune in to what Sabbi is saying. She's talking fast, in that same weird run-on chant-talk that Viv was using before.

"If we are a family, a true *family*, then we sacrifice for the family. Do you see? Do you see this truth? *Do* you?"

Sabbi turns from facing the deck below to facing her own people.

"Do you see this, my darlings?"

They nod, Viv along with them.

"Viv, it's me, Laurel. And I want you to come with me. You're not well."

Viv shakes me off.

"We're sick. We NEED more juice. We must have more Solu. Is this right?" Sabbi asks.

They nod.

"Vivika, Tom and I are going to take you off the ship and go get help. Okay? Okay, sweetie?" I say. "Can you hear me, Vivika?"

"SHHHHH!" Vivika shushes me, her eyes ferocious.

"*Vem, Juliana. Venha aqui. Me dê sua mão.*" Sabbi holds her hand out to a thin girl with caramel-colored skin.

"You had a lot of Solu, *meu querida*. More than those people." She nods over her shoulder toward the people on deck below. "That's because of *me*. I got it for you. Really, when you think about it, then, it's *mine*."

Then I see Sabbi Ribiero has a corkscrew in her fist.

Juliana puts her hand in Sabbi's left and Sabbi brings her fist across Juliana's in a slash.

"NO!" I scream and Tom lunges forward, but it's too late.

Blood sprays up, hitting Sabbi's face. Splashing over the clamoring clique of skeletons.

And they descend on the screaming girl and her fountain of a wrist.

"No, no, no, NO, VIVIKA!" I scream. I try to pull her off the bleeding girl, but Vivika turns, her muzzle red, and snarls at me.

Tom pulls me into his arms and away from them.

"We're getting off the boat now, Laurel," he whispers into my hair. "It's over. We're leaving."

"She's my best friend!" I cry. "She's my sister."

"No," he says. "She's a monster now."

"I can't leave her. I can't," I say, pleading. I have my hands on his shirtfront.

Vivika Hallerton is my best friend. I've known her since we were two years old. We played boyfriend/girlfriend as eight-year-olds. We have eaten ice cream together twenty thousand times. We've peeled sunburned skin off each other's backs.

I cannot leave her behind.

"LAUREL, we have no *choice!*"

It hurts like I've cut out a piece of my own heart, but I know he's right.

Tom leads the way, holding my hand. We weave through the addicts.

The smell of blood seems to be agitating them. I see a man with shining black eyes biting a woman on the neck.

The woman, gaunt and crusty mouthed, moans in pleasure.

I realize he's the dad from my dinner table. The woman is not his wife. I don't know why my brain makes a note of that. (Hey, that man is either making out with or about to eat a woman who is NOT HIS WIFE!)

"Tom, look!!" I shout.

There's a woman standing on the other side of the rail, about to jump into the water.

It's Tom's producer.

Tom wheels around.

"Tamara!" he hollers. "Don't!"

She looks around, her face drawn and pinched.

She takes one hand off the rail and wags her finger at him, saying, "No, no, no!"

And then she jumps.

"Jesus!" Tom howls. "Tamara!"

But she's gone.

"*There* he is!" shouts a dry, bitter voice and I see it's the man with the too-big baseball cap.

He has assembled a small crowd of skeletons and he points at Tom.

"He knew what would happen to us! He's one of them! And LOOK AT HIM!"

They do.

There's a glittering hatred in their eyes that makes my arms and legs cold all of a sudden.

"Baby Tom-Tom," a woman says, saying his name like it's a gutter curse. "You sold us out!"

"String him up!" someone shouts. "Right beside Zhang!"

They cheer.

The monsters surge forward and Tom pushes me toward the stairs.

"Find the others," he shouts.

Then he's fighting.

He punches the baseball-hat guy and kicks out at another, but they're jumping on him. Whaling on him. Biting and clawing.

"Help!" I scream. "Jaideep! Milo! Somebody help me!"

I try to pull one of them off him and *whack*. Someone hits me on the head with their elbow or their fist or, I don't know.

"HELP ME!" I scream again.

A waif with stringy blond hair and giant blue eyes laughs at me. Cackles.

I run.

Because I have a dumb idea.

I run into my room, my lungs burning.

The combination, the combination.

2-6-6-8-7.

B-O-O-T-S.

The Laurel who entered that combination was an infant, a toddler. She knew nothing.

I'm shaking and sobbing and my fingers futz it. But then I get it and the red light switches to green.

My vomit bag with ten packets (*ten* packets) of Solu. There are two more packets lying there. I'd forgotten I'd tucked them aside.

I grab them, too.

I race back to the deck.

Stupid idea, stupid idea.

I round a corner headed upstairs and I run into a tiny Latino man. He's emaciated and wearing a chef's white uniform.

He snarls at me, then he . . . he smells it.

Teeth bared, he lunges at the bag.

"No!" I shout. "It's not for you."

I take the two loose packets and throw them away from me, down the hall.

The man shoves me aside and leaps after them.

I take the stairs to the deck two at a time and burst out onto the deck.

Every one. *Every* addict on the deck turns their head toward me and sniffs.

Tom is down on the ground. He's curled into a ball, hands over his head.

The addicts who were beating him up just a second ago are now frozen. The man with the baseball cap has a rope in his hands.

Every addict eye is on me.

I figure I have about two seconds before they all swarm me.

I throw the whole bag. Away, away, away from me.

I throw the Solu into the pool.

With a shriek the addicts all scramble, scuttle, dive to the bag of Solu packets floating in the pool. I'm knocked down as some of them trample me from behind.

Head dizzy now, I crawl my way over to Tom.

He's bruised and battered, but he's alive and trying to get to his feet.

"Tom," I cry. "Are you okay?"

Horrible gurgling and splashing, wailing, cursing come from the pool behind me.

"Laurel!" he shouts.

He staggers to me.

"Laurel. How did you get them off me?"

"I threw some Solu in the pool."

The water is churning with deranged skeletons, fighting it out for ten packets of poison.

"What do we do?" I ask him. "Should we try to get them out?"

Some of them are dragging themselves out, but more are still fighting in the water. I don't want to be responsible for (seventy-five? one hundred?) human beings drowning (as de-ranged and violent as they may be).

Like he's reading my thoughts, Tom says, "Laurel. I think you need to stop thinking of them as . . . "

"As what?"

"As people."

"If they're not people, what are they?" I ask. My voice breaks. I feel like I'm losing it.

"Monsters?" Tom says. "I don't know—cannibals? Zombies?!"

"Viv is not a zombie," I protest.

I look up to the observation deck, where Sabbi and Viv and the rest of them are still bent over the fallen girl, sucking her dry.

(Vampires? my mind asks. Are they *vampires?*)

"They are past help now," Tom tells me.

Thank God for his hands on me or I'd think I'd died and gone to hell.

"TOM! LAUREL!"

It's Jaideep! Jaideep and Vihaan.

"Over here!" Tom yells and he leads Jaideep and Vihaan away from the pool, around the corner to the rear pool deck. It's abandoned—all the addicts are fighting it out on the other side.

"What happened to you?" Jaideep asks Tom, as Vihaan asks, "What is happening in the pool?"

"Laurel threw some Solu in there. A crowd was whaling on me and she saved me. They . . . they hanged Zhang and they wanted to hang me, too. Because I was the spokesperson," Tom says.

"Did you find a phone?" I ask them.

"No, it's a freaking bloodbath down there," Vihaan says.

"The first mate got his hands on a gun," Jaideep adds. His brown face is gaunt and there are dark circles under his eyes.

"Kiniana and the others should be here by now. Have you seen them?" Tom says.

"People are crazy," Vihaan says. "You would not believe the things we've seen."

"We know!" I say. "Sabbi and her group . . . They . . . She . . . "

"She killed a girl," Tom says for me. "They drank her blood—to get the Solu."

"Ah!" Jaideep exclaims, disgusted. "That's what they're doing."

He looks like he might be sick. "There's a group of them in the dining hall doing the same thing . . . "

Vihaan grabs me by the arms. "We must abandon ship," he whispers. His eyes are bloodshot. Terrified.

"But we have to make sure the word got out—" I say.

"They'll get us next!" Vihaan says.

"We can't just leave Kiniana and Milo and Anna," Jaideep protests. "What about the rest of our friends?"

"They're going to kill us!" Vihaan repeats.

I know how he feels. My brain is shouting at me: LEAVE! LEAVE! LEAVE!

But a cold, heavy dread sits like a brick in my stomach.

"But, Vihaan, if they never radioed for help," I say. "If nobody knows we're in trouble and nobody knows how bad Solu is . . . "

The three men look at me. Tom's battered face. Vihaan's flushed with panic. Jaideep's dread pale brown.

"Then Solu launches at midnight tonight," I remind them.

Tom wipes a hand over his eyes.

I see him changing his mind about something.

"She's right," Tom says. "We have to make sure the message has been sent. Then we can evacuate."

"To the bridge, then," Jaideep says.

"To the bridge," we repeat. It sounds like some weird drinking toast. But we're not kidding and we're not drinking. I wish I were drunk.

I wish I were dreaming.

(I wish I were on the beach back in Key West, talking to Tom back when my best friend was overweight and happy in her regular unhappy way.)

But all that wishing doesn't keep me from hearing the screaming, spitting, splashing from the other side of the deck.

T O M

WE GO INSIDE THE SHIP and down one flight of stairs to the part of Deck 11 that gives you access to the bridge.

The hallway is disgusting. The carpet's stained in places and littered with clothing that no longer fits, wadded and walked on. I see someone brought up their leather ticket holder—maybe they wanted to go over the guarantee on the paperwork.

I must make some sound of disbelief because Laurel says, "What?"

"The paperwork!" I say. "Can you imagine the lawsuits from this mess?"

"This is a multibillion-dollar nightmare for the Solu people," Vihaan declares. "Murders have been committed because of this Solu. People have lost their minds. People have died."

"Almstead's bankrupt, as far as I can see," I agree.

"I think he's going to prison," Laurel adds.

"I hope they throw away the key," Vihaan says. He spits on the ground.

Jaideep presses a button on the telecom touch screen next to the bridge door.

It's working, which is kind of surprising, considering the rest of the ship is shut down.

Jaideep speaks into the lens of the camera.

"Hello?" he says. "This is Jaideep Coffey, a member of the waitstaff. Requesting a word with the captain—"

Vihaan pushes next to him and edges into the sight of the lens.

"We are not addicts!" Vihaan says. "We just want to make sure that people have been warned about Solu. We are prepared to abandon ship."

There's no answer. No sound from the intercom.

No sound at all from behind the heavy gray door. It's probably solid and thick.

"Let Tom try," Laurel says. "Maybe they'll open for him."

Jaideep shrugs and Vihaan is grumbling as I come up to the front.

"Captain Hammonds, this is Tom Fiorelli. There are a few of us out here who aren't on Solu and we just—"

The door opens.

And I'm looking into the muzzle of a semiautomatic assault rifle.

"Fiorelli! Come in!" I hear the old man's voice. "Vince, let him in!"

The guard, Vince, sizes us up. He's wearing a tank top and fatigues. He's got a bristle-brush crew cut and a bicep tattoo of an eagle ripping the head off a guy with a turban.

We step past the door and into a narrow hallway. On one side is a room with a brass placard: CAPTAIN'S QUARTERS. The one on the other side says CHIEF SECURITY OFFICER'S QUARTERS.

The one to the captain's room is open.

We catch a glimpse of a beautifully decorated suite beyond the door—one that's been trashed.

There's blood on the carpet and I think I see feet, but Vince pokes me in the back with the muzzle of the gun.

He reaches in, grabs the door, and shuts it.

"Go on," he growls.

We step forward, onto the bridge.

I take it all in. The floor is cobalt blue, with rubber treads. A series of windows wraps all the way around the deck. Below them is a long, curved panel crowded with dozens of small computer screens and other panels, flashing lights, levers, buttons, all that stuff.

And they're all working. They're *working*!

Almstead stands near a captain's chair, looking like he's thrilled to see us.

And behind him, Amos and other armed guards are talking on headsets and checking some of the panels.

"I'm so happy you're all right, Fiorelli! Aren't you clever to stay alive!"

"What's happened?" Vihaan erupts as he and Jaideep enter. His eyes bulge as he takes in the scene, "Where is the captain?"

Vince looks to Almstead, who shakes his head. He pushes Vihaan and Jaideep back, hard.

"Wait!" I say. "They're our friends."

Vince checks Almstead's response again and Almstead shrugs.

Vince says, "Out!" He pushes Jaideep and Vihaan back out to the main hallway.

"Knock again on that door and I'll splatter your haji guts on the carpet," he says.

"Laurel!" Jaideep cries out as the door shuts.

Vince smashes the door with his fist. A warning blow.

Laurel's got a death grip on my hand.

If they try to take her from me . . . I don't know what I'll do.

"Say, what did you two pull over at the pool?" Almstead asks me and Laurel. His expression is polite and interested. Calm as could be. "To make them all do this?"

He gestures behind us and we turn.

The back wall of the bridge is lined with TV screens showing areas all over the ship.

There are two views of the carnage in the pool. There must be twenty people floating, dead, in the water. Blood is leaching out of them, making hideous swirls in the water. Two addicts are still duking it out in the shallow end while other addicts are in the pool—*drinking* the bloody water. The bloody chlorine water.

The screens show widespread carnage across the ship.

In the Celestial Lounge, in the casino, in the hallway outside a suite, there are people clustered around the fallen, drinking their blood.

There's an inside shot in one of the glass elevators, the glass walls splattered with blood.

There's a shot of a man in uniform putting a gun to his head.

"Well, what was it?" Almstead repeats.

"We . . . Laurel, that is, she threw some Solu in the pool and now . . . "

"How many packets?"

"Ten," Laurel says weakly.

"All that bloodshed for ten packets!" Almstead marvels. "You know, out of the passengers on the ship, we estimate . . . what is it, Amos?"

"We estimate at least three hundred dead, sir," Amos answers without taking his eyes off a small screen.

"We don't know about the crew, though," Almstead says. "Far fewer of them were taking Solu. Maybe twenty percent."

Laurel catches my eye: He is, what, crazy?

"Mr. Almstead, please, what's happening? Where is the captain?"

"Captain Hammonds and the rest of the crew up here are dead," Almstead says.

Amos steps up. "Excuse me, sir. Jack says the speedboat's here. We can move into the final phase whenever you say."

"Lovely," Almstead turns to us. "You want something done—hire a mercenary! They can do anything! They could navigate this ship, if need be. But that's not the plan. No, it's time for us to make our exit."

"So the rescue . . . ," I say. "It's not happening."

"Rich said the coast guard was on its way," Laurel sputters.

"That was, well . . . that was a lie," Almstead says.

"What about what you said about pulling Solu off the market? Delaying the launch of the product. All that stuff," I say.

Almstead nods his head, wincing. "Guilty! But those lies were all part of the plan."

"What is this plan?" Laurel asks.

"Dear girl, what's your name?"

"Laurel Willard."

"Ah, you remind me of a girl I knew when I was young. Frances McMahon. Freckles are so fetching on a young girl."

I start to talk, but he holds up his hand.

"Phase one—Create bait to lure fat, lazy Americans into a trap. Phase two—Promote the trap. Make it look safe and easy."

Almstead turns to Vince, "Go get Rich. Bring him out here."

"Rich was in on it?" Laurel asks, her voice cracking.

"No, no. He had no idea until it was too late. And please, just 'cause you're pretty doesn't mean you get to interrupt. Phase three—Spring the trap and enjoy the show! What fun Zhang and I have had, watching our creation take hold. We never thought it would act so quickly. The weight loss was like watching one of those sped-up movies. And the vampirism! That was completely unexpected!"

He gestures to the screens. "Solu works far better than we ever could have hoped."

"What's phase four?" I ask.

"Sir, *Entertainment Daily* is on," Amos tells Almstead.

"Turn it up. Look, Tom—here you are. This was phase two—you did it!"

He indicates a small screen set into the navigational panel. It's a live TV feed—*Entertainment Daily*.

Anchorwoman Kim Wooster sets up the clip: "Unless you've been hiding under a rock, you know that the new non-nutritive sweetener,

Solu, will be released to the public in just a few hours, at midnight to-night! Solu-mania has been sweeping the country. People are lined up on the streets outside drugstores and many stores have hired extra security—it's like Black Friday—but all for one product."

She winks at the camera.

"Those sexy little lavender packets of Solu. All week all eyes have been watching everybody's favorite child star turned mega-hunk who's a guest on the *Extravagance*. Here's what he had to say earlier today about the Solu Cruise to Lose!"

And then she throws it to me, on the deck of the ship.

"Turn it up!" Almstead commands.

The audio blares louder.

"Hi, I'm Tom Fiorelli coming to you from the deck of the *Extravagance*. We've seen some jaw-dropping, mind-blowing changes on this trip!"

There's some girl next to me. I guess I remember her. She's thin and pretty and probably dead by now.

"I'm talking to Julie, here. How's this cruise been for you, Julie?"

"Oh my God, just amazing. Solu is just . . . it's just a phenomenon. I mean, no one ever has to be fat again. Can you believe that?! I can eat all I want and I'm losing weight. I'm seriously losing weight! And eating like a horse! I love it!"

Ugh. I'm dizzy.

I feel this churning fritz come up from my feet. I think I'm going to keel over.

Laurel grabs my arm.

"You son of a bitch," I spit.

Almstead laughs.

On the screen, I continue my idiotic schpiel. "I'll tell you this: Everyone on board is incredibly lucky to be here. The parties have been nonstop and the weight loss is really remarkable. Solu works!"

Why did I say that stupid schlock? Why did I take this stupid job in the first place? You can see the boredom in my eyes.

I was bored. I was getting paid. I was peddling mass murder.

"Utterly convincing," Almstead says, elbowing me in the ribs. "A great job! Eh, Rich? Could Tom have done a better job? I don't think so."

We turn and see that Rich has been brought in by the guard.

Rich's face is ashy, his seersucker suit dirty and rumpled. He's obviously been crying and he obviously betrayed us.

"How could you?!" I yell. "How could you let me do that?"

"I didn't know!" Rich wails.

"But you told us rescue was coming," Laurel says.

"I had to," Rich says. "I had no choice."

"How did you not have a choice?" I spit.

"He was going to give it to my mom!" Rich cries. "He had a deliveryman with a lifetime supply, right outside her house! He showed it to me on a phone!"

Jesus Christ.

I remember the guard with Rich when we saw him on the deck. I remember how scared Rich looked.

"Now, now, children. No fighting!" Almstead says.

"What's phase four?" Laurel asks.

"Thank you! Back to the business at hand! Phase four is we leave. And then on Day Seven, Sunday morning, the ship will blow sky high. That's right, the engine room is wired to blow at six a.m., right, Amos?"

Amos nods.

"See that man there?" Almstead points to Amos. "He is an irate, bereaved ex-marine who has become more and more obsessed with Pipop. He's determined to kill me at the hour of my greatest success! And he will. Tomorrow morning the whole ship gets blown to kingdom come. And I will go down with the ship." Almstead is beaming with pride. He winks. "Not really, of course. In reality I'll be on my way to an unchartered island. They do exist! And I've bought one. Isn't that brilliant? Rich, isn't that smart?"

Vince elbows Rich with the butt of his machine gun.

"Very imaginative," Rich says.

"Amos has been blogging stark, raving mad nonsense in conspiracy theory chat rooms for months now!" Almstead continues. "And next week, as America mourns me, I'll be on my island, watching the country eat itself alive, watching my board of directors flounder and panic, and I'll just be laughing myself silly. And Amos will be off somewhere, enjoying his compensation, is that right, Amos?"

"Sir, yes, sir," Amos answers.

"Well, I can see I've shocked you," Almstead says to us. "You three look like a bunch of gaping carp."

He mimics us with his mouth open wide like a fish.

"You planned it all," Laurel says, her voice quiet.

"Yep," Almstead says. He leans toward her and spells out. "L . . . O . . . L."

I step forward. I should kill him, now. But Vince has the gun trained at our guts.

"Put them in with the others, Vince," Almstead says.

Rich jumps, stricken. "No," he says. "Mr. Almstead. No, please."

Vince pushes Rich into us, then directs us with his gun toward the door.

"It's time to wrap it up," Almstead says with regret. "But I do respect the three of you. You didn't take the bait, and that's admirable. And you were instrumental in the success of the launch. I'm sorry it has to end this way."

"But, why?" Laurel blurts out. "Why do you hate people so much that you'd do something like this?"

"I'm afraid you'll never know, will you?" Almstead says. "No one will know the truth. And if that's sad, it can't be helped. Amos, I'm ready to be away from this ship."

"Wait! Don't take us away! We're still . . . We're still . . . ," Rich stammers.

"You're still what?" Almstead asks, a dark twinkle in his eye.

"We're still useful," Rich says.

"We should do an interview," I say. I turn to Almstead. "If you don't tell your side of the story, then no one will know this was a choice you made. They'll assume it was all just some stupid accident."

Rich joins in. "It airs posthumously. You put it in a bank vault. Give directions to a lawyer to open it when you actually die. Then the world will know that you created Solu on purpose."

Almstead is considering it, his eyes glinting as he scratches his jaw.

"You kids are just stalling," Almstead says. "And, anyhow, I'll only come off like some grandstanding villain."

"I think it's a good idea," Laurel says. "You should tell your side of the story."

"Mr. Almstead, please listen," Rich begs. "People need to know that it came from you. Otherwise they won't understand about the plan. All that stuff you told me about your shareholders. All that stuff about the Oinkers of the world and how this could be a wake-up call. They need to hear they're being given a new chance. A chance to start again, because that's what it is, isn't it?"

Almstead's eyes are moist. Jeez, Rich is good. He's brought Almstead to tears.

"Yes. All right, you're on," he says. "A posthumous interview. It's very smart."

Rich nods, but ducks his eyes away. It feels wrong to pander to an old man who's insane.

But it's what we're going to do. To try to stay alive.

"You can talk about your vision for the world," Rich says. "A world with no shortcuts."

"All right, Rich, don't sell past the close," Almstead says.

Before we leave the bridge for Almstead's suite, the guards shoot round after round of bullets into the navigational equipment.

Sparks fly and tubes explode.

"Our own fireworks show," Almstead jokes.

"You ain't seen nothin' yet," Amos tells him.

LAUREL

AMOS, VINCE, AND ANOTHER MERCENARY, the skinny one with the scruffy beard, escort Almstead, Tom, Rich, and me back to Almstead's suite.

I can tell Amos doesn't like this wrinkle in the plan.

He must know that we're stalling.

Can we . . . Can we jump over the side? Can we get free somehow?

As we exit the bridge, my mind is scrambling for ideas.

I can tell Tom and Rich are thinking along the same lines.

But we don't come up with anything on the short walk down to the stairway and to Almstead's suite on Deck 10.

Through the glass doors, I can see the sky turning gold and apricot. A beautiful sunset.

I wonder, Is this my last sunset?

I feel strangely displaced from the sadness and fear I should feel.

I am somehow floating above it all.

"Mr. Almstead, we'll seat you here," Rich says. "And, Tom, this is you." He indicates the other chair.

Tom and Almstead sit down.

I stand next to Rich, who is manning the camera.

In the suite, Rich has centered the shot on two beautiful wooden chairs, upholstered in glossy, jewel-toned silk. Behind them is a coffee table with a huge, slightly faded bouquet of flowers. Pollen from the heads of the drooping, yellowed lilies is scattered on the polished surface of the table. Translucent curtains dress the large porthole windows behind the table.

You would never know about the shipwide apocalypse outside the doors.

The scrawny mercenary next to me is trembling, I realize.

I turn and look at him and I see what I missed before. He's too thin. He's on Solu. He doesn't seem as far gone as the people on deck. Maybe he's only had a few doses.

Poor thing.

"I think we are about ready to begin. Can you please clear the shot, Amos?" Rich says.

Amos is standing between Tom and Almstead, maybe a few feet in back of them.

Amos shakes his head. "Not safe," he says.

"What do you mean?" Almstead says. "What's going to happen?"

"He could jump you," Amos says, indicating Tom with his chin.

"Oh, for heaven's sake, what's he going to do?"

"He's a strong young guy," Amos says. "He could do some damage to you. And quick."

"Well, it doesn't look like a very good interview if I have to have a bodyguard watching over me," Almstead protests.

Amos grumbles with irritation. Then he walks over to me,

shouldering his machine gun, and withdraws a handgun from a holster under his arm. He grabs me by the hair and pulls up.

Fire! It feels like my scalp is on fire and I cry out (though I didn't mean to).

"Then I'll keep tabs on your girl," Amos says to Tom. He lifts me until I'm on the tips of my toes. The barrel of his handgun pokes into my belly.

"Leave her alone!" Tom says. "I'm not going to do anything."

"Not now, you're not," the marine counters. He keeps the gun pressed into my stomach.

"Is that really necessary?" Almstead complains. "I like the girl."

"Me, too," Amos grumbles, and he lets me down a bit, so my feet are resting on the ground. "But it is."

My scalp and neck are burning with pain.

"Well, let's do this, shall we?" Almstead chirps. "I'm not getting any younger!"

Rich counts down. "Five, four, three, two . . . "

(I am in a sick parody of a studio audience.)

"I'm Tom Fiorelli and I'm here with Timothy Almstead, the CEO of Pipop and the man behind Solu."

"Hello, everyone," Almstead says.

"We are recording this interview on the evening of June twenty-sixth, less than six hours before Solu will be released across the country. And yet, you, the viewer, will not be seeing this until a time after Mr. Almstead's death. Mr. Almstead has agreed to speak with me in order to set the record straight about Solu and his role in its creation and distribution."

"Well said, Tom. I like how seriously you're taking this."

Almstead turns to the camera.

"Howdy, folks. I imagine that a lot of you are angry at me.

Maybe you think that Solu was a terrible mistake. That we got the formula wrong, something like that.

"Nope. It was on purpose.

"You see, as the CEO of Pipop, I've been under attack for years. Fat people blame me and my soft drinks for causing their fatness. People with no self-control whine about how addictive the drinks are.

"And then some sicko hick tried to shoot me! All because his fat, lazy wife drank herself to death.

"I got fed up with it, frankly!

"When Elise Zhang told me her discovery . . . I saw a way. A way to teach you all a lesson! Why do we hate fat people, Tom?"

"I don't hate fat people," Tom says.

"Oh, you're lying." Almstead waves his hand like he's shooing away a fly.

"We hate them because they have no self-control. All of us regular, thin people have to watch what we eat and the oinkers of the world just gobble down whatever they feel like and it chafes at us. It's not fair! What I say is . . . "

Almstead looks right into the camera, a sneer of a smile on his face. He leans forward in his chair.

"You want to be out of control? *Really* out of control? Have some Solu."

I shudder. Amos pokes me with the gun barrel.

Almstead is insane.

Even if Tom, Rich, and I die, making this tape is worth it. The world has to see him for who he is.

"Mr. Almstead," Tom says. "Can you tell us how you got Solu past the FDA?"

"Lord, boy, didn't you read your talking points? Solu is not a drug. It's not regulated by the FDA. It's a nutritional supplement.

"As for the formulation, it was a happy accident. See, Solu's made from a combination of plants. There's something called bitter candyfruit that grows all over in Europe and some Indian herb called bacopa, naturally sweet, the both of them. Together, they made a pretty good sweetener.

"Dr. Zhang brought it to me, first just as a sweetener. But when we tested it on rats, they dropped weight. Within days, they'd go from fat rats to skinny. To dead. And the rats couldn't get enough of the stuff.

"I knew we had something big on our hands.

"And the great thing about Zhang was, she wasn't attached to humanity, per se. I mean, she was much more interested in the effect of the formulation than anything else. You should have seen her on this cruise, 'Mr. Almstead, the subjects are demanding more Solu!' 'Mr. Almstead, the subjects are losing their inhibitions!' 'Mr. Almstead, they're raving mad!'

"She kind of scared me, the way her eyes lit up when she was talking about 'the subjects.'

"She should be here with me now. I bought her her own island to live on—but she was out watching the rioting and a group of them caught up with her. Too bad."

Tom clears his throat.

"Are you worried about what will happen to the Pipop Corporation when people learn how dangerous and damaging Solu is?" Tom asks.

Almstead leans back.

"Pipop's gonna go under. And I'm glad," he says. "The godforsaken shareholders! They're as bad as the customers. They wanted continual growth. 'Conquer new markets. Create new products.' But when the chips were down, when the politicians started legislating against our company, did they stick up for me? No! Did they use their Washington connections to fight back? No!

"They're fat and lazy, too! Just want more money, more money. Feeding on my daddy's company. I'm hoping they'll all go to jail!"

He hoots with laughter.

"That would show them!"

It feels like this interview is coming to an end.

Oh God. I glance around us. Amos still has his handgun pressed into my belly. The scruffy guard is to my right, next to Rich. The other one, Vince, is near the door.

I need to come up with a *plan!*

I need to think.

Tom asks, "What do you see happening when the product hits the stores tonight?"

"I see a whole lot of waddling oinkers lining up for an easy fix. And they'll get a fix, all right."

Tom shifts in his seat.

"But . . . Mr. Almstead, surely . . . surely you can't believe that people deserve to die because they're a little overweight. I mean, these are good people you're talking about. They didn't do anything wrong."

"How do we know they're good? I mean, look at you and Laurel and Rich. You're all smart, healthy young people—none of you took it. You didn't fall for the trap because you're not fat and lazy."

Tom is grinding his jaw. I can see the muscles in his jaw rippling.

"Aha! I see your disapproval there, Fiorelli," Almstead continues. "If anyone should feel bad, it's me. I'm the one who's going to be looked down on throughout history as some kind of a genocidal maniac. That contempt for me you have—everyone's going to feel that way. But after a hundred years or so, they're going to respect me and what I'm doing for the world. Solu is going to cleanse America of the fat and the lazy. Can you imagine it?"

Tom starts to speak, but Almstead holds up his hand.

"My father brought Pipop to the world. And I'm bringing Solu. He made a contribution and I'm making a contribution," Almstead says. He snaps his fingers at the tattooed mercenary. "Vince, there's a black metal briefcase in my closet. Bring it here."

Vince hustles off.

"I want to show you something, Tom," Almstead says.

Vince returns with the case.

Almstead snaps it open.

The eyes of the scruffy guard next to me open wide. His nostrils flare.

Inside, on a bed of foam, is one single can of soda. I bet I know what the sweetener is.

"Take a look at this," Almstead crows.

He removes the soda. The design of the can is a play on the distinctive looping purple-and-white Pipop banner.

This is Solu-pop.

A can of Solu-pop.

"See? Here's the perfect marriage of my father's contribution and mine. Solu-pop. It's a prototype.

"I know we'll never get a chance to produce it, but I couldn't resist. We had to make it pretty concentrated to be sweet enough. Probably ten doses in this little can."

Tom looks away in disgust.

Our time is running out.

Suddenly Almstead has a brainstorm. "Say, would anyone like to try it?"

Tom scoffs in disbelief. Rich gestures at him to play it cool.

The skinny guard next to me, he raises his hand slowly.

I gasp.

The guard looks to Amos, for permission.

"Are you kidding, Jensen? You've seen what it does."

Jensen shrugs. "I feel . . . I don't care. I want it."

Amos shrugs—his body language saying, "It's your funeral."

Almstead holds the can out to the scruffy guy.

His hands are shaking as he steps forward.

This is my chance. This is my moment, and for a second, I am paralyzed.

"WAIT!" I say.

Everyone looks at me, surprised. (As if a floor lamp started speaking.)

"You need a glass and ice," I say. "You have to do it right."

They all boggle at me for a moment.

"This is a historic moment, guys. We have to do it right."

Almstead beams at me.

"Good idea!" he says. "Just like a lady to think of something like that! The goodities and niceties!"

I bustle forward.

"Tom, get the guard a chair," I instruct. "And you should introduce him properly. We're making television history here."

Tom is looking at me with a "What the hell are you doing?" look on his face.

Almstead beams at me as I take the can from him.

"Aren't women wonderful? A different breed entirely!" he says.

I cross behind the men, into the kitchen of his suite.

I take a tall glass from the shelf.

Tom introduces the guard, whose name is Jimmy Jensen.

The fridge is dead, but I find some ice in a melting clump in the ice drawer.

I need to be very careful.

I pop the top on the can.

In the other room, I hear the guard gasp.

Jensen smells it.

I pour the soda over the ice.

I stop, my hands shaking. Maybe . . . maybe this is not going to work.

I thought Jensen would jump up by now.

Then I hear it. A sound like thunder. Thundering feet and screaming. The shrieking of the survivors on the ship.

"What on earth are they going on about now?" Almstead says.

I step back into the living room. Almstead, Tom, and the addict mercenary turn toward me.

Jensen licks his lips.

I step closer.

The sounds from the hallway grow louder and louder.

They smell it.

I dump the soda and ice over Almstead's head.

"Hey!" he protests.

Suddenly there's a loud *bang* on the door.

Voices screaming: "YOU HAVE IT. SOLUSOLUSOLU! GIVE IT TO US. LET US IN! LET US IIIINNNNN!"

Addicts. At the door.

They smelled the Solu.

(I knew they would.)

They smelled it through the door—through the hallways and corridors. Through the metal hull of the ship.

The suite's door explodes inward.

Tom stands and Amos hits him on the head with the butt of his gun. Tom drops!

Addicts swarm inside. First they hit the floor, licking and lapping. Then they smell it on Almstead.

And they jump him. Lick him, suck his hair. They bite him. They tear at him.

They're pulling, trying to get him away from one another.

They rip him apart.

His screams are horrible.

I'm pushed, thrown down to the floor.

They're stepping on me, crushing me.

The smell is overwhelming. Blood and innards and bowels.

Ragged, dirty skeletons. Shoving and shrieking and clawing their way to Almstead's bloody bones and guts.

"Tom!" I scream. "Rich!"

I try to stand but I can't get up. I can't even get to my hands and knees.

The swarm is kicking, shoving me back, and then I feel my back to the wall.

I push with my arms and legs, pushing against the wall. I manage to get to my feet.

Where is Tom?

A sweating teenage boy in filthy underwear shoves against me to get forward.

I have to get to Tom.

TOM

THERE'S A *SNAP* AND A *ROAR* of pain that brings me to my senses. My face is pressed to the ground and people are crawling over me.

My ankle is broken.

People are swarming on top of me, scrambling over me, and my blasted ankle is broken.

I look down, and oh God, the shape is wrong. There's a lump of bone jutting out above my ankle bone. Not breaking the skin, but wrong wrong wrong.

I retch; I can't help it.

It's the pain and the sight of it. The agony is surging through me. Feels like a buzzing swarm of flies in my blood, lifting and settling.

There's a high heel embedded in my forearm.

A scrawny, screaming harpy is standing on my arm and her heel is piercing my flesh.

I have to get up. NOW.

That a-hole hit me on the head with his gun. I remember.

"Laurel!" I shout.

God, she got Almstead. She killed him.

I try to stand up. My ankle screeches STOP. But I can't stop. I have to get up.

I shove and elbow addicts off me. They're feeding on a bloody, meaty something. A skeleton.

I have to stand on my left leg. I use the muscles of my left leg to haul me up.

I do a one-legged leg press for my frickin' life.

The pain rushes up and I'm going to pass out but I just lean to the side, into the mass of wriggling addicts.

"Laurel!" I croak. The room is spinning.

An electric pain flares and I look down to see an addict woman pressing the high-heel puncture wound on my arm.

It's Lorna Kreiger.

Lorna Kreiger is digging her finger into the hole.

"Get away!" I shout.

She smells the blood on her fingers and grimaces, like she's smelling bad milk. There's no Solu in my blood—so she's disappointed.

I don't see Laurel anywhere. I can't find her.

Then there's machine-gun fire.

It's Amos. He's firing into the crowd, into the addicts coming through the door.

"OUT OF THE WAY!" he shouts.

He is shooting his way through the crowd, trying to get out of the room.

Now the screeching addicts turn on one another—drinking the blood of the fallen.

This is hell. This is a living hell.

Blue blips of light swoop and flock in my vision.

I tell myself, *You pass out, you die.*

And thank God, thank God, I hear Laurel's voice.

"Tom!" she sobs. "Tom!"

She's climbing over the addicts. She's crawling over them; her arms reach out to me.

"You did it!" I say. "Laurel, you did it."

I pull her to me and she shoves and kicks her way down till her feet hit the floor.

I'm so happy to see her. So relieved she's all right. I want to hold her, but I can barely stay up. Only the press of addicts is keeping me upright.

Laurel wipes my face and I realize she's wiping away my puke. Once I would have been embarrassed. Now I'm just thankful we're both alive.

"Are you okay?" she shouts.

"My ankle's snapped," I tell her.

She looks down.

"Oh, man," she says.

Someone crashes into me and I try not to scream like a girl.

The insane, churning mill of addicts presses in on us from every side.

My ankle is screeching nonstop—like the pain is the sound made by bones rubbing together.

"We have to get out of this room!" Laurel yells.

I try to keep myself vertical, but they're all over us. They are thickest at the door, shoving and climbing over one another.

A skeleton draped in hanging folds of skin grabs my hair and tries to crawl over me. A naked woman covered in red marks—bite marks—puts her bare foot on Laurel's shoulder to push off. We're getting buried alive in bodies.

Then *RATATATATAT*.

Rich is holding a machine gun and firing into the ceiling.

"Everybody down!" he shouts. "Get down or die!"

They cower. They cower for a moment and Rich holds his hand out to Laurel.

"Come on, you two, let's get the hell out of here!"

Laurel kicks her way out and I follow the best I can, leaning on her and dragging my right leg. I can't hold it up high—the pain won't let me. It catches on people's limbs and I nearly black out over and over again.

The hallway is glutted, but with some more fire from Rich into the ceiling, we make it out of the press of bloodthirsty skeletons.

I lurch, falling facedown onto the floor. I'm not going to be able to get up. I'm not.

The floor is cool under my face and I close my eyes.

Laurel and Rich drop next to me.

"We made it," Rich says. "We're alive. We're alive!"

"Tom broke his ankle," Laurel tells Rich. "He can't walk."

"I thought we were all going to die," Rich continues. "Laurel, you were amazing! And I got you guys out of there! This gun is amazing!"

"Rich! Tom broke his ankle. Look!"

Only now does Rich look at me.

"Oh no, no, no. Is that his bone? That is disgusting."

Face pressed against the floor, I glare at him.

"We'll get you some help," Rich says. "Can you walk?"

"No," I say.

Not "I'll try." Not "maybe."

Just no.

I just can't.

My whole body is starting to shake. And I'm cold, I realize. Very cold.

"Leave me," I say.

"Not in a million years," Laurel tells me.

"Not on your life," Rich says simultaneously.

So they drag me.

Rich loops a piece of discarded clothing from the floor under my arms. He takes one sleeve, Laurel takes the other and they drag me down the hall.

Some addicts dodge past us, hoarding pieces of cloth. They snarl and dart at one another like wild dogs.

If they notice us, they don't show it.

The business center is on the same deck as Almstead's suite.

That's lucky.

Stairs would kill me.

Rich and Laurel drag me to the far hallway wall and leave me there, propped up against the wall. We can hear people, sane people, trying to break down the doors.

"Thank God, they're still alive!" Laurel says.

She's sweaty and dirty and there's blood smeared all over her. I hope it's my blood—I don't want addicts to smell Solu-tainted blood on her and attack.

"You okay?" she asks me, bending to brush the hair out of my eyes.

"Yeah," I lie.

"Think I should shoot it open?" Rich asks us. He's nodding toward the doors.

There's a length of chain looping through the elegant brass door handles. It's locked with some kind of digital combination padlock.

"Hello!" Rich shouts. "This is Rich Weller. Are you guys okay in there?"

Laurel rises and goes to Rich's side. "Jaideep? Are you in there? Milo? Kiniana?"

"Hello?!" It's Jaideep, along with a chorus of others. "Yes, we're here. With lots of others! The guards put us in here. They may come back!"

"Stand back," Rich shouts. "I'm going to shoot the door open. Everyone get clear."

There's clattering and shouting from within, as they scramble to get out of the way.

RATATATATAT.

Rich blasts away the chain and the handles until the bullets run out and the gun *clicks* empty.

The doors swing open and our friends pour out of the room. Other non-addicts are with them. There must be at least eighty people.

More than I hoped.

Jaideep rushes to Laurel.

"We thought you were dead!" he says. He sees me.

"Oh no! Tom!" He and Laurel come to my side.

"Everyone make your way to Deck Six," a black crewman in uniform shouts. "We're going to evacuate the ship."

There are a couple of men in uniform. They must be from the bridge, I realize. They are taking charge, which is good.

"He broke his ankle," Laurel tells Jaideep.

"Yes, I see that." He says, eyeing my ankle with a grimace. "We need a medic! Kathlyn!"

A Filipino woman rushes to us and looks at my ankle.

"Get him a wheelchair," she tells Jaideep. Jaideep nods and rushes away. The woman turns to leave.

"That's all?" Laurel asks. "Can't you . . . fix it? Make it so the bone isn't sticking out like that?"

"We will get him to a doctor. We need to do X-rays, and setting an ankle is delicate business."

"Can you give him something for the pain?" Laurel asks.

"Yes, yes. I'll give it to him on the lifeboat," she tells us. "And I can put a cool pack on it in the boat."

Around us, crew members are springing into action.

The medic, Kathlyn, is swept up in a group headed for the stairs.

Jaideep comes back with the wheelchair. Vihaan is on his heels.

The two of them struggle to lift me into the chair. Laurel holds it steady.

They jolt and jostle my leg. Waves of nausea alternate with shocks of pain.

Putting my ankle in the leg brace thing nearly takes me down. Jaideep is rolling me down the hallway when we hear an air horn.

It gives one long blast, then seven short ones.

"I cannot believe we are hearing that sound," Jaideep says. "The signal to abandon ship."

"Not even over the PA," Vihaan adds. They both shake their heads.

"What has become of our beautiful ship?" Jaideep sighs.

"ABANDON SHIP!" Vihaan yells off into the hallway.

"ABANDON SHIP!" Jaideep echoes.

LAUREL

WHEN WE DID THE MUSTER DRILL, half the passengers were on one side of the ship and half of them went to the other.

I stood on this deck with 250 other people, all of us wearing life jackets, feeling goofy, shifting from foot to foot, and waiting for it to be over.

Now there are . . . maybe 120 of us, all told? We are the people who did not take Solu. Everyone looks beaten, bloodied, and ragged. The injured are hanging on to the able-bodied.

There are a lot of crew members among our ranks, helping people with life jackets. It makes sense that there are more clean crew members than passengers—they were *supposed* to not take Solu.

The lifeboats hang just above us, from big mechanical braces.

I see a crew member on the rigging near the lifeboats, moving levers. The first of the three boats lowers down.

Everyone cheers.

Rich is standing with Tom and me.

Vihaan and Jaideep went to make sure everyone has a life jacket.

After everything that has happened, after the mistreatment

they experienced at the hands of the crazed passengers, they and the other crew members are still doing their jobs.

It's amazing.

They are evacuating us, calmly and professionally, just as they must have practiced a thousand times.

Jaideep even found Tom a bottle of orange juice, to get his blood sugar back up, and has wrapped him in a shiny, reflective blanket.

"I sedated her!" an anxious voice cries. "Please, she's just a child!"

A bossy woman is arguing with one of the crew members. A sleeping form lies on the deck at the woman's feet.

"We are not allowing any addicts on the lifeboat."

"She's twelve years old!" the woman begs.

She removes a large emerald ring from her hand and presses it into the crewman's hand.

"Please!"

The crewman blows out an exasperated breath and puts the ring firmly back into the mother's hand.

"We will bind her hands and feet," he declares.

"Yes! Fine! Anything!"

I can't help my curiosity. I step forward as the woman pulls her daughter onto her lap.

Her skin hangs in folds off her emaciated frame, but her sleeping face is the same sweet girlish face I remember from the day I practiced my guitar on the upper deck.

It's Claire. The girl who took selfies with Tom.

"It's okay, baby," the mother croons to her daughter.

"I'm going to find my wife!" a short man yells. "Wait for me!"

"If she can come, then I'm going to get my brother!" a woman insists.

The crewman holds up his hands.

"I made an exception because this girl is twelve years old and she's already sedated! No other addicts may be brought on the lifeboat. Not a one!!"

Other passengers become agitated.

"I'm not getting on the boat with one of them!" a tall, jowly man with a face like a pug says. "They're animals!"

Some other passengers agree, but the crew member gets up in the man's face. "You don't have much of a choice. In an emergency situation, you do what we say or get left behind," he tells the man.

That shuts him up.

Night has fallen and the sea is nothing but a black expanse with twinkles reflected from the full moon.

Below us, other crew members are being evacuated from a lower deck.

Men roll these large canisters out into the water and then pull on ropes attached to the canisters. They pop, and a full life raft inflates by itself, with a roof and everything. These are round and have an orange tent top.

We are getting into lifeboats; they have hard bottoms and tops. They are much bigger and have an engine, Jaideep told us.

From below I see all these kitchen workers and cleaning people piling into the life rafts. Must be at least two hundred of them. They fill three rafts.

The passengers cheer for them and some of the workers wave to us.

I remember Anna said something about a barricade.

Good for them.

"Hey, look!" a passenger yells.

Far off in the water are lights. Little lights.

"Hey! Over here!" some of the passengers start shouting, waving their arms.

But I know what they are—they're taillights.

"It's the guards," I say. "Almstead's guards."

"They got away," Tom says.

"I hope they rot in hell," Rich says. "When we get to the shore, the first thing I'm going to do is give their names to the police."

Wind whips up from the dark water, lashing my hair across my face just as my stomach bottoms out.

"Rich." I grab his arm. "What time is it?"

He checks his watch.

"It's nine thirty."

"Then there's still time! Solu is released at midnight. If we can get word out, they can stop the release! There's still time!"

Tom looks at me. His face is gray. "You're right," he says.

The first lifeboat is now locked into place against the railing. People are eager to board, scrambling across onto the boat.

"Slowly, now," a crewman shouts. "One at a time!"

Some people have some of their belongings. One guy is carrying a bottle of single malt scotch.

"We can help with Tom," Jaideep says, coming over.

"Wait," I say. "We can't get on that boat. We have to warn the mainland. We have to get the word out."

Rich eyes the lifeboat with longing.

"We must get ashore. Then we will put the word out," Jaideep says.

"But how long will that take?" I ask.

Jaideep shrugs. "It could be as many as six or eight hours. We don't know exactly where we are."

"That's not good enough!" I shout. "There must be a radio—something!"

Rich puts a hand on my shoulder. "Laurel, you know the mercenaries shot up the bridge. You saw it yourself."

"It'll be okay," Jaideep tells me. "These lifeboats have a beacon. We will likely be rescued soon."

Rich pushes Tom's chair toward the lifeboat. I trail behind.

"But no one knows the ship is in trouble," I protest. "Almstead saw to that."

"Laurel, we don't know! Okay?" Rich snaps. "The sooner we get off the boat, the sooner we can get the word out!"

I can't stand still—I'm pacing back and forth.

We can't just get on a lifeboat and let midnight come and go. People are buying up all the boxes. They will buy enough doses to get fully addicted—all at once. They could binge on Solu and become monsters in even less than the six days it took for the people on board to succumb.

It's our turn to board, but I can't. I won't.

"Come now, we will carry Tom across," Jaideep tells us.

"Keep moving!" people shout from behind us.

I step out of the line, pushing Tom ahead of me.

"Board the boat, Laurel," Rich insists. "The sooner we board, the sooner we get somewhere with phone service!"

A man with a leg wound asks Jaideep to help him.

Jaideep gets under the man's shoulder and helps him walk. Together they step onto the lifeboat and they step inside the craft, ducking under the roof. For a second, Jaideep is a dark silhouette against the orange emergency lights inside the lifeboat.

Then he disappears inside.

There's almost no one left on the deck now.

"Time to board the lifeboat," says a crewman. "You need to get on. Right now."

"But we haven't warned the mainland!" I shout. "We have to warn them!"

"All communications are down," the crewman says. "There's no way to contact them."

"Time to let go, Laurel," Rich says. "You've done enough already. You can't save the world."

I push Rich away.

"What about flares?" I ask the crewman.

"No one's looking for us," he snaps. "They won't see a little flare in the water."

"Laur . . . ," Tom says. "Laurel!"

He grabs my hand.

I bend down.

I'm ready for him to tell me to chill out, too. I know he's wanted to get off the ship all day. He probably wishes we'd done it much earlier.

"We can't just abandon ship, Tom! We can't. There has to be a way to get the attention of the mainland."

"You're right," he says. "And there is."

"Come on, man," Rich moans. "Can't we just get off this god-forsaken ship?"

"Listen," Tom says. Rich and I lean in close. "The ship is rigged to explode tomorrow, right? So I blow it now."

Yes.

Tom continues, "You guys will all be on the lifeboat—you'll motor away. Someone will see a huge ship on fire. It will be too big to miss. They'll come and then Laurel, you and Rich, will tell them all about Solu. About Almstead, about his plan, everything."

"It's a great plan," I say.

Tom sits back with a grimace. "Good," he says.

"Except I'm going to be the one who blows it up," I tell him.

"No!" Tom says. "Laurel, that's not the idea!"

"We are leaving now!" The crewman shouts. "Get on board or be left behind."

Jaideep comes out of the lifeboat's shelter and motions to us. "Laurel, Rich, Tom! Come on!"

"Guys, just come now," Rich pleads. He walks backward toward the rail. "Your plan sucks. Please come."

"Laurel, go," Tom says to me. "Go with them. I can handle this."

"No. We'll do it together. You need my help. Okay?" I squeeze his hand. "Okay?"

"Okay," he says. "But I don't like it."

"Rich, you have to tell them everything. About Solu. About Almstead. The plan doesn't work if you don't tell them."

There are tears streaming down Rich's face.

"Oh, don't you worry. I'll get the message out," he says. "I'll tell them how you saved us. Everyone will know about you two."

Rich crosses the threshold onto the lifeboat.

"Mr. Fiorelli? Miss?" the crewman calls. "WE ARE GOING TO LEAVE YOU!"

"Go ahead!" I yell back. "We're staying!"

The crewman detaches the lifeboat from the side of the ship and closes the gate on the boat.

It starts to lower automatically from the side of the ship.

Jaideep lunges for the rail as the lifeboat sinks out of view.

"Miss Laurel!" he yells. "Come with us! No!"

He doesn't understand why we're not coming and there's panic in his eyes and it just gets me. A sob comes up. I try to choke it back.

"Nope. None of that," I say aloud. "Let's get to work."

TOM

LAUREL STARTS UNBUCKLING the life jacket Jaideep gave her.

"Guess you won't need that, huh?" I ask.

"Nope," she says. "Not if your plan goes right."

"You know, I always wanted to do an action movie. Save millions of lives. Blow up a ship," I say.

"Well, you're doing it," Laurel says. She pushes me back toward the entrance to the main hall.

"Didn't quite see myself doing it being pushed in a wheelchair by a pretty girl, though," I say.

"Maybe the movie features a disabled guy?" Laurel says.

I laugh. "Oh God, how are you still funny?"

She reaches forward and kisses me on the back of my head.

"I got a tour on the first day of the cruise," I tell Laurel. "The engine room is on Deck 4. We go through a door marked RESTRICTED AREA. It's at the end of the casino."

"Off we go," she says.

She eases my wheelchair over the bump as we cross the threshold between the deck and the ship, and it jars my ankle.

I inhale sharply through gritted teeth.

"How is it?" she asks.

My ankle has swollen to three times its size. It's so big and bloated and bruised I'm worried the flesh will split open like an overripe plum.

"It's grotesque," I answer.

"How's the pain?"

"It's okay," I lie. "But I'm a little worried about the stairs."

"Yeah, I was thinking about that, too," she tells me.

The engine room is two flights down.

We reach the staircase.

Laurel helps me stand, then carries the wheelchair down the stairs, so it waits for me on the landing.

What follows is agony, one stair at a time.

My right thigh shakes violently as I try to hold the damaged foot off the ground. Laurel supports me under my left arm and I'm clinging to the railing with my right.

"I'm sorry I'm so slow," I gasp. Sweat is pouring off me.

"It's okay," Laurel says. "It gives the people on the lifeboat time to get away safely."

Pain, pain, pain.

We get to Deck 4 one step at a time.

"Hey, look at that," I say.

This is the deck all those kitchen workers evacuated from. It has a door that essentially opens right up onto the sea—it's where the boats dock when they pick us up for excursions to shore.

The door is standing open, just opened right up to the water level—maybe five feet above it.

A life raft is bobbing there, tethered to the ship by a long cord.

It has an emergency light in it that illuminates the whole raft from within. It's glowing orange.

The kitchen workers must have not needed this one.

Laurel and I exchange a look.

"Maybe," I say.

"Maybe," she answers.

Now my teeth are chattering and I'm shaking.

"I'm worried about you," Laurel says.

"We're going to blow up the ship," I remind her. "I can make it that far."

She peers into my eyes, examining them as if I might have a concussion.

I cup her face in my hands.

Laurel is so beautiful she shines like the moon. Her pale skin glows in the murky light of the hallway.

"Don't go into shock," she tells me. "Because I'm too scared to be alone."

"I won't," I promise her.

Laurel wheels me into the ship.

We're close—all we need to do is cross through the casino and the boutique area to get to the engine room.

But it doesn't make it any easier that it's so dark and foul inside the ship. The only light comes from some emergency lights running along the edges of the carpet, showing you how to get out.

The casino is empty. Most of the tall leather stools overturned. A few tables have been upended and chips are scattered across the floor like confetti.

"Almost there," Laurel says as she navigates my chair around a bank of dead slot machines.

Then there's a rustling ahead of us and a male voice grunts, "Dude! It's mine! MINE!"

A figure moves ahead of us, followed closely by two others. They are all clutching at something.

There's a sharp, husky laugh. My hackles go up.

"We share everything. That's what a family does. You should know that by now!"

Everyone in America knows that accent—it's Sabbi frickin' Ribiero.

Laurel freezes. I can hear her breaths coming fast and anxious behind me.

The three of them cluster by a window and in the light of the moon I see Sabbi, next to Luka Harris. It's got to be him—no one has that hair but him. But his body is unrecognizable. He looks like a cadaver.

And of course they're with Vivika.

They're huddled around a long shredded piece of dark fabric. They are sucking it.

Laurel's friend's face is bone hollow. Her cheeks sunken. Her eyes huge in their dark sockets.

Sabbi looks even worse. She's even thinner than Viv and her skin is waxy and taut.

"Go back," I whisper. "Go backward."

But Laurel, ARGH, Laurel clears her throat.

"Viv?" she says softly.

All three look up sharply.

"Vivvy, sweetie, is that you?"

Sabbi straightens up from her crouch.

"Ha!" she shouts. "It can't be my Tomazino!"

Sabbi stalks toward us through the fallen stools and tables.

"Stay back!" Laurel shouts.

I grab at the wheels of my chair, trying to move forward, but Laurel's hauling me backward.

"Forward!" I say to Laurel. "We can't stop."

Sabbi walks after us. Talking to me as Laurel wheels me backward.

"Tom, do you see what I did for you? To be pretty for you—to be thin, like you want me? I got down to nothing!"

She holds her arms out and cackles.

"Look at me! I shrunk down to a size *zero*. A size *dead*! I am all bones now and I hope you are happy!"

She takes three giant steps and jumps at me, shouting, "Kiss me! Kiss me like you did!"

I put my hands up to block her and I push forward, toppling out of my chair.

She's on me, her mouth on my mouth. She smells like a slaughter-house and the pain from my *ankle*—

"Kiss me!" she demands and darkness flashes, slashes, tears through my vision and takes me down, down into a hole.

LAUREL

"TOM!" I SHOUT. "TOM!"

Sabbi is on top of him, kissing him, and he's unconscious.

"Get off him!" I scream. "You can't have him, you skinny bitch!!!"

She looks up at me and snarls.

So I stomp her with my boot. Right in the hip.

I hear a crack, but she spins and grabs me by the leg.

I fall back and hit my head on the edge of a fallen table.

Then she's on top of me. I try to get out from under her, but Sabbi pins my arms under her knees.

"You!" she spits. "You fat, ugly nobody! I got your friend! She's mine now!"

Sabbi's face is inches from mine and her breath smells like rotten blood and animal guts.

"I win. Ha-ha." She puts her hands around my throat. I try to roll her off me, but my head is reeling.

Her arms are shaking but she squeezes.

Everything goes flashy in my vision.

I see a shape moving behind her.

It's . . . It's Viv.

Something shines in her hands. A shard of glass.

"GET. OFF. MY. FRIEND," Viv grunts and chops down with the glass, stabbing Sabbi in the back of the neck.

Sabbi's eyes go wide in shock.

The thin finger of glass protrudes from just under her chin.

I gasp.

The air hurts my throat.

I gasp for air.

Viv pulls Sabbi off me.

"Viv," I sob. "You saved me."

But she's not listening.

She's drinking.

She's lapping at Sabbi's blood like a thirsty dog.

When I can breathe again, I get my hands under Tom's arms and I pull.

It's so hard to get him into that chair. He's so, so heavy.

With Tom out cold, I am making a new plan.

"Vivvy, can you help me?" I ask. "Can you?"

But she and Luka Harris, who scuttled forward like a rat, are feasting on blood.

I get Tom on the chair. I'm sweating and shaking, but I finally get him on the chair.

I pull him back, back toward that door open to the water. Toward the life raft.

I kneel at the door that opens onto the ocean and grab the cord. Fist over fist, I draw the life raft closer to the open door.

"You've got to go," I tell Tom's unconscious body. My voice is shaking. "It's better this way. No reason for me to drag you along." (Except that I'm terrified—but how much comfort could an unconscious boy in a wheelchair really provide?)

"I hope you won't be mad at me. Well, I hope you'll live. That's the first thing, and that you won't be mad at me; I guess that's irrelevant."

I realize I'm rambling, but it helps to fill the (dead, ominous, eerie) silence with chatter.

"There's a chance you'll make it. Slim chance, but why not?"

I tie off the raft as close as I can get it to the door, securing it to one of the T-shaped cleat things just below the door on the outside of the ship.

I pull Tom's body from the wheelchair and get it headfirst as close to the door as I can.

I sit on the edge of the doorway next to him, then slide out and down into the raft. There's a pretty steep angle because of how I tied it and I slip-slide down.

Now I have to pull Tom's unconscious body in with me. Hard to do with my feet slipping on the slick, drawn-up floor of the raft.

"Sorry . . . about . . . this . . .," I say between heaves and then Tom's body comes free of the ship and slides down on top of me. I struggle to get out from under him and it's awful and funny and horrific because I keep slipping as I try to stand.

I grab on to a set of nylon grip straps lining the roof of the tent and use them to haul myself back up to the opening.

"Core strength," I pant. "I should have worked on my core strength more," I say to no one conscious. I can see provisions tucked into bags attached to the walls of the raft. There's food and water in there. Maybe he will be okay.

I grab on to the cleat and use it to heave myself up onto the ship.

Tom just lays there in the bottom of the boat. He looks so defenseless and broken. (No "looks" about it—he IS defenseless and broken.) I almost can't bear to leave him.

"I wanted to introduce you to my parents," I say with a sobby kind of a laugh. "I think they would really like you. And I wanted to see them and tell them about everything that happened and about poor Viv. But none of that is going to happen. I'm not going to see them again."

I wipe away my tears with the back of my hand.

"Because people will die if Solu gets out. That's why."

I'm panting and cursing and crying as I untie the ropes I used to tie the raft to the ship.

I give it a shove and a kick and then I try to shove it again, but it's out of reach.

"Good luck, Tom," I tell his sleeping form. "Good luck and good luck and good-bye."

The raft bobs on the waves, the sea taking it slowly away from the ship.

I hope the blast will push the raft farther away, and not suck it down to the bottom of the ocean. I hope Tom will survive. But I can't worry too much about it. I've got a flare to light.

I avert my eyes as I pass Viv and Luka in the casino. They don't notice me. Too much blood leaching into the carpet.

I find the door marked RESTRICTED AREA and I push through it. The corridors are painted flat gray and lit by yellow emergency lights set in the ceiling.

I follow them down the hall, and when the hallway branches in two, I head to the left. Of course, this seems to be the wrong choice. I find myself in the ship's laundry room.

I backtrack to the intersection and go the other way, only to find myself back at the door leading to the casino.

A half laugh, half sob rips out of me.

"I'm lost!" I say. "Of course I am!"

But I try the only other way to go and then I see it: a door marked ENGINE ROOM.

The door is open because from what I can tell, the center to the doorknob—the part that locks it—has been removed with some sort of high-tech drill. (Hi there, Amos and company.)

I'm in.

The massive engine room is eerily silent.

Giant ducts and pipes crisscross, connecting the engines. A series of machines the size of refrigerators lines one side of the passage. On the other are what look like rectangular tanks. Thick ducts and valves everywhere.

And running in a loop around the perimeter of the floor are ten small packages of what must be explosives, connected with shiny copper wire.

I wipe my hands on my pants. (They're shaking.)

The wires connect to an iPhone.

It's just sitting on the floor.

I drop to my knees in front of it.

"God," I say, because I have to say a prayer. Because I need courage. "Thank you for my beautiful life. I was so lucky. Thank you for my mom and my dad and for all that they gave me. Thank you for my friends. For Viv. I hope you can forgive her. Thank you for Tom. Thank you for Bach, just for the world, for the beach and for delicious food and for all the love that I got to feel."

And I take the iPhone into my shaking hands and press that familiar round, slightly concave button.

ENTER PASSWORD, the screen blares.

I need to pick something that is most certainly *not* the password.

And then it will detonate the explosives.

I gulp.

Then I press in 2-6-6-8-7.

B-O-O-T-S.

WRONG PASSWORD, it flashes, then, ENTER PASSWORD.

I do not stop to think.

I enter 2-6-6-8-7.

WRONG PASSWORD.

ENTER PASSWORD.

Again I type in B-O-O-T-S.

And the iPhone's face resets.

It's a countdown. Sixty seconds.

That was easier than I thought it would be, I think for a second.

Then I come to my senses—I set it down and I *run*.

I race through the casino and when I get to the open door, I see the raft.

It's floating off a ways. Not very far. (Probably not far enough.)

I kick off my boots and I dive.

TOM

I WAKE WITH A START and everything is orange. I'm in some sort of tent? No. Water's rolling beneath me. For a second, all I know is that everything is wrong. Then I remember: Laurel. Sabbi. The ship.

"NO!" I shout, because I realize where I am.

I'm in a freaking life raft.

"Laurel!" I yell. "LAUREL!"

I flip over, which wrenches my ankle. Hot pain sears up my leg. Using my arms, I belly-crawl across the smooth, yellow floor to the opening in the roof overhead.

I pull myself up on the side of the raft, coming up to kneel on my good leg.

The raft is floating maybe a hundred feet from the ship.

She's swimming hard.

"Come on!" I shout. I reach out my arm.

She swims for all she's worth.

I reach out, my ankle shrieking but there! She reaches for me, fumbling, her arm wet and slippery, and I get a good hold on her wrist and pull with everything I've got as—*BOOM!*

Everything is white-hot light and a wall of sound.

I pull Laurel over the side of the raft to me and—*BOOM!* A second explosion splits the air and we're hit with water.

The raft tips; Laurel and I slide down it, back through the open doorway, into the part of the raft that has a roof. And then the raft goes end over end like we're in a washing machine.

Water pounds us from every direction, and there's the feeling of falling. The raft being sucked into a giant vortex of dark, churning water.

We hit something—a part of the ship, maybe—and the raft absorbs the hit. We're scrunched together, heavy rubber against my face for a split second and then the raft regains its shape.

I sputter and gasp—trying to get air.

My lungs are burning. My ankle's bleeding. Bone through the skin. I can feel the joint sickly loose now.

Then we're spit back up, the whole raft, into the night air. We're spit back up on a wave that carries us away from the wreckage.

The waves churn and spin us. But I hold on to Laurel.

We choke up seawater. We gasp. We puke up seawater.

We slide all over the life raft. There's nothing inside except us and the soft sides.

But eventually we are floating. Bobbing on the waves.

Laurel says, "Tom." She says it over and over. I answer her with, "Laurel."

There's blood and water in the raft. It sloshes back and forth as choppy waves roll under the raft.

Laurel crawls-paddles through the water to the edge of the raft and looks out.

"What—" I sputter. "What do you see?"

"The ship is a flare," she says. "It's a flare."

"We did it," Laurel says.

Her hair is plastered to the sides of her face and she's shaking.

"You did it," I tell her.

She crawls back to me.

We lie there, huddled together, looking up at the inside of the life raft.

The smell of burning ship fuel wafts across the water.

We bob on the waves.

My leg throbs in constant agony.

We're all washed out. Nothing left. Nothing but the instinct to cling.

After a good long while, we hear choppers.

LAUREL

AT FIRST I DON'T KNOW WHERE I AM.

There's a window with glass slats. Outside I see the tops of scrawny palm trees and I can hear street noise and the sounds of televisions blaring and chattering.

It smells like cheap gasoline and grilled chicken and frying bananas.

Everything on my body hurts. I can't even lift my head, the pain is so severe.

There's an IV in my hand.

I'm in a hospital, I realize. A hospital in some country that is not America (which is why it doesn't smell like a hospital).

"Tom," I croak. My throat is dry and scratchy. "Tom."

No one can hear me. I need to know if he is alive. And no one is coming.

I lift my head (agony) to see if there's a nurse call-button thingy. There's none.

"Tom," I repeat. "Somebody!"

The walls are painted a mint green and the equipment is mismatched new and old.

There's a TV. On it I see the news. The anchors are a Latino man and a Latino woman. The sound is off.

I wonder where I am. (Will anyone ever come?)

I hear a fuss in the hallway. The sound of people talking in Spanish. And Tom! I hear his voice!

"Tom!" I call.

And he bursts in.

He's dragging his leg, which is in a plaster cast, and he staggers to my bed.

"Laurel!" he cries and we're kissing and trying to embrace and I forget the pain I'm in because it feels so good to touch him.

Two small nurses are tutting and fussing in Spanish. They demand that Tom return to his room. (Fat chance, nurses.)

"*El canal Americano!*" he says, pointing to the TV. "*Por favor, el sonido! Por favor!*"

One of them shakes her head in disapproval but marches over to the TV, changes the channel, and cranks up the volume. The two nurses argue for a moment, pointing at us, and they must decide to leave us alone for a minute because they turn and go.

"Look," Tom says, as if I need to be told.

It's one of the networks and two news anchors are reporting, a gray-haired man and a pretty black woman.

"Search-and-rescue teams from Honduras and Nicaragua have been combing the seas for survivors. We have word that at least seventy-five people have been rescued, but no crews have been able to speak to any of the survivors yet," the man says.

Footage of helicopter rescues show on screen. There's our raft—I think it's our raft. And a shot of a stretcher being airlifted off. I think it's me on the stretcher!

The anchorwoman takes over.

"Thanks, Jim. Now, the authorities have not confirmed this, but we have received an e-mail from a Private Amos Lancaster, formerly of the U.S Marine Corps, claiming responsibility for the attack. He wrote to us—"

An excerpt from his e-mail shows on the screen.

> Timothy Almstead is dead now and he deserved it! I
> blame Pipop for the downfall of America. No one can
> resist it and all that sugar has poisoned us all. I look
> around and see poison everywhere. Every store, every
> second of the day we're surrounded by it. It has to end
> somewhere! I blew up that ship to fight back! Everyone
> should join me and fight back!

The man, Jim, talks: "Wow, Sabrina, what a tragedy for Timothy Almstead, the president and heir of the Pipop empire, to have worked to bring Solu to the market and have this happen on the day the product is launched!"

"I agree, Jim," Sabrina says. "Stores across the country sold out in a matter of hours."

They cut to a Greenway Superstore. Happy, smiling shoppers with arms full of lavender boxes wave and mug for the camera.

"Now we're getting word of a new development," Sabrina says. She's reading from a piece of paper that's just been handed to her. "The authorities are asking people to temporarily refrain from taking Solu. Huh. Apparently, the passengers from one of the lifeboats are claiming it is not safe."

"Solu is not safe?" Jim repeats.

Sabrina makes a little embarrassed face.

"Uh-oh!" the anchorwoman says. "That's a little late for a lot of us. I'm already on my third packet of the day, and I have to say . . . " She winks. "I'm feeling *fantastic*."

ACKNOWLEDGMENTS

What a pleasure it is to collaborate with the smart and talented people at Feiwel & Friends, Macmillan, and the Einstein Literary Management. I feel an enormous debt to the editorial, design, publicity, marketing, and sales departments for all the hard work that went into this book, as well as to my savvy and hardworking agents.

A brief laundry list of gratitude:

Holly, Jean, and Dave! Anne Heausler!
Susanna, Sandy, and Molly R-L.!
Molly Brouillette! Mary, Allison, Ksenia, Nicole B., and Brittany!
Liz F.! Kathryn!
Rich Deas and KB!
Angus!
Vannessa, the other Holly, Jenn, Mark, Claire, and Jennifer!
Lauren! Nicole L.M, Anna, and Christine!

I really mean those exclamation points. Those are sincere and exuberant exclams from the heart!

Another set of earnest exclamation points to my extraordinary and generous beta readers, Kristin Bair and Wendy Shanker. Thank you!

I dedicated this book to my father, Kit Laybourne. Dad, you have an irrepressible creative zeal and I'm so glad it rubbed off on me. Thank you for taking me on a luxury cruise to the Caribbean to do research. Wow—was that fun! (And a shout-out to all the friends we made on the cruise, crew and passengers alike.) Also, thanks for taking me to all those B movies over the years. They rubbed off on me, too.

Now, *Sweet* is hardly an issue book, but there are some important subjects that come into play. Just to be very clear, I, Emmy Laybourne, am a believer in fat acceptance and shame-free body love. I also have personal experience with food addiction (sugar, to be specific). You can read more about my personal feelings on these subjects on the page for SWEET at emmylaybourne.com. There, you'll also find links to articles I find relevant, as well as information on the books and tools I use to combat my sugar addiction.

Lastly, I want to thank my beloved children, Elinor and Rex. I feel so unbelievably lucky to be your mom. And thank you to my husband, Greg, for taking such good care of me and making me laugh and letting me love you so much. I kicked sugar and now you are my sweetener of choice.

sweet

BONUS MATERIALS

A CONVERSATION WITH EMMY LAYBOURNE

In addition to being the kind of thriller your fans have come to expect after the Monument 14 trilogy, *Sweet* illuminates some serious issues: body image and fat shaming; nutrition and obesity. Why did you decide to write about these issues?

With *Sweet*, the premise of the book came first. It's often this way with me. I'm hit with a flash of an idea. In this case it was, "What about a book about a substance that seems harmless, but turns out to be highly addictive?" And then I thought, "It seems as safe as sugar or caffeine, but is actually so addictive, people will do anything to get their hands on it once they're hooked."

Once I was developing the premise, I realized that if I made the substance a weight-loss drug, I could also investigate issues of body image, nutrition, and our obsession with weight. These are such important issues right now and I have so much to say, I feel like I could write another book just filled with my own experiences and opinions! Obviously, we don't have room for that here, but let me just touch on body image. I'm fascinated with how we perceive our bodies. Start with the fact that each of us is amazingly lucky to be alive. I watched a great TedX talk by Mel Robbins. She said the chance of you being born YOU is 1 in 400 trillion. Let's go with her numbers. Can you imagine that? 1 in 400 TRILLION! Can you get your mind around a number that big? I can't. Yet, here I am and there you are, both of us miracles. And the tragedy is, somehow, we've been turned against our beautiful bodies. We've been made to feel like we're failures if we aren't in a certain proportion. Well, friends, I blame the media! I do. Every day, from the big screen to the small screen, from billboards to glossy magazines to the devices we carry around in our back pockets, we are bombarded with images of an ideal body that is not realistic. Allow me to blow your mind one more time. I read a great statistic on anad.org—the type of woman's body that we see portrayed in the media as being the ideal is only possessed naturally by five percent of American females. Five percent! And here we are, all beating ourselves up because we don't look like 'em! So, ahem, you can see I'm passionate about this issue.

Laurel, one of the protagonists of *Sweet*, is at ease with her not-magazine-perfect body. Do you think she is the exception or the rule?

Ah, Laurel Willard! She was so much fun to write. Laurel has definitely got her share of insecurities, but her weight simply isn't one of them. And I tell you, it felt downright revolutionary to write a character who didn't hate her body fat. It was crucial for the book to have a grounded protagonist who has balanced feelings about her body because most of the other characters in the book are so focused on weight loss—and some of them really hate fat people. Laurel loves and accepts her body the way it is—and that's a very powerful position to be in.

Girls need this power! (Remember how I said I could write a book with my opinions on this stuff? Here I go again. . . .) For centuries, society has given girls messages, not just about how their bodies should look, but about how small their lives should be. Look nice, play nice, take care of everyone around you, be good—all in all, don't take up too much room. Loving your body the way it is? It's a great place to start. It's a revolutionary act.

Tom, another protagonist, works out strenuously and monitors his food intake with the help of his trainer. Why did you decide to give him these issues?

Yeah, Tom does have some food issues, doesn't he? As a child, he was a compulsive overeater and now he's probably a little too rigid about how he eats, and he exercises a LOT. I think it's a bit unusual for guys to be depicted as having eating disorders in YA, but guys are definitely not immune to the pressure to have a perfect body. Another study I read on anad.org said that one half of girls had reported using unsafe techniques for losing weight, and that one third of boys said they do it, too. *One third* of the guys surveyed reported skipping meals, fasting, using laxatives, or vomiting to control their weight!

Food is tricky, isn't it? We need to eat it at least three times a day. We want to eat delicious things that make us feel good. But we also have cravings that lead us far away from what our bodies need to be healthy and fit. And the junk food, aargh, it's everywhere! Tom's lucky. He has a trainer who's also a nutritionist that he reports to everyday. Part of Tom's job, as a celebrity, is to look terrific, so he works hard at it. For the rest of us non-celebrities, it's not so easy. But it's crucial to feed your beautiful, miraculous body the stuff it needs to be healthy. You know, lean protein and vegetables and fruit and that quinoa stuff that everyone is in love with all of a sudden.

The passengers who ingest Solu become almost zombie-like—the walking hungry. What made you decide that Solu would have this effect?

Continuing our discussion of eating disorders from the last question, I will confess—the truth is that the idea for the way the passengers would react to Solu came from my own lifelong addiction to sugar. I've written a special letter to the readers of *Sweet* on my Web site (emmylaybourne.com), so check it out if you'd like to hear more about my experience. But to make it simple, most people can handle consuming sugar. I can't. (I used to steal money off my parents' dresser and sneak out of school to buy candy. And this was in New York City—in the late 70s!) As an adult, I've used nutritional rehab and a lot of support to kick the habit, but I remember how much of my time and energy I used to spend obsessing about sugar. When I was developing the idea for *Sweet*, I knew I could describe addiction well! At first, I wasn't 100 percent sure that raging addiction was the right effect for Solu to have on people, but then I got the idea for the corkscrew scene and I got goose bumps. When you give yourself goose bumps, you know you're on the right track!

Why did you decide to set *Sweet* on a cruise ship instead of, say, in a hospital or clinic?

There are two reasons I set *Sweet* on a luxury cruise—one served the plot and one was entirely self-serving!

In terms of story, I knew I had to figure out how to contain the epidemic. I didn't want to write a giant sprawling story trailing a dozen of characters through, say, downtown Detroit. I wanted a close, controlled environment. And once I hit on the idea of it being a luxury cruise, I liked that many of the passengers affected by Solu would be glamorous and rich, maybe even snobby, so their fall would be even more pronounced.

Setting it on a luxury cruise was self-serving because: RESEARCH! My dad treated me to a cruise of the western Caribbean on the *Regent Navigator*! Oh my goodness, we had the best time. The rooms were gorgeous (we each had our own, of course, because sharing with your dad? Gross). The food was delicious. And the crew and staff were so warm and sincere. I had written a first draft of the book before we went on the cruise, and I vastly expanded the role of Jaideep after going on the cruise simply because the wonderful staff we met were such an important part of the experience.

Once the crew and staff found out I was researching a book, they were happy to share insight about how the ship functioned and what their responsibilities were. The only awkward moment was when I asked the first mate, "Now, if you were going to blow up the ship, how would you go about it?" He refused to answer. Can you believe that?!

What has been the reaction among readers to the body-image issues raised in *Sweet*?

I've been getting tweets and e-mails from readers saying they are recognizing themselves in the characters of Laurel and Viv. One reader said the conversation Laurel and Vivika have about weight made her cry. Laurel asks Viv, "Why do we have to be thinner, thinner, thinner all the time?" And Vivika grabs her belly and says, "Because when people see this, they see weakness. And I don't want to be seen as weak." The reader said that she feels exactly the way Viv feels and that reading it was therapeutic. That made me feel really terrific.

When I first came up with the idea for *Sweet*, I thought I was writing a pop-horror book. It turned into something cooler, I think. I like to give my readers a guarantee: It's the only Romantic-Comedy/Adventure/Horror/ISSUE book set on a cruise ship about celebrities who start drinking blood you'll ever read. If you can give me an example of another, well, dinner's on me!

RESOURCES

Eating disorders, and more generally, body image issues, affect people of all genders everywhere. Help yourself. Educate yourself.

The following links provide more information, resources, and support for those fighting eating disorders and body image distortion.

MORE INFORMATION

anad.org/get-information/about-eating-disorders/eating-disorders-statistics
nationaleatingdisorders.org/general-information
eatingdisorderhope.com/treatment-for-eating-disorders/special-issues/teen-adolescent-children
nimh.nih.gov/health/publications/eating-disorders-new-trifold/index.shtml#pub3
nlm.nih.gov/medlineplus/eatingdisorders.html
nedic.ca/know-facts/overview

SUPPORT

theprojectheal.org
thebodypositive.org
proud2bme.org

FASHION

alreadypretty.com
thecurvyfashionista.com

SOCIAL ACTION

adiosbarbie.com
girlsforachange.org
about-face.org

FOURTEEN KIDS. ONE SUPERSTORE.
A MILLION THINGS THAT GO WRONG.

Keep reading for an excerpt of the first book in the
riveting MONUMENT 14 series.

CHAPTER ONE

TINKS

YOUR MOTHER HOLLERS THAT YOU'RE GOING TO MISS THE BUS.
She can see it coming down the street. You don't stop and hug
her and tell her you love her. You don't thank her for being
a good, kind, patient mother. Of course not—you launch yourself down the stairs and make a run for the corner.

Only, if it's the last time you'll ever see your mother, you
sort of start to wish you'd stopped and did those things. Maybe
even missed the bus.

But the bus was barreling down our street so I ran.

As I raced down the driveway I heard my mom yell for my
brother, Alex. His bus was coming down Park Trail Drive,
right behind mine. His bus came at 7:09 on the dot. Mine was
supposed to come at 6:57 but was almost always late, as if the
driver agreed it wasn't fair to pick me up before 7:00.

Alex ran out behind me and our feet pounded the sidewalk
in a dual sneaker-slap rhythm.

"Don't forget," he called. "We're going to the Salvation Army after school."

"Yeah, sure," I said.

My bus driver laid on the horn.

Sometimes we went over to rummage for old electronics after school. I used to drive him before the gas shortage. But now we took our bikes.

I used to drive him to school, too. But since the shortage everyone in our school, everyone, even the seniors, took the bus. It was the law, actually.

I vaulted up the bus steps.

Behind me I heard Mrs. Wooly, who has been driving the elementary–middle school bus since forever, thank Alex sarcastically for gracing them with his presence.

Mrs. Wooly, she was an institution in our town. A grizzled, wiry-haired, ashtray-scented, tough-talking institution. Notorious and totally devoted to bus driving, which you can't say about everyone.

On the other hand, the driver of my bus, the high school bus, was morbidly obese and entirely forgettable. Mr. Reed. The only thing he was known for was that he drank his morning coffee out of an old jelly jar.

Even though it was early in the route, Jake Simonsen, football hero and all-around champion of the popular, was already holding court in the back. Jake had moved to our school from Texas a year ago. He was a real big shot back in Texas, where football is king, and upon transfer to our school had retained and perhaps even increased his stature.

"I'm telling y'all—concessions!" Jake said. "At my old high school a bunch of girls sold pop and cookies and these baked potatoes they used to cook on a grill. Every game. They made, like, a million dollars."

DAY 1

"A million dollars?" Astrid said.

Astrid Heyman, champion diver on the swim team, scornful goddess, girl of my dreams.

"Even if I could make a million dollars, I wouldn't give up playing my own sport to be a booster for the football team," she said.

Jake flashed her one of his golden smiles.

"Not a booster, baby, an entrepreneur!"

Astrid punched Jake on the arm.

"Ow!" he complained, grinning. "God, you're strong. You should box."

"I have four younger brothers," she answered. "I do."

I hunkered down in my seat and tried to get my breath back. The backs of the forest green pleather seats were tall enough that if you slouched, you could sort of disappear for a moment.

I ducked down. I was hoping no one would comment on my sprint to catch the bus. Astrid hadn't noticed me get on the bus at all, which was both good and bad.

Behind me, Josie Miller and Trish Greenstein were going over plans for some kind of animal rights demonstration. They were kind of hippie-activists. I wouldn't really know them at all, except once in sixth grade I'd volunteered to go door to door with them campaigning for Cory Booker. We'd had a pretty fun time, actually, but now we didn't even say hi to each other.

I don't know why. High school seemed to do that to people.

The only person who acknowledged my arrival at all was Niko Mills. He leaned over and pointed to my shoe—like, "I'm too cool to talk"—he just points. And I looked down, and of course, it was untied. I tied it. Said thanks. But then I immediately put in my earbuds and focused on my minitab. I didn't have anything to say to Niko, and judging from his pointing at my shoe, he didn't have anything to say to me either.

From what I'd heard, Niko lived in a cabin with his grand-father, up in the foothills near Mount Herman, and they hunted for their own food and had no electricity and used wild mush-rooms for toilet paper. That kind of thing. People called Niko "Brave Hunter Man," a nickname that fit him just right with his perfect posture, his thin, wiry frame, and his whole brown-skin-brown-eyes-brown-hair combo. He carried himself with that kind of stiff pride you get when no one will talk to you.

So I ignored Brave Hunter Man and tried to power up my minitab. It was dead and that was really weird because I'd just grabbed it off the charging plate before I left the house.

Then came this little *tink, tink, tink* sound. I took out my buds to hear better. The *tinks* were like rain, only metallic.

And the *tinks* turned to TINKS and the TINKS turned to Mr. Reed's screaming "Holy Christ!" And suddenly the roof of the bus started denting—BAM, BAM, BAM—and a cob-web crack spread over the windshield. With each BAM the windshield changed like a slide show, growing more and more white as the cracks shot through the surface.

I looked out the side window next to me.

Hail in all different sizes from little to that-can't-be-hail was pelting the street.

Cars swerved all over the road. Mr. Reed, always a lead foot, slammed on the gas instead of the brake, which is what the other cars seemed to be doing.

Our bus hurdled through an intersection, over the median, and into the parking lot of our local Greenway superstore. It was fairly deserted because it was maybe 7:15 by this point.

I turned around to look back in the bus toward Astrid, and everything went in slow motion and fast motion at the same

DAY 1

time as our bus slid on the ice, swerving into a spin. We went faster and faster, and my stomach was in my mouth. My back was pressed to the window, like in some carnival ride, for maybe three seconds and then we hit a lamppost and there was a sick metallic shriek.

I grabbed on to the back of the seat in front of me but then I was jumbling through the air. Other kids went flying, too. There was no screaming, just grunts and impact sounds.

I flew sideways but hit, somehow, the roof of the bus. Then I understood that our bus had turned onto its side. It was screaming along the asphalt on its side. It shuddered to a stop.

The hail, which had merely been denting the hell out of our roof, started denting the hell out of us.

Now that the bus was on its side, hail was hammering down through the row of windows above us. Some of my class-mates were getting clobbered by the hail and the window glass that was raining down.

I was lucky. A seat near me had come loose, and I pulled it over me. I had a little roof.

The rocks of ice were all different sizes. Some little round marbles and some big knotty lumps with gray parts and gravel stuck inside them.

There were screams and shouts as everyone scrambled to get under any loose seats or to stand up, pressed to the roof, which was now the wall.

It sounded as if we were caught in a riptide of stones and rocks, crashing over and over. It felt like someone was beating the seat I was under with a baseball bat.

I tilted my head down and looked out what was left of the windshield. Through the white spray outside I saw that the grammar school bus, Alex's bus, was somehow still going. Mrs. Wooly hadn't skidded or lost control like Mr. Reed.

Her bus was cutting through the parking lot, headed right for the main entrance to the Greenway.

Mrs. Wooly's going to drive right into the building, I thought. And I knew that she would get those kids out of the hail. And she did. She smashed the bus right through the glass doors of the Greenway.

Alex was safe, I thought. Good.

Then I heard this sad, whimpering sound. I edged forward and peered around the driver's seat. The front of the bus was caved in, from where it had hit the lamppost.

It was Mr. Reed making that sound. He was pinned behind the wheel and blood was spilling out of his head like milk out of a carton. Soon he stopped making that sound. But I couldn't think about that.

Instead, I was looking at the door to the bus, which was now facing the pavement. How will we get out? I was thinking. We can't get out. The windshield was all crunched up against the hood of the engine.

It was all a crumpled jam. We were trapped in the demolished sideways bus.

Josie Miller *screamed*. The rest of the kids had instinctively scrambled to get out of the hail but Josie was just sitting, wailing, getting pelted by the ice balls.

She was covered in blood, but not her own, I realized, because she was trying to pull on someone's arm from between two mangled seats and I remembered Trish had been sitting next to her. The arm was limp, like a noodle, and kept slipping down out of Josie's grip. Trish was definitely dead but Josie didn't seem to be getting it.

DAY 1

From a safe spot under an overturned seat, this jerk Brayden, who is always going on about his dad working at NORAD, took out his minitab and started trying to shoot a video of Josie screaming and grabbing at the slippery arm.

A monster hailstone hit Josie on the forehead and a big pink gash opened on her dark forehead. Blood started streaming down over her face.

I knew that the hail was going to kill Josie if she kept sitting there out in the open.

"Christ." Brayden cursed at his minitab. "Come *on!*"

I knew I should move. Help her. Move. Help.

But my body was not responding to my conscience.

Then Niko reached out and grabbed Josie by the legs and pulled her under a twisted seat. Just like that. He reached out and pulled her two legs toward him and brought her in to his body. He held her and she sobbed. They looked like a couple out of a horror film.

Somehow Niko's action had broken the spell. Kids were trying to get out and Astrid crawled to the front. She tried to kick through the windshield. She saw me on the ground, under my seat, and she shouted, "Help me!"

I just looked at her mouth. And her nose ring. And her lips moving and making words. I wanted to say, "No. We can't go out there. We have to stay where there is shelter." But I couldn't quite piece the words together.

She stood up and screamed to Jake and his people, "We've got to get into the store!"

Finally I croaked out, "We can't go out! The hail will kill us." But Astrid was at the back of the bus by then.

"Try the emergency exit!" someone shouted. At the back of the bus Jake was already pulling and pulling at the door, but he couldn't get it open. There was mayhem for a few minutes; I don't know how long. I started to feel very strange. Like my head was on a long balloon string, floating above everything.

And then I heard such a funny sound. It was the *beep-beep-beep* sound of a school bus backing up. It was crazy to hear it through the hammering hail and the screaming.

Beep-beep-beep, like we were at the parking lot on a field trip to Mesa Verde and the bus was backing up.

Beep-beep-beep, like everything was normal.

I squinted out, and sure enough, Mrs. Wooly was backing up the elementary–middle school bus toward us. It was listing to the right pretty bad and I could see where it was dented in the front from smashing into the store. But it was coming.

Black smoke started pouring in through the hole I was looking through. I coughed. The air was thick. Oily. My lungs felt like they were on fire.

I should go to sleep now was the thought that came into my head. It was a powerful thought and seemed perfectly logical: Now I should go to sleep.

The cries of the other kids got louder: "The bus is on fire!" "It's going to explode!" and "We're going to die!"

And I thought, They're right. Yes, we'll die. But it's okay. It's fine. It is as it should be. We are going to die.

I heard this clanking. The sound of metal on metal.

And "She's trying to open the door!"

And "Help us!"

I closed my eyes. I felt like I was floating down now, going underwater. Getting so sleepy warm. So comfortable.

And then this bright light opened up on me. And I saw how Mrs. Wooly had gotten the emergency door open. In her hands she held an ax.

And I heard her shout:

"Get in the godforsaken bus!"

DAY 1

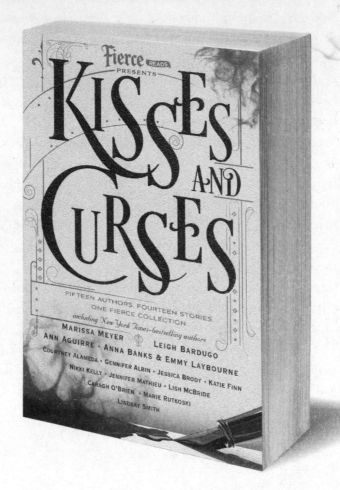